Hard to Resist

Shanora Williams

Cover Design by Stephanie White of Steph's Cover Designs

Acknowledgments

Goodness, where do I start with this one. *Hard to Resist* was an experience. It is my first Contemporary Romance and I have to admit that writing it was amazing. I'm beyond words with this book. I'm completely speechless.

I give my honor to God for blessing me with this amazing talent. Without him, I'd literally be nowhere.

To all that supported me throughout this process, thank you so much! It truly means a lot to me and to know that you were all impatiently waiting cracked me up, made me nervous, but kept me going all at the same time.

Especially, Stina, who is my loyal beta-reader. I love seeing her reactions.

I could relate so much to this book because not only was it fun, but it dealt with the way that I felt. There are events in this book that I won't mention exactly but that are related to me. Natalie and I have a ton in common which is why her story was so hard to get out. I had written two books before finally combining the two stories into one. That's how *Hard to Resist* came about. I've thought on this story for years and it finally clicked.

Kim Bias for helping a sister out with re-writes and construction. For making things clearer for me that I looked over. It seriously helped so much! I felt honored that she went over the book with me – especially since she doesn't usually do it with authors. Her comments and critique helped a ton. She is one awesome lady!

I have to thank my family for supporting me, my boyfriend for keeping me inspired, and of course my readers. The support and love that you show is just . . . wow. Mind blowing. I can't thank you enough.

Thanks to Stephanie White for being the creator of my lovely cover. I love the magic you create!

Dedicated to my Juan Carlos. Without you, I wouldn't have been able to write this book. I love you. Forever and always.

Chapter One

Graduation Night

"Are you ready?"

I sighed, reaching for my clutch to pull out some of my best lip gloss. I bought it every time I would go to Victoria's Secret. It tasted just like peppermint and the only reason I kept buying it was because Bryson loved to suck it off of my lips. I shivered, thinking about Bryson and his velvety tongue. Whenever he would tease me, use his tongue to trace my lower lip, it would be to die for. When he would use that same velvety tongue to caress my ear lobes—oh, God... I was in heaven.

I smeared some gloss on my lips then turned to look at Gracey as I pushed the visor of the car back up just as she was pulling hers down. "You're asking me if I'm ready but you keep checking your face," I teased, my lips hinting at a smirk.

"I know, I know." She sighed then reached to fluff her glossy black hair. "There's just this guy that's going to be here. I met him at a party last week. He's really hot—but I forgot his name." She glanced at me before her eyes drifted to look through the windshield.

"Does he just want your thong?" I asked.

She grinned. "I don't know. Maybe I just want his dong!" We both burst into a fit of giggles, clutching ourselves but making sure that we didn't destroy our makeup with our corny tears. "But at least you won't have to worry about that."

She was right. I didn't have to worry about sex that night because Bryson was there. He was my boyfriend and, technically, I could have sex with him whenever I wanted and not feel guilty about it. Just thinking about him made me grin.

"Gah, you look like a love-struck idiot when you smile like that," Gracey muttered beneath her breath, pushing the visor back up and opening the passenger door of the car. She climbed out and shut it behind her but I continued to grin as I climbed out of the driver's seat.

I placed my lip gloss in my clutch before turning to face Gracey in her bright orange, skin-tight mini dress. She could have passed for a stripper (especially since her boobs were extra perky and her make-up was a bit dramatic) but she was still gorgeous. Gracey's skin was flawless with a beautiful light-brown tint to it. Her complexion could have been compared to the color of mocha. She had brown freckles, beautiful hazel eyes, and a body she loved to work out with.

I locked the car up then walked around the hood to meet her. She studied my creamy white mini dress briefly before turning to face the large mansion that was just a few yards ahead of us, swarmed by cars. "I envy you tonight," she hissed as we began to walk for the house in our stilettos.

Chuckling, I asked, "Why?"

"Because, you look beautiful and if you want *some*, you can get some without even trying . . . unlike me, where I have to work for it, you don't."

I laughed again. "Oh, trust me, Gracey. It's graduation night. I'm sure whoever this guy is that you're trying to sleep with will be drunk enough for you to drag upstairs and hump for a little while. He won't mind."

"Euch." Gracey's face pinched. "Don't make me sound like a tramp."

"I'd hate to burst your bubble but..." She scowled and I gave her a teasing grin. "I'm only kidding, Gracey. I love you, and after four years of working our asses off, we deserve a little fun. High school would have been hell without you."

"Same here. I wouldn't have survived biology or history without you as my study buddy."

I nodded and began to smile but that smile evaporated as we approached the large oak door. Gracey looked at me, wide-eyed, and we both could tell it was really going down inside. We could hear it, feel it. Most of the students of West Ashley High School of South Carolina were there. We had all graduated and we were all partying with no regrets.

"You ready?" I asked, looking at Gracey who was tugging her dress down.

"Been ready." Reaching for the door knob, she swung the door open and it was just like a jungle-gym inside. As soon as we stepped in, people were making out, red cups were spread all over the floor. The lights were dim and the thick stench of sweat and beer filled my lungs. I tried my hardest not to breathe it in as I shut the door behind us. I spotted couples on the staircase to my right. They were making out and some I would have thought were having sex by the way their legs were intertwined and their tongues were lodged down each other's throats.

"I see him!" Gracey yelled over the music. The song changed and as it did, the lights went out, the room grew darker, but the flickers of various colored rave lights began to shine. "I'll find you later, kay?" she shouted, already drifting away from me. I nodded, watching as she met up with a tall, fair-skinned guy with cropped hair and his lip pierced. He had on a tight black T-shirt, skinny blue jeans, and his arms were toned, as if he worked out every day. He really was hot and now I can see why Gracey was so ready to be all over him.

I pulled my phone out to text Bryson immediately. I knew he was there because he'd told me he was going to help set up the DJ stand. The guy hosting the party was Bryson's best friend, Mark. Bryson was always there, holed up in Mark's room when he wanted to make an escape.

I waited ten minutes. I'd even grabbed a drink. But I didn't get a text back. It wasn't like Bryson to hold off on texting me—although lately he'd been drifting away from me more and more. I looked towards the spiral staircase again, figuring if he wasn't downstairs, he was most likely upstairs.

I pushed through the thick crowd, passing by people with their plastic red cups in hand, until I was near the staircase. I hopped up the stairs quickly, stepping between the couples having *make-out-sex* until it was clear. The music had grown quieter up there but the bass was thumping against the soles of my feet. I passed by the first four rooms until I reached the last one. The last room was Mark's room and if Bryson wasn't in there, I didn't know where the hell he could have been.

I knocked on the door and heard stumbling of some kind. *They're in there.* I knocked again but no one answered so I twisted the knob, stepped inside, but as I did my heart failed to beat.

I clutched the door knob, staring in horror and choking on my next breath, wishing I had never gone upstairs. My hands began to tremble but I couldn't pull my sight away from it.

Bryson hopped from the bed quickly, reaching for his jeans to tug them over his legs. "Nat," he breathed, staring at me with wide eyes.

I remained speechless, looking from him to the blonde bitch lying on the bed with a smirk. It was Sara Manx. I hated her with a passion. She'd always been trying to find a way to get between Bryson and I and I guess she'd found a way because there he was, just lying on top of her, sweating like he'd just ran for an hour on a treadmill.

I couldn't even speak. I didn't want to. I wanted to pretend none of it had happened. I spun around and began to march down the hall but he caught me by the hook of my arm. I shoved him away, feeling my chest tighten. Tears pricked and stung at my eyes but I wasn't going to let Sara get to me. She wanted this. She wanted to see us fight and to see us unhappy. And, to be honest, she'd won.

"Nat, please," Bryson begged but I pushed against his sweaty, bare chest harder.

"Fuck you, Bryson! How could you do this to me—with *her*?" He clutched my wrists, forcing me to look him in the eye but I couldn't. He had the most beautiful emerald green I'd eyes ever seen but I began to hate them. I began to despise everything about him. I told myself he wasn't worth the tears and that I didn't need him, but it was a lie. Bryson and I had promised to grow old and happy together. To have children and to raise them correctly. He'd promised me so much. A beautiful wedding, a romantic honeymoon—all of it. But that had all gone down the drain. That promise was no more.

"Let go of me," I growled through my teeth.

"Nat, I'm sorry!" He removed one of his hands from my wrist to cup my jawline but I pulled away.

"Don't touch me!" I hissed, feeling the tears ride along my cheeks.

"What the hell is going on?"

I spun around to face Mark who was looking at us both with wide eyes. I jerked away from Bryson while his guard was down and stomped around Mark. I figured Mark knew something about this whole ordeal. He had too. They're best friends. Bryson tells Mark everything.

"Natalie," Mark called after me as I clambered down the stairs. I ripped my clutch open to pull my keys out. I then pushed through the crowd, searching for Gracey who I'd found on the dance floor. I gripped her wrist and drug her out of the room.

"Hey—Nat! What are you doing?" she whined over the music. I ignored her. I continued to push through the sea of bodies, not caring about who I'd hit or what elbows I was throwing to get them out of my way. I just wanted to get the hell out of there. And fast.

I finally reached the door and stepped out into the night air. I continued to drag Gracey down until I was at the last stoop. But as I reached the bottom, I couldn't hold it in anymore. I fell against Grace's shoulder and her whole body tensed before she wrapped her arms around me.

"Hey, Nat, what's wrong?" she asked, her voice lowering to a coo. She pushed me back by the shoulders to take a look at my face. She studied the grief in my eyes, the hurt taking over every single one of my features. "What did he *do*?" she growled.

"I caught him cheating on me . . . with Sara Manx."

She gasped, her eyes wide. Bewildered. "*Sara Manx*! What the fuck is his problem?" She pulled her hands away from me to turn around and march up the stone steps. She gripped the door knob, pushed in, but as soon as the door was open, Mark was stepping out, his eyes still wide and confused.

"What the hell are you doing? *Move*," Gracey scowled, trying to push Mark aside.

"You're not going back in there to cause drama, Grace." Mark's voice was humble. He looked up from her eyes and spotted me, the helpless, idiotic girl that'd just been cheated on. He shut the door behind him but gripped onto Grace's wrist and dragged her down the stoop.

Mark, let go of me," she grunted, struggling to pull her arm free. He ignored her with his eyes still on me. There was no point for Grace to fight. Mark was like a brick wall. He'd finally decided to release Grace as he stopped less than an inch away from me.

"Did you know about this?" I asked, taking a step back.

"Natalie, I swear to you, I didn't know," he said. "Bryson is a fucking idiot. He knew that if he would have told me I would have told you so he kept it to himself." He reached for me and pulled me in by the shoulders for a tight hug. Mark always did have comforting hugs. "Nat, you're my best friend. I would never allow anyone to cheat on you—not even Bryson. I promise I didn't know."

I nodded against his chest, feeling the tears building up within me. My throat scratched from holding the tears in so I released them. I choked on each sob, still disbelieving he'd really done this to me. Four years with him, and that's how it had ended? Four years, and all I get is a shattered heart in return?

Chapter Two

One month later

Shoving the last suitcase into the trunk feels unbelievably odd. I sigh, glancing down at my white Camry. After dumping Bryson, I've never felt so bad. Mom says I'm running away but I don't think of it that way. I think of it as getting a new start. Leaving has to be the best thing because at least when I leave, I'll have many things to do to occupy my time. My mind will be distracted and living with Harper will be a blast.

Harper has been my best friend since we were younger. She's two years older than me and we're like sisters. She moved to Miami, Florida during my senior year to go off to a real college and I haven't seen her since. Her parents rented her a condo there and I'm beyond ready to see her. I told her about Bryson and she immediately told me to come down. I'll be staying with Harper for a few months—until I can find a job and arrange enough money to live on my own. I may even go to a community college down there. I just can't continue to stay here. Bryson tries to come to my house every day just to apologize and it annoys the hell out of me. One day, I'll probably end up going to jail for strangling his ass.

Nothing he says can make up for what he did to me. Ever since the night of the graduation party, I've shut my emotions off. I've stuffed them in a jar and sealed that jar tight. I won't be opening that jar for a very long time. Maybe never again.

He's a fool if he thinks I'll talk to him. He blows my phone up constantly. He even tries to get Mark to speak for him but Mark's on my side. Mark doesn't condone cheating and I hate that I blamed him for covering up for Bryson. Mark was furious, especially since Bryson had sex on *his* bed with *Sara the Slut*.

"You all set, Natty?"

I turn around quickly to face my dad. He looks like he hasn't caught any sleep in days, but it's most likely because he and my mom have been arguing a lot lately and he's been sleeping on the sofa. People tell me my father and I look alike but I believe they only say it because we have the same chocolate-brown eyes. My mother, on the other hand, we have the same button nose, the same plush, pink lips, the same almond-shaped eyes, and the same silky red-brown hair.

"Yeah," I sigh, turning to face him. "I'm all set. I should get out of here while it's still early, huh?" I ask, forcing a smile.

He nods, sighing as well. "You should. Eight hours is a long drive. Might as well knock 'em out." He looks me over, his eyes clouded with worry as I clutch my keys in hand. I know that look all too well. It's the look he always gives me when he thinks I'm reminiscing or that I'm still torn. It happened a month ago, but every day he worries himself about it. "You go down there and have some fun with Harper," he says, raking his fingers through his dark hair. A few streaks of grey fall onto his forehead and he brushes them away.

"I'll be fine, Dad. Promise."

"I trust that you will. Your mother said to call her as soon as you hit Florida."

"Yeah, I know. I'll call her. She should be off of work by then." He nods, looking me over again. He then stretches his arms outward, his signal for me to walk into them and give him one of his famous bear hugs. I grip onto him tightly and he sighs, rubbing my back.

"I love you, Nat. Have a safe trip."

"I love you, too."

He releases me, then presses his lips together. I head for the driver's side of the car and he watches me hop in. "If you get lost, use the GPS!" he calls before turning for the house. "It's a 2012 version with TTS and hands-free calling so if you get lost, call for help."

"I will!" I call back, even though I don't know what the hell he's talking about. I peer out of the window and watch him nod slightly. I wait for a moment, but he remains in the center of the driveway. I know he isn't going to go in until I'm out of the neighborhood, so I crank the car, blow a kiss at him, and then pull out of the driveway, making my way to a new destination. To a new place I hope won't linger on depression, heartbreak, and pain.

****

Eight hours later and I'm in Miami, Florida. I release a huge breath of relief as I cruise through the city. Nightfall has just hit and it's a Friday night. The streets are far from clear but they amaze me. On every corner is a night club with lines that extend from the door to the end of the block. I pull my cell out and dial Harper's number. She answers after the second ring.

"Natalie! Are you here?!" she screams.

"Yes I am. I'm driving through the city right now. I'm near some club called "Da Bump." What road do I turn on?"

"Oh! I know where you are! At the end of the street, you'll see a tall white building. My condo is in the Infinity Condominiums at Brickell. You can't miss it unless..."

Harper's voice continues to chime in my ear but I slam on my brakes, my body jerking forward quickly. The wheels of my car come to a screech as I toss my phone to the passenger seat, breathing heavily and gripping the wheel with broad eyes. As I glare through the windshield, I spot someone tall in a black muscle T-shirt staring right back at me, his eyes wide as well.

His hands are firmly planted on the hood of my car and, luckily, I missed him by what looks like almost an inch. My heart starts to settle but the beats are still heavy. I climb out of the car and rush to the hood but as he stands up and looks down at me with warm grey eyes, I gasp. He's beautiful. His face is ridiculously stunning. Chiseled perfectly. His dark-brown hair is cropped and tousled, yet extremely delicious.

"Are you alright?" His deep voice is almost a purr, humming throughout me, making every part of me flutter softly like the wings of a gentle hummingbird. I continue to stare at him. His broad chest, his jeans that are fit to him snuggly. My gaze meets his again but this time there is a hint of a smile on his lips. He tilts his head, crossing his arms across his sculpted chest while looking me over. He licks his bottom lip before speaking again. "Are you okay?" He narrows his eyes innocently.

I nod stupidly, feeling my hair shaking against my shoulders.

His chuckle rumbles and I liquefy as my bones turn into Jell-O. "I'm sorry I ran out like that. I thought I could make it across before you rolled past. I guess I'm not as fast as I thought. That was a close one though, huh?" He grins but I continue to stare at him, my face still dumbstruck. How can a beautiful man like him be so simple? So casual? I've never seen such a person. Most gorgeous men like him are usually cocky and a stunt like this would have ticked them off. Cocky people usually blame the whole world for their idiotic actions. He steps in closer and I inhale sharply, forgetting to breathe. "You alright? I'm sorry..." He reaches his hand towards me to try and touch me—to most likely see if I'm still breathing—but I take a leap back, shaking my head, finally breathing again.

"I'm alright—I'm fine," I breathe. "I'm just glad I didn't...run over you."

He raises both his eyebrows. "Oh. Good." He then sighs, rocking on his heels and tucking the tips of his fingers into his back pockets. "I guess I'll just be on my way then." He gives me a charming, heart throbbing smile and to my surprise, I haven't fallen backwards from a mesmerizing heart attack. His smile is dazzling and his teeth, perfect. Everything about that face of his is perfect. He's undeniably handsome and he has charm, something I should steer clear of because he knows he the shit. "Again, I'm sorry," he murmurs, his lips quirking up at the corners, his eyes scanning me once more. "Have a great night."

I remain glued in my tracks and although people are beeping and yelling for me to get the hell out of their way, I'm frozen. Stuck. How in the hell can he do this to me? I don't even know him. His beauty can't cause me to go this numb with adoration... can it?

His footsteps fade and I finally find the will to tear the soles of my sandals from the asphalt and march for my open car door. I have to get to Harper ASAP.

Chapter Three

"OH MY GOSH!"

My body is squeezed tightly as Harper wraps her thin arms around me. I giggle as I hang onto her while she bounces up and down like a six-year-old doped up on sugar. After a minute of hugging, she pulls away to look me over. "You look amazing, Nat! I've missed you!" She tugs me by the arm to get inside before slamming the door behind us.

"You look even better!" And I'm not kidding. Harper is gorgeous, and always has been. But unlike four years ago when her hair touched her shoulder blades, her straight blonde hair has been cut and layered to touch her shoulders. Her hair fits around her oval-shaped face beautifully. Her makeup is casually done (like how it always was) and she's still in shape—still the skinny-mini who won't gain a pound, no matter how much she eats. There's more of a rosy red tint to her cheeks and her smile seems brighter. I have to admit that due to my "depression" I had ended up gaining at least five pounds. But Gracey dragged me to the gym every day for a whole month before she ended up getting grounded.

"Were you going somewhere?" I ask, studying her skin-tight plum dress. There's a cleavage V on the front that cuts down to the middle of her stomach, revealing way too much skin. It's a club dress. She can't possibly be trying to go out tonight... *not tonight*. "Harper," I groan as she grins widely, revealing a full set of square, white teeth.

"Please, Nat," she begs, batting her heavily mascaraed eyelashes. "You really need to have some fun tonight. It will be a way to celebrate your arrival. I know the manager of the club and he gave me a pass to drink free. Just pretend you're twenty-one." She winks. "Besides, I'm not letting you wallow in self-pity tonight—at least not on my watch—so, come on. Let's get dressed," she insists, eyeing the suitcase in my hand.

"Sorry to tell you, Harp, but I don't own any more club or party dresses. I gave them all away."

She narrows her crystal-blue eyes at me. "I know you're lying," she accuses, "and even if you didn't, I have plenty. Come on," she demands again, gripping onto my wrist and dragging me past her brown leather sofas to get to her bedroom. "Let's get you dolled up." I groan as she leads the way towards her room. There is no way of winning with Harper, but she's right.

As soon as all of my things would have been unpacked, I would have curled up with a container of butter pecan *Haagen-Dazs* ice-cream and watched movies all night. I would have been a complete fat and lazy ass woman but I would have settled with it. I guess I do need to get out. I need to follow my own advice because tonight marks my new start. I'll live it up, have fun, and I won't think about Bryson Daniels... the guy who ripped and tore my heart to pieces.

****

An hour later and we're inside a night club called *LIV*. It's pretty live. People are everywhere, dancing, grinding, and partying with the night theme.

"Isn't this great?" Harper asks, handing me a shot glass full of some sort of vodka. I grab the glass from her, nodding my head.

"It's amazing. I'm glad you talked me into it!" I shout over the bass.

"You deserve it!" she shouts back. She raises her glass to clink hers with mine. "This is for fun tonight. No worries!"

"To fun!"

Our glasses clink again and we toss our drinks back quickly. My face pinches but I take it like how I used to during spring break. Drinking was never a problem for me. I loved to drink whenever I went out. It loosened me up a lot and made me feel like a free woman.

Now that I think about it, maybe more drinks are what I need. Harper and I walked to this club so we wouldn't need a ride. We can easily walk back home. There's nothing holding me back from getting wasted. I've had two shots already. Two more and I'll be the next thing closest to a free woman. "I'm gonna go grab another shot."

Harper grins, handing me the extra platinum drinking pass the club manager had given us. I was completely surprised when he had let us in so easily. Harper must have done something really dirty for him to accept me into his twenty-one and older club. He couldn't keep his eyes off her. "While you're at it, make the hot guy on the wall to our right buy you one. He won't stop looking at you."

I frown slightly, looking from Harper to the tall, broad body. My eyes widen as his meet mine. He's already staring at me, his lips hinting at a smile. His arms are folded across his chest and the sole of his right foot is pinned against the wall behind him. On his right is another really hot guy with long and wavy sandy-blonde hair and a lip piercing but that guy can't even compare to the one staring at me. It's the same guy from earlier. The one I almost ran over. I tear my gaze away to look at Harper who is now looking at me inconspicuously.

"Do you know him?"

"Nope." My lips pop.

"He seems interested. You should give him a dance, at least."

"Not right now," I murmur. "I'm gonna go get us some more shots." She nods then makes her way towards the dance floor. I can tell the drinks are already getting to her. She's already had two rounds of tequila and three shots of vodka. It's probably best if I don't bring her a shot back. I head for the bar, pushing through the crowd until I spot the glowing countertops. I spot an open seat and rush for it but before I can get to it, someone steps in my way, blocking me from taking it.

"Oh, I'm sorry," the person says.

"I was going to sit there—" My mouth clamps shut as *he* stands before me again. He tilts his head softly, gazing down at me with his hand placed on the bar stool. His lips are still hinting at a pleased smile and his grey eyes are still warm, still beautiful and surrounded by lush eyelashes.

"This is the second time you've almost crashed into me. We should be more careful," he says, leaning down so I can hear him over the music. I inhale, taking in his scent. He smells delicious and fresh, like the aroma of masculine body wash with a hint of spice. He has the natural scent that always makes a man smell completely irresistible.

I continue my gaze at him but take a step back to get some space between us. He takes a step back as well, but it's only to offer me the bar stool behind him. "By all means."

With a sigh, I step past him and sit on the stool. I can still feel him hovering behind me, waiting to say his next pick-up line. His body is close. His breath is warm as it trickles across my bare shoulders, causing the hairs on my back to prickle. "You don't mind if I sit with you, do you?"

I shake my head. "Free country."

He chuckles, stealing the seat on my right. Good thing my hair is covering my face, otherwise he would see how scarlet I am. It's suddenly grown hot and I'm not sure if it's because of the shots of alcohol, or if it's because he's that damn hot and can change the atmosphere from casual to steamy. What in the hell is going on with this guy? How can he affect a girl like this—a brokenhearted one at that? I shouldn't care.

"Would you like a drink?" he asks.

"I'll be fine getting my own."

I sneak a peek at him but he's already looking at me, his eyes soft and not phased at all by my response. "That's weird because most girls who come here beg to have their drinks bought for them. What makes you any different?"

I frown, turning to look at him. "Don't compare me to other women. I'm not them."

"You're not?"

"No." I scowl, turning away from him and his cocky demeanor. No wonder he's making me feel this way about him. Perhaps he is cocky in his own way.

"I must be making you mad. I'm sorry. I can just tell you're not from here."

"Oh yeah," I sigh. "How?"

"Well, for one, I saw your license plate." He smiles broadly. "And two... well, look at you." His eyes travel from mine to my lacey pink halter-top and black mini-skirt. My clothes are tight but nowhere near as skin-tight as Harper's are on her. "You're dressed, stating that you only show a certain amount of skin and if anyone wants to see the rest, they have to work for it. Most of the women from here, they'll wear almost nothing. Your sense of style, on the other hand, amazes me." I roll my eyes then lean forward to flag the bartender down. He's trying to run his game on me. *That's most definitely not gonna work.* He chuckles again, raking his fingers through his hair. "You're tough," he admits. I eye him briefly, forcing myself to keep my mouth sealed. "I guess that's what's reeling me in."

He observes every inch of bare skin on my body. He stares at my legs the longest before returning his gaze on mine. "Has anyone ever told you how rude it is to stare?" I snap.

"I didn't think admiring was the same thing as staring."

Heat forms in my lower belly, sneaking its way between my legs. I flush and tear my gaze away again. I definitely need another drink. The bartender finally comes up to me and I show him the pass before ordering another round of shots. The sooner I'm away from this guy, the better. The bartender pours two shots quickly and I reach in my bra for a bill as a tip but the hot guy beside me places a ten dollar bill down on the counter before I can even get to it. "Consider that an apology."

He stands from his stool, looking me over once more before turning and making his way through the crowd. I watch until he disappears within all of the bobbing heads and stretched arms before I turn to grab my shots quickly and chuck them both down, back-to-back. I slam the glasses down then rush for the dance floor to do something I know I'll probably regret tomorrow.

But this is my new start and I might as well take advantage of it. If I think about it too much, it won't be fun. Another techno song plays loudly as I push through the crowd until I see him. I catch his wrist and spin him around and he stares down at me, his eyes wide and sparked with confusion.

"I'm Natalie," I breathe. "Dance with me?"

His head tilts, eyes gleaming. "Nolan," he murmurs, leaning in to place his lips against my ear. Unexpected heat drowns my entire body as he pulls back but grabs my hand to turn me around. The music seems to get louder, my mind is swimming, and here I am, dancing with a really sexy *Nolan* guy. I start to dance like I never have before. The drinks are really getting to me now. I'm not Sober Natalie who would usually tell this Nolan guy to fuck off or to leave me alone. Right now, my broken heart no longer matters. All that matters is if I'm having fun. And I am.

Nolan leans his head down as I tilt mine back, still grinding and moving with the music. My hips are glued between his as his hardness presses into me, turning me on even more. At least I can still turn men on.

"What made you change your mind?" he asks, his voice humming into my ear drum. He places his hands around my waist as I continue to move, twisting and dipping my hips with the bass of the music.

"Life's too short."

His chuckle rumbles from the heart of his chest. He then spins me around to face him and we both stop moving, staring into one another's eyes. "What do you say we go talk over some drinks?"

I nod quickly then turn and stand on my toes to look over the crowd for Harper. I see her dancing with some guy I'm sure she doesn't know.

Nolan grips my hand and leads the way through the crowd. I bite back on a smile as we reach the stairs and he begins to walk up, still holding my hand. Why is this so exhilarating? I can't believe I've actually caught his attention. This guy wants to chat and drink with *me*. I have to do this. I'm having too much fun to try and stop it and, for once, I could give a shit less about Bryson. Bryson can kiss my ass.

Nolan continues to lead the way through various leather couches. The lights are still dim and I have to admit I'm feeling every shot of alcohol I've taken. I'm getting lightheaded, giggly. All I want to do is dance, move with the rhythm of the beats.

I shut my eyes briefly, enjoying the bass and letting it drum through my blood as I bob my head. It isn't until Nolan has squeezed my hand when I realize we're sitting.

"Are you okay?" he chuckles.

I giggle. "You want me to be honest?"

"As honest as you want to be."

"I feel great. I feel *free*."

"Am I making you feel that way already?" he teases. He leans in closer with his hand still glued to mine.

"Maybe."

"A "*maybe*" is good enough with me when it's coming from someone like you."

"What's that supposed to mean?" I ask, smirking.

"It means you have thick skin. For a second, I felt like giving up. That's never happened to me... with *any* woman before."

"So you're saying you pick up a lot of easy women from clubs?" I look him over this time, narrowing my eyes playfully.

"Not as many as you're thinking, I'm sure. And to be honest, it's not that hard when all of them are coming for the same thing." His smile is deliciously wicked and my heart stumbles over the next beat as another wave of heat works its way between my legs again.

"How do you do that?" I try to murmur to myself.

"Do what?" he asks. I blink quickly, pulling my hand away. If there's one side of being drunk I don't like, it's the fact that I don't hold my tongue. I always say what's on my mind and do what I feel is right. I'm careless when I'm drunk. Nolan looks at me, his clear grey eyes confused. "What am I doing?"

I shrug. "I don't know. When you smile I feel all girly and weird—" I pause as he flashes another smile and once again I liquefy. "See!" I shriek over the music. "That!" I point out.

He chuckles again, holding his hands up innocently. "I'm not doing anything. I'm just being myself."

"Yourself?"

"Myself," he says coolly, smirking. "Would you like another drink?"

"Sure," I nod and he stands from the silver sofa.

"I'll be back. It will literally take me, like, two minutes. Just don't leave." His face grows serious, his eyes hardening a bit. He thinks I'm going to bail on him? Maybe he really is into me. But I don't need him to be into me right now. I don't need him to feel anything towards me. I just want a one-night-stand, no feelings involved.

I fix my mouth to speak on it but he's already making his way towards the bar, his hips swinging in a manly, seductive way. I sigh, slouching back against the leather sofa, staring up at the dim lighting above me.

What the hell have I gotten myself into?

Chapter Four

As soon as Nolan unlocks the door of his apartment, our lips lock and we barge in, not giving a damn about who sees. He groans, slamming the door shut behind us. He stumbles over a few things on the floor, reaching to pull my shirt over my head. I reach down to grab the hem of his shirt and pull it over his head, allowing our lips to part for only a few seconds before devouring them again as soon as his shirt is off.

He stops abruptly as his body is forced to fall down and land on the sofa behind him. I climb on top of him, raking my fingers through his silky hair as he presses his fingers against my bare skin.

"Hey," he breathes as I begin to kiss his neck.

I ignore him. Right now, I've never been so turned on. Outside of us making out, I really can't think about anything else and that's exactly how I want it to be. He switches roles, picking my body up effortlessly to lay me down on his sofa. He dips down, placing his lips against mine before dragging feathery touches on my cheek, my ear, my neck. I moan, grazing my fingernails through the creases of his muscular back. I reach to unbutton his pants but he reaches down to stop my hand.

"Hey," he says again, this time through a soft chuckle. "Are you sure about this?" His voice is deep, husky. Another huge turn-on.

"Yes," I whisper, nodding my head and still trying to unbutton his pants. His hand remains gripped around mine. I pull away and place my hands on his warm chest, deciding to breathe his fresh, masculine scent in instead. I pull him down against me and he grunts, laughing again. His lips hover above mine and I lean up, begging to feel the light brushing of his lips, but he pulls back. "What are you doing?" I snap.

The moonlight is filtering onto his face from the balcony window. He smiles, his teeth flashing and causing my skin to melt against my bones. "I can't, Natalie."

What the hell? Just seconds ago we were making out. He was enjoying this—every part of it. What man wouldn't want to have sex with a drunk girl? Isn't that what he kept buying me drinks for? I sit up quickly, pulling away from him. "Why not?" I ask defensively. Am I really that hideous that he wanted to change his mind? Does my breath smell bad? Am I not perfect enough for him? I thought I had him in the bag.

"Don't take it that way." He perks himself up to sit down beside me. "I feel bad—and that's the thing. I'm not supposed to feel anything for you."

"What do you mean? You've literally just met me. We both want the same thing." I inch away from him a bit, my face in a tight grimace.

"Exactly, I've just met you, yet, I know nothing about you," he says, shaking his head. "Look, if I sleep with you tonight, I know you'll consider it a one-night-stand and never answer my calls in the future. You'll regret meeting me. When I call, you'll think all I want is sex and I don't want you thinking like that. It'd be nice to… try something else for a change."

What? But that's exactly what I was aiming for. No feelings, just sex. "So what are you saying?" I ask. "Because that's kind of what I was going for."

He tilts his head, his eyes narrowing. "Just *sex*?"

"Yeah," I say through a forced, breathy laugh.

"You think that's all that I want from you right now?— after out walk on the beach, which—by the way—was less than an hour ago."

"I was hoping so."

Nodding his head, he sighs as he leans against the sofa. He folds his arms across his broad chest and faces forward, not bothering to look at me. I sit back with him, confused on what else to say. Why would he expect more from me? I don't need more right now. I just need to be myself—to be free.

"I take it someone's hurt you before. It's the only reason a girl would want "*just sex.*" If she's been hurt or if she's a prostitute." He turns to look at me, his mystic eyes sparkling from the streaks of moonlight again. "Which one are you, Natalie?"

My heart pounds heavily as I look away from him. I squeeze my hands together, feeling the tears begging to be shed. But I won't release them. I won't let the memories of Bryson take over me and my emotions and ruin my night. I turn to face Nolan again. His eyes are soft, begging for an answer. "I shouldn't have come here," I mumble, standing to snatch my shirt off the floor.

"Whoa—*what?*" Nolan stands from the sofa quickly to get to me. "What do you mean? You don't have to leave, Natalie."

"I know, but you want more and I can't give you more—" I break off as I tug my shirt over my head. I stare into Nolan's eyes and a swarm of guilt overwhelms me. "Nolan, I can't give you more right now. To be honest, all I wanted tonight was to forget about my problems—to just have fun with someone else for a change."

"I can provide the fun. You don't have to leave."

"But with that, there's a price to pay. I—I can't do it with you right now. You hardly even know me."

His mouth opens again, as if he wants to speak, but after a moment it snaps shut. Although Nolan and I did hit it off tonight during out little walk on the beach, I can't do that to myself.

He's a great person, inside and out. Harper ditched me for the really hot guy that had come with Nolan to the club so we bailed as well. I know I said some things I shouldn't have that probably led to why he wants something more with me, but now I regret being so drunk and stupid. Now I regret chasing after him, dancing all over him, and leading him on. I chose him because I thought he would keep it at a distance. I was dead wrong.

I grab my shoes then head for the door. "You're not from here, Natalie." Sighing, he reaches for his keys that he tossed on the coffee table when we first got in. "At least, let me take you home."

I turn to face him, nodding.

He marches through the living room, still shirtless as he steps past me and opens the door. Not once does he look back at me as he makes his way down the hallway with his head down, raking his fingers through his hair before he meets the stairs. With an aggravated groan, I clutch my keys in hand before shutting the door behind me.

Chapter Five

A banging noise startles me and I'm not sure if it's my throbbing skull or something else entirely. The banging happens again and I groan, removing the white sheets from over my face. The sun blazes through the window, blinding me at first sight. I can't believe I got that drunk last night. I can hardly remember a thing—well except the part where I pretty much rejected Nolan, flat out.

I still can't believe that happened.

The banging is louder this time and along with it is the sound of Harper's voice. "Nat! Let me in! I lost my key!"

I perk myself up, shielding my eyes from the sun as I swing my legs around and drop my feet on the floor. My bare feet drag along the carpet before pressing against the hardwood floorboards that lead me to the door. I unlock it, swing it open, and my hangover subsides, my eyes broadening at the sight of Harper.

My mouth gapes, disbelieving how matted her hair is. A pair of dark, bug-eyed sunglasses are covering her eyes but I'm sure her makeup is ruined. "What in the hell happened to you?" I ask as she steps past me.

A low, aggravated groan is her response. She tosses her clutch on the sofa then heads for the balcony window to shut the blinds. "There's too much sun today. My fucking head hurts," she growls.

"Someone's grumpy." I make my way towards the sofa to slump down.

"Beyond it," she mutters before sitting down with me. She snatches her sunglasses off and I was right. Her eye makeup is completely ruined.

"Want some coffee?"

"That would be amazing," she breathes.

I nod, pressing my lips together before hopping from the couch to get to the kitchen. I'll wait until later for her to spill the beans. Harper usually tells me when something is wrong without the need to ask. The only time she won't tell me something right away is if she's ashamed of what she's done. I figure she's done something terrible. Harper is beyond a party animal and when she's drunk, it's worse.

"Nat, what do you say we go to the beach later on today?" she asks from the living room.

The beach? I'm not really up for that. "I haven't unpacked, Harper."

"Screw unpacking, Natalie." Her voice sounds closer and it isn't too long before she's prancing her way into the kitchen. "You're going to be with me for months—plus you don't even have that much to unpack. Why are you making excuses for yourself?" Her eyes thin into slits as she folds her arm. "You should be more than ready to get out and live it up."

I shake my head, forcing myself to keep my eyes from her as I start the coffee machine. I search through all the cabinets to look for the ground coffee but she steps past me, reaching into a cabinet beside me to pull a can down.

"Nat." Her voice is stern. I hate when she gets all serious on me. But I can't say I didn't see it coming. She told me before I had even arrived that she would come up with a million ways to get me to stop thinking about Bryson. I guess taking me out is her strategy. "Talk to me," she begs as her eyes soften but it's hard to fall for it this time because her smeared makeup makes her look like a night-demon.

I snort a laugh, peeling the top from the coffee can.

"What in the hell is so funny? I'm being serious."

"No—it's not that," I say, still sneering. "It's just... well... you look like shit, Harp."

Her face depresses while she reaches up to smooth her matted hair. "I know. Don't remind me," she groans.

"What happened to you?"

She thinks on it, her glass-blue eyes zoning in on me. "I won't tell you unless you promise to go to the beach with me."

"Oh, we're bargaining now?" I raise an eyebrow, placing the lid down to cross my arms.

"If it will bring some life into you." She studies my eyes, pressing her dry lips together. "Nat, I know you're still hurt. I know you want to forget about him, but you never will if you're stuck inside wallowing over him." I look away from her, forcing myself to hold back on the tears that are threatening to spill. My throat lacks with moisture and my hands turn into fists beneath the pit of my arms before I turn away from her. "Natalie, please. I'll beg you if I have to." I take a peek at her and now her eyebrow is raised, letting me know she will beg without holding back. I know better than to test Harp. She's always been a person of her word.

"Damn it. Fine," I groan.

"Yes," she breathes out victoriously. "Trust me, I will get that fucker off your mind one way or another." Clutching my wrists, she turns to make her way out of the kitchen. "Come on. We have to freshen up—and I have to find some damn Advil. We can catch some Frappuccino's from Starbucks on the way."

"Oh—that reminds me, Harp."

She continues to drag me along and doesn't stop until she's in her bedroom. "What?"

"I don't have a bathing suit."

Her lips stretch to reveal all of her pearly white teeth. "Stay here," she says before rushing away from me to get to her closet. She steps back out within a second with a teal and white two-piece bikini on a hanger. The tags are still on it and it seems a size too big for her. "It's for you. Your favorite color!"

"*What?*" I shake my head. "You bought me a bathing suit?"

"Hell yeah. I knew you weren't going to bring one or buy one so I picked one out for you. Grace told me you weren't planning on wearing one. I swear I love that girl," she sighs. "I have to tell you, though, I'm glad you're still the same size."

"Harper, that's a bit too much."

"That may be so," she quips, "but at least I was thinking about you. Consider it a gift for your arrival." She grins then steps forward to hand me the bathing suit. "I'm sure it looks better on. Go try it."

I frown, clutching the hanger in my hand as I turn for my bedroom. "Right after a shower," I mutter.

***

"Harper, what in the hell is this?" I hiss as soon as our feet touch the sand. Loud music flows with the wind, along with millions of colorful beach balls being tossed in the air.

Harper glances over her shoulder, giving me her famous pleading eyes. "I knew if I said it was a beach *party*, you wouldn't have come."

"Harp—"

"Nat!" She turns to look at me, her pleading eyes now scolding. "You're going to have fun with me. Fuck Bryson and screw your self-wallowing. The old Natalie is still in there somewhere. All she needs is a few drinks and she's as good as new." I press my lips together, scowling at her with demented eyes. She shrugs. "Give me the devil eyes all you want. You know it's true."

She grabs my hand, then leads the way towards the crowd. I guess Harper is right. I need fun. I need to forget. I still feel guilty about last night—about Nolan. I know he'll never forgive me, but my only hope is I never see him again. I guess that's why I'm so bothered about being at this beach party. Because I know he might be around. He seems like the type who knows about every party or event that goes down.

The music grows louder as we hit the edge of the crowd. Harper releases my hand and I step to her side as we stick together, pushing through to get to the center. I've been to a beach party once before and it was the best party ever. It was during spring break of my senior year. So many people were there, the bands were great, and the drinks were fantastic. Of course, we were under age and the police came as soon as they heard the noise but it was amazing. But that's one of the memories I have to bury because when the police showed up, I was with Bryson and we ran away together. We made love that night, too.

The memory attacks my heart, wrapping around it and squeezing like the grip of an anaconda. I force myself to think of something else and luckily I can because we've stopped in the center of the whole crowd. Everyone rocks together heavily, jumping up and down, rocking side to side to the band on stage.

"We should get some drinks," Harper shouts, standing on her toes to find the nearest bar. She spots one, points at it, and then grabs my hand again before pushing through the sea of bodies until we're clear. The bar is small and set in a tiki-hut theme. The bartender happens to be a beautiful guy with a firm, tanned chest, blonde hair, and a pair of blue swimming trunks on. He flashes a smile at us as we reach the counter.

"Hi," Harper breathes as she studies him. She bats her eyelashes and his lips hint at a small smile.

"Hi, ladies. What can I help you with?" he asks, pulling the rag away from the counters.

"We'd just like a few shots, if possible," Harper says.

With a flirtatious tone, he asks, "How many, exactly?"

Harper looks from him to me. I sigh, sitting on the stool as I hold up two fingers. "Two for me."

"Two for me, too," Harper mumbles.

"What kind of vodka?"

"Um... how about you choose for us," Harper says, her eyes brightening against her newly applied makeup. She looks at me for reassurance.

I nod as the bartender reaches for four shot glasses from under the counter. He turns to grab a bottle of clear liquid, pours some into each glass, and then slides them towards us. "All yours, ladies." He winks, screwing the cap on the bottle again. A few more customers step up to the counter and he leaves us for them.

"He's hot, huh?" Harper turns to look at me as soon as he's out of ear shot.

"Very." I nod. The guy really is hot. His body is sculpted perfectly, his smile is dazzling. He has the simple charm girls would love—but who knows what his background story may be. He could be a player, a cheater, or even just a natural born heart breaker. I shake my head, reaching for a glass quickly. Ever since Bryson cheated on me, I've made it a bad habit of believing every guy on earth is a low-down dirty dick.

I chuck my drink back and my face pinches as it burns the heart of my throat. I ignore the burning as I reach for my second one, knock it down, but this time it isn't as rough.

"Natalie, slow down," Harper complains, her eyes narrowing at me before she takes a look at my empty shot glasses.

"Why? Isn't this what you wanted? The party Natalie?"

"Yes, but—" Her eyes widen as she looks over my shoulder. Her mouth gapes and her face turns pale, as if she's just seen a ghost. Studying the horror in her eyes, I frown before turning around to see who she may be looking at.

At first I don't see anyone, but when I spot the molded tan chest, the soft grey eyes, and his hair, which is most likely slick from water, my heart fails to beat. He's talking to some girl, but I'm not paying attention to that. He looks un-fucking-believable. With a shirt, he was already hot, but without one... all I can think is the word *damn*. His abs are glistening, shining from tanning oils. His white swimming trunks hug his hips and the bulge between his legs that I had a feel of last night seems extremely large today. He flashes a sparkling smile at the girl he's talking to and she grins, most likely melting to the core because I'm melting just by staring at him.

"It's him," Harper mumbles. She grabs her shot glasses, chugs them down, slams some money on the counter, and then heads for the crowd again. "Come on, Nat!" I hop from my stool to rush for Harper, but before I can meet with her, her face is struck with horror again as she stares off to her left.

A guy with black swimming trunks on, long and wavy sandy-blonde hair, and a nipple piercing makes his way towards her. I stop in my tracks, taking in this familiar stranger. The ring in the bottom right corner of his mouth gives depth to his full, pink lips. His dark eyes are hooded, soft as he stares at Harper and his lips are graced with a sweet smile. What is Harper so afraid of? Why does she look like she's watching someone being brutally murdered? She finally tears her gaze away from him to look at me, her eyes begging for help but I'm too confused to know what she needs help from.

"Harper," the stranger finally says, craning his arms around her waist to pull her in. Her smile is forced, but I can tell she's enjoying his touch, his body, and everything else about him. Her eyes shut briefly before she opens them again and pulls away.

"I wasn't expecting to see you here," he says. I continue to stare at the familiar stranger but as he continues to chat with Harper, I realize who he is. He's the one Harper was dancing with—the one who was standing against the wall with Nolan last night.

Oh, shit.

I turn to my left slowly to see if Nolan is still around and it's just my luck he's disappeared. I sneak my way back towards the bar, turning slowly to retrieve my seat, but as I spin completely, someone catches me and holds me back by the upper arms before I can clash into them. Their hands are strong and their arms look somewhat too familiar. My eyes travel from the length of his arms, up to his broad chest, until I finally reach sight of the lips that were pressed against mine last night.

"Natalie?" I finally look into the grey eyes I'm not too pleased to see. He sounds surprised to see me.

"Nolan," I breathe, pretending I'm glad to see him.

He releases his hold from my upper arms to cross his, along with a smirk. "Now I see why you rejected me last night."

"What do you mean?"

"You're a party girl."

I shake my head. "I'm actually not. I just tend to get dragged to these kind of events."

"No one forces you to go anywhere, Natalie. Just like I didn't force you to come to my apartment last night." He tilts his head, his glassy eyes gleaming. "Or to have sex with me."

"Okay—please just stop." I shake my head swiftly. "If I've upset you, I'm sorry, but I told you I can't."

"Well, can I get a little bit more depth of why you can't?"

"What do you mean *depth*?" I snap, my forehead creasing heavily.

"Of why I was rejected—of why you wanted *just sex* from me." He presses his lips firmly, waiting on a response. "I can understand continuous *just sex* with the same person, but *you* requesting a one-night-stand... that's what completely catches me off guard."

"It's a very long and personal story—"

"You know, I thought about it last night," he says, cutting me off mid-sentence. "And I think I know what it is because I've experienced what you're going through."

"What are you talking about?"

"You know exactly what I'm talking about. You're heartbroken and you're keeping your guard up."

He stares at me, his eyes firm with confidence. "And how would you know that?" I ask.

"Well, I was just hoping you weren't a prostitute," he sighs. "I would much rather you be a brokenhearted girl than a night streaking whore. I can't get through to a hoe, but a broken heart— well, those can be easily mended with time."

"That still doesn't change anything, Nolan."

"I know." Then, unexpectedly, he pulls me against him, placing a hand against my hip while his other hand slides under my hair to hold onto the nape of my neck. He tilts my head back gently, moving his lips in closer to mine. "But I can make you change your mind. I can make you reconsider." His lips inch closer but I pull away, refusing to let him kiss me. But he obviously has other plans because his muscles tighten to keep me in his grasp. His teeth sink into his bottom lip and just by his hold and his seductive eyes, my body is melting cell by cell. "I've already had a taste of your lips last night, Natalie. Why not do it again?"

"I was drunk," I mutter.

"But you liked it. You said it." He pulls back to study my eyes. He's right. I did love the plushness of his lips, the taste of the alcohol on his sweet tongue. He tasted delicious. But I'll never admit it to him.

"I have to get back to Harper." He releases me but his chest is close to mine.

"I don't think Harper needs you right now." He folds his arms and looks past me.

I turn around quickly only to spot Harper now making out with the guy who caused her face to look like a blank sheet of paper just a few moments ago. *Damn it, Harp!*

"What is up with you two?" I snap.

"We're just ourselves, and you party girls hate it."

"Ugh, whatever." I begin to turn and walk off, but he catches my arm to reel me back in. His head tilts as he studies my face, slithering a hand on top of my shoulder. Leaning in, he places his lips against my ear. "One chance, Natalie. That's all I'm asking for. If you don't like it, then I'll leave you alone for good because at least I had the opportunity of getting to know you." He pulls back and my skin pricks. It's even hotter now. "You can't just reject me like this. I'll only continue to find you." A smug smile creeps across his lips. *Hmm... Sounds kind of stalkerish.* "So, what do you say?"

I pause, hesitating on my answer. I know he won't leave me alone. Even if I were to say no, he'll keep popping into my life. He knows where Harper and I live. I can't hide out at her place. There's nowhere I can go and nothing I can do about it. Harper will continue to drag me out and I'll continue seeing this beautiful man who will keep begging me for a chance.

"Just one chance?" I finally ask.

"Only one." He smiles as he releases me.

"Fine. Only one. But don't expect much from me."

"Oh, I already know not to expect much from you. I don't expect to get anything from you, actually." I cringe. *Ouch.* Harsh, but true. "We'll go as friends—if that'll help."

"Yeah," I breathe. "As friends sounds much better."

He nods, his lips pressing together. "Alright. What do you say I pick you up around seven tonight? When the party's clear we can take a walk on the beach, catch a bite to eat... something simple."

I nod, biting on a smile. To be honest, that sounds amazing. He isn't trying too hard to do this. He wants it to be casual with no feelings involved. I'll accept his offer, although I already know he'll try to make his move a few times. But it's only one time. After tonight, I won't have to worry about him anymore.

"Okay." I grin.

Chapter Six

I'm still debating on whether I should wear more than mascara and lip gloss. Those are my casualties. I wear nothing more than that. No foundation, no eyeliner... just mascara and lip gloss. Gracey always told me I never needed the extra stuff. She reminded me every day that I was beautiful. I won't be a Debbie-Downer and say I'm not. I just don't like to make it an obvious fact. Not everyone may think of me as pretty or beautiful. But I can tell you right now Bryson did.

I hate how I'm thinking about him, but when I feel like I'm at my lowest, memories of him telling me how gorgeous I am flood my mind. But I couldn't have been gorgeous enough because he cheated on me—with someone who can't even compare. Sara Manx was truly hideous and she hid behind so much make up that she could have turned into a bag of makeup herself.

"No one is going to choose her," Sara hissed to one of her friends as I passed by. A smug smile tingled at my lips as I looked over my shoulder.

"Maybe we should take classes on whispering, huh, Sara?" I stopped in the middle of the school hallway to face her.

"Maybe we should take classes on being an interesting girlfriend, huh, Natalie?"

I cringed, but scowled. If there was one thing I always worried about, it was being a boring girlfriend to Bryson. I felt so uninteresting because he was my first at everything. He took my virginity, he had my first kiss. He was my everything. I guess that's why I was so in love with him. "You're a bitch, Sara. You're the one who's not gonna win." I felt so immature for arguing with her. If only I'd known how stupid I was making myself look.

"I look better, though," Sara countered. "I mean, really. Look at you," she scoffed, looking me over in my loose blue jeans and grey hoody. "You look like complete shit. Like a bag of fucking garbage. I don't know what Bryson's thinking. I could do him so much better." She flicked her blonde hair over her shoulder, then turned to look at her friend. "Come on, Danielle. We've got a pageant to practice for." Sara looked over her shoulder to scowl at me once more before walking away.

I shook my head as I turned around. I don't know why I had let Sara get to me like that. She was a bitch and she was obviously jealous of me. She would say anything to get under my skin. But this time she really had me because I knew Bryson could do better than me.

Bryson was perfect in so many ways. He had the perfect smile, the perfect cropped black hair that would be perfectly untamed. He had the sexiest body I always found myself drooling over. If someone were to ask me to describe him, I would start with his height. Bryson is six-foot-three. I find the height of a man the most appealing. He has to be way taller than me. It's a must when choosing a guy. His hair was always gelled in style. His eyes are a bright green I'd always fallen in love with— especially with his long eyelashes. He had the best abs from working out every single day and his smile could make a girl tumble over and collapse. Every feature on his face was beyond perfect.

Which is why I drove to his house immediately for comfort.

I banged on the door and he swung it open. He was in the middle of playing his XBOX with Mark but when he saw it was me, he told Mark to shut the game off and to go downstairs.

"What's the matter, Nat? What happened?" he asked, leading me towards his bed.

"Sara—I fucking hate her," I growled.

"What happened?" he asked with a small smile. I could tell that he was trying not to laugh at my childish reply. But he had the right to laugh. I was being immature and idiotic, if I say so myself. He laced his fingers through mine and tilted my chin. "What did she say?"

"You know how I feel like I'm not enough for you, Bryson?" His eyebrows elevated. "She reminds me of that every single day. I hate how she can get under my skin like that. Anything she says about our relationship negatively just kills me."

"Why?"

"Because sometimes I feel like what she says is true."

"Well it's not," he mumbled. He reached forward, running the back of his hand across my cheek. "I love you, Natalie Fiona Carmichael. Nothing will ever change that—not even that crazy bitch Sara." I giggled lightly before he slid in and placed a soft kiss on my lips. "Nothing will tear us apart. You're more than enough for me. Sometimes I feel like I'm not enough for you, but if we feel the same way about each other, it must mean we really are in love, right?" His next kiss was a passionate one. He pulled me in closer, cradled me in his arms, and then laid me back. It wasn't too long before we were making out and after making out, we made love—or so I

*thought it was love. To me it was love. To him... I'm
not quite sure what it was called.*

Tears prick at my eyes as I try to rid my mind of
the memory. I try to shake it off but it's just too
damn hard. That night, Bryson and I made incredible
love. I can't even describe it. Every position was
heaven to me. He knew exactly how to please me.
And I guess that's what I'm afraid of with Nolan. I'm
so torn because I feel like Bryson is the only one
who really knows me.

I don't want to be learned about by someone
else. I don't want anyone to realize how much of a
bitch I am, how stubborn I can get, how terrible my
flaws really are, or how hard it is for me to make
friends. Harper has been my friend since the
sandbox days and the only reason Grace and I are so
close is because she was my lab partner in biology
since freshman year.

Bryson really understood me, personally and
mentally. Which is why it's so hard to let him go. I
want to let go, but I don't want to move on from
how comfortable I was with him. I'm so confused
that I feel terrible for myself.

I can't gain feelings for someone else, especially
for someone like Nolan. He's stunning, and to catch
feelings for someone like him is pretty much asking
for my heart to be ripped out completely. It can't be

shattered any more than it already is. I can heal myself if I just do what Harper is doing. If I go out, party, get drunk, then I'll forget. I won't have to worry when I'm not sober. If I can, I'll become an old drunk hag who doesn't give a shit about her life or her appearance...

Ugh. Okay. Who the hell am I kidding? I would never stoop that low. I'm not that damn broken to just lose track of myself.

"Nat!" Harper screeches from the living room. I blink rapidly, snapping back into reality as I place my mascara down on the bathroom counter and rush for the living room.

"What?" I ask quickly. As I round the corner, I spot her standing in the middle of the living room staring at the screen of her phone. Her eyes are wide and her face is just like how it was earlier: as if she's just seen a ghost. "What's going on?" I ask as I step to her side.

She groans before finally looking at me. "It's the guy from the beach! He said he won't stop texting or calling me unless I agree to go on a date with him."

I frown. "The hot guy with the nipple and lip piercing?"

"Yeah," she breathes. She slumps down on the couch with another groan. "His name is Dawson.

But I can't go out with him." She shakes her head swiftly.

I sit down with her. "Why not?"

"Because—I just can't, Natalie." Her phone buzzes and as she checks the screen, she lets out a low growl. "See! This is why! He's too clingy when he doesn't know shit about me! I could be a killer for heaven's sake!"

"Well maybe he wants to get to know you. What exactly is he asking for?"

"He just wants to go on a date with me. But Nat... I've been in Miami for way too long. I pretty much know a guy's motive when I see them coming. I can't take a date seriously here. I moved here to have fun and to party my ass off for my college years. I'm still young and I'm not tired of going out yet. But Dawson... he's different. He's not like them and it's hard as hell to read him."

"It's just one date, Harp. It can't be too bad. Just tell him what you've told me."

"I have!" she wails. "I've told him I'm not interested but he always does something that will make me momentarily change my mind —just like earlier at the beach. I told him to stop talking to me, but then he just... kissed me... and I *liked* it."

"Wow," I breathe.

"Yeah. I don't wanna get fucked over again. Even thought I can't read him, he seems like *that* kind of guy." Harper's head lowers as she stares at her phone. Harper and I are in the same situation, but unlike me Harper decided to live it up after her heartbreak instead of wallowing about it.

Harper's heart was broken by a guy in high school and ever since then, she hasn't dated anyone. She doesn't want to believe in true love but we both know it's out there. We were both fooled by love completely. We were blinded and we didn't even realize how deep we were until it ended. "But I knew you and that hot guy from the club had something going on. I'm not stupid," she mutters.

"It's not like that, Harp." I sigh. "Trust me. After this one date, there will be no more. I can't get too caught up with a guy like him. You saw him. He's too beautiful to only want me."

"You never know," she chimes. "He may actually want someone to settle down with."

"Well, that's the thing. I don't want to settle down again... especially right now."

"You just don't want to 'cause you're still stuck on Bryson the Shitbag."

"You're one to talk!" I say, pinching her thigh playfully. "You don't want Dawson because you're still stuck on Bobby the Dickhead."

She frowns. "I'm not stuck. I just don't wanna fall again. I can't. With Dawson, I'll have no other choice. We really hit it off the other night but… I don't know. I can't. I'm afraid."

"That's the same way I feel about Nolan."

"Well maybe you could both just be friends with strong benefits," Harper inquires. "I've been thinking about doing that with Dawson. He was extremely, *extremely*, good in bed." Her eyes expand as she looks at me.

"No," I shake my head. "Because when the benefits fade, that's when love shows up. I can't afford it." I hop from the sofa to make my way towards the bathroom. "I have to finish getting ready," I call over my shoulder.

But I'm honestly not going back to just get ready. I still have two hours left. I'm really going back to reminisce about Bryson the Shitbag. He may have been a Shitbag afterwards, but before he was rather amazing.

Chapter Seven

About two hours later and Nolan is knocking at the door. As soon as I swing it open, my immediate reaction is to smile.

"Hi." I grin.

"Hi." He grins back. My eyes travel from his dark hair and his beautiful, chiseled features, down to his yellow muscle T-shirt and dark jeans that are snug on his hips. I happen to stare at his chest the most. Even with his shirt on, I feel like I'm staring at the abs I saw earlier this afternoon.

"Are you ready?" he asks, clutching his keys.

"Yeah." I nod as I tear my gaze away from his lean body. "Let me just grab my phone and my wallet."

"Your wallet?" His eyebrows pull together. "What do you need your wallet for?"

"Um, to pay for my food," I mumble with a hint of sarcasm.

"I'll be damned if I let you pay for *anything* while you're with me. Come on," he demands, cocking his head to the right.

"Nolan—"

"Natalie." He raises an eyebrow as his smile fades. "I'm serious. Bring your pretty ass on."

I choke on a laugh, staring at him with bewildered eyes. "I'm still bringing my wallet—I always do. Just in case." I grab it, then head out the door before shutting it behind me and locking the condo up.

"Okay." Nolan sighs, following after me to get to the elevator. "But if you try to pull it out and pay for *anything*, I'm tossing it."

I press the down button belonging to the elevator before I turn to face him. The doors shoot open immediately and we step into the cart but my eyes don't drift from his. "What is up with you? What's wrong with me paying for myself?"

"I asked *you* to come out with *me,* which means *I'm* paying. First impressions, and all." The doors of the elevator slide shut but my gaze doesn't tear away from his. Pressing his lips together, he forms a dazzling smirk. His smirk causes me to whip my head. That smile... I can't fall for that smile. It's enough to knock the wind right out of me. "So, I guess I'll start with the small talk," he says, shifting to lean against the silver walls of the elevator. "How has your day been?"

"Great," I breathe.

"Just great?"

"Just great."

Just as he nods, the elevator stops and the doors shoot open. He holds a hand out, gesturing for me to step out before him. I walk out, making my way towards the glass door but before I can grab the handle, Nolan stops me by the hook of my arm. "Natalie," he says, turning me around to face him. He pulls me against him and our bodies plunge. The heat radiates from his chest, seeping through my thin white blouse. His scent fills my lungs, making me want to mold with him even more. "I didn't want you to come out with me if you weren't really up for this." His eyes are serious as he stares into mine. "I don't want you to think you're doing me a favor."

"I know I'm not doing you a favor," I retort.

"Really?" he asks rhetorically. "'Cause you're acting like I'm dragging you out with me. If you want, we can turn around. I can let you go back up to your condo and we can forget all about this whole thing. You won't have to worry about me anymore."

I shake my head, feeling the guilt take over. "It's not that, Nolan. You don't understand how hard this is for me."

"I can't understand if you don't tell me what's really going on with you."

I groan. I can't tell him. If I start to tell him, I'll never stop. It'll be enough to make him run away and forget about me for good. Hmm... Maybe it's exactly what I need to do.

"How about this?" he says. "You take this night seriously and I'll help you forget about whatever it is that's bothering you. Honestly, you won't be able to have fun if you're stuck on something that's irrelevant. I want to have fun tonight—as friends. Like I said."

He places a hand on top of my shoulder and squeezes it lightly. I stare into his grey eyes that are now begging. Ugh. Why is he so damn beautiful? I have no choice but to say yes.

"Okay. I'm sorry," I mumble as I pull away from him. I force a smile as I turn to grab the door handle. A deep chuckle comes from the heart of his throat as he follows me outside. I can give a guess at why he's laughing.

Because I'm a brokenhearted broad who doesn't know what to do with herself.

Chapter Eight

With every push, every stroke, I was suffocated with desire. He kept going harder, faster, way too quickly for me to keep up. I was worn out but I was enjoying it. I ran my fingers across the beads of sweat on his chest with one hand while the other was braided through the locks of his hair. He kept grunting. I loved when he groaned while staring into my eyes. He was beautiful in so many ways possible.

"I love you," Bryson murmured huskily before leaning down to place his lips on my ear. His tongue began to play with the lobe of my ear, tickling its way down to my neck. From that moment on, I knew I was his forever.

He kept plunging into me, keeping my hands locked above my head. The heat of his lips was still hovering above mine but he didn't stop... and I knew he wasn't going to for a while. It was beyond late and the night was still, but our moans, groans, and the slightly creaking bed filled the silence. I loved the noise we created. It was harmonious. I asked him if he wanted to play music but he refused. He said the only thing he wanted to hear was the pleasure of my moans.

That was my first time, but the first time is one I'll never forget. There was just something about it—something that was telling me he actually did love me. But how did it all change? Why would he flip on me like that? It's crazy how I thought we were actually going to last. I never thought anything would get between us. Apparently, I had it all wrong.

"You're awfully quiet." I turn quickly to look at Nolan who already has his eyes locked on me. I was so out of it that I didn't even realize the car had stopped. We're now sitting in the parking lot of a familiar restaurant.

My head whips to look at Nolan but there's something blocking me from seeing him. A warm wetness prickles at the rims of my eyes and now I realize what's blurring my vision. My tears. "Hey," he breathes, unbuckling his seatbelt and reaching for me quickly. I keep my eyes away from his and decide to stare at my lap instead. I blink quickly, fanning the tears away. I can't cry in front of him. He'll definitely think I'm crazy. Well, maybe I am.

After a few moments, the tightness in my throat ceases and my vision is no longer blurred.

"I'm fine." I look up slowly to meet his eyes.

His remain confused. He looks me over for another few seconds before letting out a heavy sigh. "Is it me?" he asks.

"No!" I shake my head as the abruptness in my voice catches us both off guard. "I'm fine. I just need to eat... I guess."

"You guess?" One of his eyebrows shoots up. "Natalie, what is going on with you?"

I shake my head, feeling the tremble threatening to take over my bottom lip. I seriously can't hold this in anymore. But if I tell him, what will he think of me afterwards? He may regret this date and even regret meeting me. My emotions are completely fucked up right now. Nolan's sigh cuts my train of thought off. "Look, let's just go eat. Okay?"

I nod, but I don't think he sees because he's already turning to get out the car. His door shuts behind him and I let out a deep breath of relief. *Just stop thinking about him, Natalie*, I tell myself. I'm telling it to myself but it's impossible. I've been telling myself this for a month and at one point, it worked but it lasted for no more than a few hours. I had to start writing poems one day. Writing poems are my escape. Every emotion I feel, every ounce of pain, heartache, and the agonizing fear that I may be alone forever is what I would scribble out. The writing picked up after Bryson and I broke up. All the poems I'd written about my relationship with him before (when we were happy) are now stored away in the back of my trunk. When I would read over them, I wanted to rip them to shreds and throw them away, but then I thought about it and I couldn't do it. I just couldn't come to grips with letting go. I needed something to hold on to.

Writing the heartbreaking poems was the worst, but it brought out a lot within me. I had unleashed a load of untamed emotions. I jotted them all down on paper. At times, I didn't understand what I was writing but after I would re-read it over a million times, I would know what I was getting at. My poems only prove how confused I really am about all of this. Those poems are deep and writing them only makes me wallow in grief about him. I wish he didn't matter to me. I wish there was no such thing as a broken heart. I never wanted to have one, which is why I worked so hard to keep our relationship going.

It isn't too long before Nolan swings my door open, scaring the hell out me. "Are you just going to sit in here?"

I reach for my wallet quickly before stepping out with him. He shuts my door behind me but he doesn't bother to make his way towards the restaurant in front of us that I now realize is *Steak 'N Shake*.

I turn to face him. "Are you not hungry?"

"We're not going in there until you tell me what that was about." His face hardens as he lifts his left leg up to place the sole of his shoe against the passenger door of his red Mustang.

"Does it really matter?" I grumble.

"It matters completely, Natalie."

Ugh. Why does he have to say my name like that? Why does he have to pose like that against his car? He truly does look like he could belong in a Hollister magazine. "We should just eat." I turn to make my way towards the restaurant but he steps around me, stopping me from taking my next step.

"Natalie." His hand sneaks its way up to brush a strand of hair behind my ear. He studies my face, eyes wide. He scans me as he breathes softly and a small smile spreads across his lips. His head angles in a way that confuses me on whether he's pleased or aggravated. As he stares at me, I can feel the sincerity radiating from his body. "Who's hurt you?" he murmurs, his lips extremely close, and to my surprise, it isn't uncomforting.

"No one," I lie.

"I don't believe you." His arm then hooks around my waist. "To be honest, I'm starting not to believe anything you say."

"Well," I breathe as I find the will to pull away from him, "if you think I'm a liar, why are we on a date?"

"Number one," he chuckles, lifting a justified finger. "This isn't a date. You made it very clear a date isn't what you wanted." My face falls as I stare into his eyes. "And number two, I never called you a liar. Now you're just putting words into my mouth."

My mouth clamps shut as his lips form a smug smile. I can't believe this. He's completely shut me up. That's a first. I usually want the last word in everything... but I can't now. I can't get the last word because he's right. I'm considering this a date, but he's not. He's doing just what he said.

"Can we just go eat?" I snap.

Nolan stares at me for a few moments before he finally turns around. He lifts a hand, gesturing for me to walk ahead of him. I press my lips together as I step past him and make my way up the path leading to the sidewalk. As I meet the glass door, Nolan beats me to it by rushing forward to swing it open.

"First impressions, and all," he says, wiggling his eyebrows.

I fight the urge to smile back before stepping in. There's just something about him. He's so simple it kills me. I suppose I could go along with this. He's says it's not a date, but I know it's what he's aiming for. I have to give this a shot. I only have *one* life to live and I'm only going to be sharing *one* night with him. Why not make the best of it?

As soon as I step inside, a young, skinny guy with shaggy brown hair greets us. "Two?" he says. My eyebrows pull together as I stare into his eyes, confused by what he means. "Never mind." His cheeks burn a bright scarlet. "Right this way."

He leads us towards a corner booth located against the wall. No one else is around the area and it's a good thing because I don't want anyone to hear me spaz out on Nolan if he tries anything silly tonight.

I slide against the seat of the booth and Nolan sits across from me. His masculine fragrance whiffs past my nostrils and I breathe him in, allowing his scent to fill my lungs. He smells so delectable.

"Can I... um... start you off with some drinks?" the waiter asks.

"Is this your first day?" Nolan asks him.

With a wary smile, the young waiter reaches up to rub the back of his neck nervously. "Yeah. I'm kinda nervous."

Nolan nods. "I see. Don't worry. I'm not the type to cause a hassle." His eyes lower as they meet mine. "But her on the other hand... her outer shell may make you a bit frustrated." He quirks a smooth smile but I look away quickly at our waiter whose nametag reads *Michael.*

"Michael, I'd love a strawberry milkshake please. And don't worry," I say, looking from Michael to Nolan. "I'll be as sweet as candy. I always am. Some just try to have too much at once."

Michael nods quickly then looks at Nolan. "And for you?"

"I'll take what she's having." He winks. My eyes roll slightly.

"Be right back," Michael says then dashes away between the booths and tables.

As Michael disappears, I avoid immediate eye contact with Nolan. Nolan's sigh causes me to look up. I notice he's already staring at me—into my eyes—as if he's been waiting this entire time for me to look his way.

His head tilts. "Are you always this down?" he asks.

My eyebrows stitch. "I'm not down."

"Why did you have tears in your eyes, then? I'm pretty sure they weren't tears of joy." My chest tightens as I look away. "Seriously, Natalie. When I asked you to take this night seriously, I meant that. I want all or nothing."

"I can't give you my all, Nolan."

"Well… not exactly your all but, something more than what you're giving me now."

"What exactly am I giving you right now?"

He chuckles softly. "Um, let's see…" He places a hand on his chin, pretending to think. "Oh, yeah! That's right!" His hand jerks away from his chin so his fingers can snap. "Nothing! You're giving me nothing. No effort, no interest. Absolutely nothing. What changed from the night at the club?"

"Nothing changed. I was drunk that night. You can't expect me to act like I'm still some drunk and horny bitch."

His eyes broaden and it isn't too long before a smile snakes its way across his lips. "You'd be surprised how I feel when I hear you speak that way to me. I could take you out to my car right now and you wouldn't stop me." The spot between my thighs tightens as I stare at him. His lips are still quirked up as he observes the way my body has just tensed, his hand on his chin again. "See," he says. "There's my point. You want to hold off on me, but you can't."

"I can," I counter with a shake of my head. "I can hold off on whatever I want."

His eyes narrow softly as he nods. "Okay, if that's true, how about you spend tomorrow with me as well—after I get off work."

"What?" My curls flop as I shake my head again. "No. You said one night. This is it. After tonight there'll be no more. You promised."

"One: I didn't promise," he says, matter-of-factly. "And two: it doesn't have to be a date, Natalie. We can do what we're doing now. Have dinner and milkshakes... as *friends*."

"I know being friends isn't what you really want. I'm not stupid," I say in a near growl.

"Trust me," he sighs, pulling his hand away from his chin. "I know you're not stupid. If you were, those panties would have been mine already."

My mouth gapes, more heat sliding from my lower belly to the center of my legs. There's a flutter in my stomach but I force myself to turn the butterflies into knots. I shut my legs and at the moment I'm very thankful that I'm sitting because my knees would have buckled by now if I were standing. "Stop doing that," I hiss.

"Stop doing what?" he asks, his eyebrow rising smoothly.

"You know what you're doing."

He fixes his mouth to speak again but before he can, Michael steps up to the table with our milkshakes. "Here you are," Michael says. I can tell he's a bit more relaxed now since he knows we aren't a load of stuck-up and rude customers." Have you decided on what you want to eat yet?"

I shake my head. I've completely forgotten about the menus in front of me and even about eating in general because of my mini banter with Nolan.

"This may seem inappropriate," Nolan starts, eyeing me with his soft eyes. *Oh, no.* I gulp down the lump in my throat and force myself to look away. I know what he's about to say. I can pretty much read his mind. "But Natalie looks *delicious* tonight. I could *eat* her for hours. Any way you could put her on a platter for me?"

Shit. He's done it. Instead of heat this time, the spot between the middle of my legs moistens. I feel the warmth dampening my lace panties. Visions of Nolan's full, pink lips on my sweet spot makes my legs slightly tremble with pleasure beneath the table. Visions of him going for hours makes me crave for him even more.

"Um..." Michael is just as shocked as I am by Nolan's remark. His cheeks are red again and I'm sure mine are, too. Mine are on fire. "I'll give you two a minute," he says then rushes away again without looking back.

As Michael disappears into the kitchen, I try to pull myself together. I breathe through my nostrils and although I can feel Nolan's eyes on me, I manage to control myself. I can still feel him smiling sheepishly. He's done this on purpose.

"Agree to go on a real date with me tomorrow and I'll take things slowly, otherwise I'll show up at your doorstep and ask you every day. If I have to, I'll come in with you. I'll do *anything* to get to know you—anything to know what really goes on in that head of yours. Just give me a chance. A *real* chance. It's all I'm asking."

A low groan rumbles from the heart of my chest. I've already told him I can't give more. A date with him will only lead to more dates. Spending time with him will only lead us into trying to work things out. Although I don't like the feeling of being single, I definitely don't like the feeling of trying to commit to someone else so soon. I've learned my lesson on committing and it won't be happening for a while. And to be honest, I don't know anything about Nolan. I don't know his background, what he's been through, how he sees me. I don't know what he wants. I feel like he wants something other than *more* from me. But what could be more than *more*?

I look up at Nolan briefly then down at the whipped cream topping my milkshake. I wrap my hand around my glass but Nolan's hand stops me from moving any further. He places his on top of mine, grips it lightly, and I look up. His smile is humble and beautiful as it graces his lips. While softening his eyes, he studies every feature of my face. "Let's go for a walk on the beach. Get some fresh air. I'm sure that will open you up a bit."

I nod because taking in the beach breeze at this intense moment sounds fantastic. I could use a walk, considering the fact that my legs are crossed tightly to avoid any more dampness within my panties. "Sure," I breathe before pulling my hand away from his.

Chapter Nine

I gulp the night air down as I meet the shore. My eyes shut briefly as I allow the breeze push my hair back. It feels nice. Everything about beach weather makes me content, which is a part of the reason why I decided to move here with Harper. I love it at night especially because it's never too hot or too cold. This is one thing I won't let Bryson ruin.

Bryson always used to take me on beach trips. Sometimes he would do it for occasion and sometimes he would do it just for the hell of it. Myrtle Beach was only a few hours away from us so that's where we usually went. He would have a few older friends rent a hotel for us, gather a bunch liquor, and then we would drink until we couldn't even walk. Going to the beach drunk at night was the best. At night, no one would be around and it would be completely dark unless the moon decided to be close. Those beach nights were amazing to me. It sucks that memory has to be trashed as well.

"What are you thinking?" a soft voice murmurs from behind. Nolan steps to my side, his fingers tucked in his front pockets. His shoes are slightly buried within the sand.

"My past," I say softly. Somehow that response just slipped out. I suppose I could give into Nolan just a little. Just enough to the point where I can get some things off my chest.

"What about it?" he asks.

My head lowers as I let out a soft laugh. "Believe it or not, when I come to beaches this late at night, I think way too much."

"There's nothing wrong with thinking too much. I think a lot, too."

I look up at him but he's already looking down at me. "Why do you do it?"

Sighing, his eyes move from me to the massive body of water ahead. "I think about my past a lot, too. I think about my mom, my dad, my brother. My ex…" His voice lowers as he says his last sentence.

"Your ex?" I frown and now I want him to look me in the eye. "Why your ex?"

"Same reason you think about yours." I cringe. "The memories," he adds.

I tear my gaze away, refusing to look at him now. Is it really that obvious I think about Bryson constantly? It can't be. "What do you think of when you think about your ex?" I ask, turning to look at him slowly.

"How much I can't stand her guts. How bad she hurt me. How dumb I was to believe she actually loved me." Nolan's features fall as he pulls one of his hands out of his pockets to rake his fingers through his hair.

"Oh," I mumble. "I'm um . . . I'm sorry." My eyes soften naturally. I feel terrible for Nolan. But if he's heartbroken and still thinks about his ex, why does he want to get to know me so badly? "So if you feel that way, why do you want to go on a date with me again? What makes you think I wouldn't do the same thing?"

This time he turns to look at me. He presses in, thinning the gap between us. Reaching a hand up, he caresses my cheek gently. His touch is soft, caring. It causes the hairs of my spine to prick. My eyes shut briefly, actually admiring his touch. It isn't too long before his other hand wraps around my waist to pull me in and seal the gap completely. My eyelids fly open and I look up into his eyes. They're still gentle as he plays with the hairs behind my ear. My chest molds with his and my heartbeat thuds against my rib cage quickly as his lips inch in closer.

"I've wanted to kiss you again since the first night that I met you," he murmurs, the heat of his lips growing nearer.

"Why?" I ask softly.

"That first kiss was amazing," he breathes. I smile, and my cheeks spark. "Everything about you amazes me. What drew me in most was your stand-offish personality. I could see the hurt within you—I could feel it—but I tried to ignore it. Still am trying."

"I'm sorry for throwing myself at you," I blurt out, shaking my head. It's the first thing to come to mind. I've been thinking about how immature I was since last night.

His laughter is silent, but causes his shoulders to shake. "Don't apologize. I was actually kind of glad you did. But I have one question..."

"What?"

His head lowers and his lips are less than an inch away now. Although they aren't touching mine, I can feel them. I want to kiss him so damn bad. I want to drown with his lips and have him hold me as we kiss on the sand. I deserve to be held by someone that actually seems interested in me. "Can I kiss you again?"

He smiles and my head bobs up and down quickly before I wrap my arms around his neck and reel him in. I groan as his full, plush lips press against mine. I swear they feel amazing. The only person I can compare his lips to are Bryson's but Bryson has nothing on the way Nolan is kissing me right now. Nolan has a need, a want that I want to take advantage of at this very moment.

Nolan pulls his lips away to pick me up in his arms. He rushes toward the parking lot that's a few steps away, but I'm so dazed I refuse to fight it.

Placing me on the hood of his car, he parts my legs and maneuvers his way between them. He lays me down, placing light kisses on my neck and I groan as I clutch his firm forearms. The heat is spiraling; my panties are beyond damp right now. It's amazing how I don't even have to be drunk or in a stupor to want to go through with this. I want him to slide his way into me while pinning my arms above my head. I want him to go for hours and suffocate me with the hardness of his body. I want him to take advantage of every part of me. This is pure lust but this lust is truly hard to control.

Nolan's lips trail down to the curve of my white blouse but just as he is about to reach my breasts, he pulls away and just like the night I first met him, I frown. Why does he always do that? Why does he always fucking stop?

"Go on a real date with me please, Natalie." His husky voice makes my legs tighten around him. His hands are firmly planted on the hood of his car above me. His grey eyes are soft and glistening as he stares down at me. I observe his full lips, his broad chest, and his dark hair barely touching his forehead. He truly does look good right now. We could go for hours if he would just shut up about going on a date and just go through with it.

"Fine," I snap. I reel him back in but he pauses. He pecks my lips twice, looks into my eyes, and then pulls away.

"I always thought it was the men who were horndogs," he says, tugging his shirt down and adjusting his jeans.

"Are you kidding me?" My eyes thin into slits. "I'm practically giving myself to you but somehow you always find a way to stop. What is *wrong* with you?"

He chuckles, head shaking.

"Are you gay? Bi?" I ask in another snap.

That catches his attention. His eyes meet mine again, only this time they're hard. He glares at me and I spot his jaw tick way too many times to count. Then, grabbing me by the ankle, he slides me down the hood of his car. Good thing I have jeans on otherwise the slide would have been a little rough. Nolan picks me up in his arms again then sets me down in front of the passenger door. The gap closes between us when he crushes my lips with his.

A moan throttles in my throat, the fire burning me from head to toe. He picks me up by my waist but his lips don't bother to pull away from mine. His tongue lodges into my mouth quickly as I wrap my legs around his waist and my back presses against the cool window. *Damn he's really good with his lips.* Something hard and thick presses between the middle of my legs but when I realize what it is, I can't help but feel even more turned on. My panties are drenched entirely. I may have to get rid of these.

Nolan finally pulls away but before he does completely, his teeth sink into my lower lip and he tugs at it. I moan again before he pulls away to place my feet back on the ground. I'm surprised I can actually stand right now. That kiss was fucking amazing.

"Still think I'm gay?" he asks, his lips hinting at a sneer.

I press my lips together and pull them in to unnoticeably savor the taste of him. Chuckling, he digs in his front pocket to pull his keys out. "Come on. I know you're hungry. What do you say we go back to your place and make sandwiches?"

"Sure," I manage to breathe. How can I breathe? He's sucked all of the breath right out of me. I step back so Nolan can open my door then climb in before he shuts it behind me.

Right now, all I can think is... *damn*.

That was mind-blowing. Nolan must be a pro in this department. He's testing my limits, seeing how far I will go. He knows I will go all the way so what in the hell is he waiting for? Why is he trying to hold off? I'm practically begging him to bang me.

As he climbs in the car, his lips are still graced with a gentle smile. He starts the car, turns the headlights on, and then pulls out of the parking lot.

"I don't understand you," I say with a shake of my head.

"What do you mean?" He turns to look at me briefly before his eyes meet the road again.

"You've had two chances to have sex with me, but you didn't take them. You'll make out with me but that's as far as you'll go. Why?"

A small chuckle is his response.

I frown. "Are you a virgin?"

"Far from that, Natalie."

"Then what is it?" I snap. He really has me frustrated, both sexually and mentally.

"I don't want to be on the list of your regrets. I want to be the good guy. What can I say?" He shrugs, smirking.

"I wouldn't regret you, though."

"Are you sure about that?" he asks as we approach a red light. He turns to look at me, pulls in me in, and then kisses me. My legs quiver as he sucks my bottom lip then plunges his tongue into my mouth again.

"This part of you will only last for so long. I want to go on a real date and learn more about you. You can learn more about me as well. If you agree and things go well, then we can talk sex, but until then, I'll only continue to tease you. That's how people get hurt. When they rush into the sex."

"Why? I don't get it."

"Because I want *more* with you." His eyes darken just a bit, causing me to shudder only slightly. "Natalie," he breathes, taking his clipped tone down to a murmur, reaching to cup my cheek. "We've both been hurt before. Do you really think I'm that inconsiderate to put someone through the pain I've felt? There's something here for you. I told you this. As you sit beside me, as I speak with you, as you *breathe*, I know this can go far. Please. Just one date. One *real* date."

I groan as his eyes plead for him. Oh, how can I deny those eyes. "Fine."

He smiles. "I hope you're actually doing this to get to know me and not just for my dick," he quips.

My cheeks flush but two can play at this. "Maybe I want both."

Nolan lets out an obnoxious laugh and somehow it causes me to laugh as well. He has a contagious laugh. I've never heard him like this before. It's actually adorable. "Once I really know you, then I can really get to know *her*," he says, his eyes traveling south. The light flashes green and he presses the gas but I squirm as another flood of warmth destroys my panties.

Chapter Ten

As soon as we arrive at the condo, it's pitch black inside. I flip the light switch of the living room on and the spotlights above Harper's brown leather sofa's cascade and brighten it a bit.

"Cool place," Nolan says from behind me. Sighing, I place my wallet on the glass coffee table. I then turn to face him but he's now less than an inch away from me. Does he not realize how close he is? "Are we here alone?" he asks, raising a smooth eyebrow.

My breath hitches as he stares down into my eyes. My eyes lock with his quickly and I try to get myself to look away but I can't. His are beautiful, garnished with long, butterfly eyelashes that seem to touch his masculine cheekbones every time he looks down. My gaze travels down to his perfect nose, his full lips, and then his broad chest. The height of him is the biggest turn on. He towers over me and I love the feeling. It feels as if I'm being protected.

"We are," I say as I finally look away. "But nothing is going to happen so get your mind out of the gutter."

"Hey." He lifts his hands as if he's surrendering. "I'm just asking. You're the one staring holes right through me."

I bite back on a smile. "You were staring, too."

"I'll admit I was. Who wouldn't stare at you?" He steps in again but I take a step back as I shake my head.

"So, turkey or ham?"

"I'd prefer *Natalie* on my sandwich," he murmurs. My skin tingles gently. He looks me over, scans me with wide, grey eyes. "Ham," he finally says through a chuckle. "Come on, Natalie. Take a breather. I'm just kidding around with you. You don't have to be so tense."

"I'm not tense," I argue. I truly have a bad habit of making myself sound so immature—especially when I'm dealing with Nolan. He brings out the kid in me which is good at times but right now, it isn't and that's mainly because he gets a kick out of my reactions.

Still grinning, he says, "Okay."

Spinning around, I make my way toward my bedroom. "Let me just change into something comfortable," I call over my shoulder.

"Yeah."

I trot off to my room feeling the urge to just slam my door behind me. But I don't. I hate the fact that he's making me feel this way. I hate the fact that my horniness has made me agree to go on a date with him. I know very well a date isn't what I need. It's only been a month and if I fall into his sticky web, I may get caught up and hurt once again. I don't like the feeling of being hurt. I don't want the remains of my heart to be evaporated. Bryson has already caused enough damage. I definitely don't need anymore.

Nolan says he's been hurt, but I'm sure he's hurt plenty of girls as well. He said on the first night we met that he picks up lots of women from clubs. How does he feel after he's fucked them? What does he do if they want more from him? Does he just ditch them and never speak to them again? I'm sure he refuses to give them anything more than his penis.

So that leaves me with one mind-boggling question: What does he want with *me*?

To be honest, I can't even compare to the other girls of Miami. They're beautiful and well-tanned. I love the beach, but I don't look like I belong on one. I don't have that perfect beach body or the perfect wavy hair. I don't lie around to get tan and toasty on my front lawn. I'm not like Harper who can wear skin tight clothes and get away with it. I'm practically average.

As I pull my shirt over my head, I hear footsteps making their way toward my room. I turn around quickly to the sound of the creaking door only to spot Nolan leaning against the frame with his arms crossed. I fold my arms over my chest immediately, scowling in his direction.

"What in the hell are you doing? Get out!"

He smirks and right now I want to smack that beautiful smile off his face. "Checked the kitchen. Wanted to tell you there's no bread to make sandwiches."

My eyes narrow. "You couldn't have waited until I was dressed?"

"Not really. I sort of missed you." His grin causes my heart to double in speed.

"A bit clingy, aren't we?"

"I'll be as clingy as I have to be if it means I get to see you like this every time." His eyes roam my body deliciously.

"Nolan, please just get out. It's not really comfortable to change with you just standing there."

Nolan's smile fades but his eyes don't drift from mine. While unfolding his arms, he walks toward me quickly. His body presses against mine and we land on my bed with a loud *flop*. He stares into my eyes for a brief moment and before I can ask him what the hell he's doing, he presses his lips against mine. His tongue slips into my mouth and out of habit I braid my fingers through his hair.

I don't think I'll ever understand why he insists on making out with me but not going through with anything. I want him to just fuck me already. At least if we do it, I might not have to worry about him anymore. It's like he's trying to purposely make me sexually frustrated.

His hands touch me gently from my face to my shoulders and then down to my chest. One of his hands cup around my breast and I groan as I wrap my legs around him to pull him in closer. He sucks on my bottom lip before letting go and kissing me again. I swear I love when he does that. I feel the warmth and wetness building up within me. We literally could go for hours if he would just let it happen.

He finally pulls away and we both pant uncontrollably. "I want you to get comfortable with me," he says against my lips.

"I can't," I mumble.

"I want you to," he demands as his eyes harden. "Why?"

"I don't know." His head shakes swiftly. "I want to start something with you and see how far we can take it."

I frown. "You mean a relationship? You want me to commit myself to *you* already?"

His lips press and there is a brief pause before he nods. "It doesn't have to be right away. We can date like we did tonight if that'll help you get comfortable with me. We don't have to rush it."

I pull away from him to sit up. "I don't get it."

"What is there not to get, Natalie?" His voice cranks in volume, his grey eyes beaming holes through me. "It's obvious I want you, and I find it beyond obvious you want me. You can only resist my offer for so long. I want you to fall for me, just like I want to fall for you. I can already feel it happening." He runs his hand over his face, obviously aggravated. "I just—I wanna change."

My head whips to look at him. "What do you mean '*change*'?"

He rubs the back of his neck nervously. There's a still silence in the room and his mouth twitches, as if he doesn't want to speak on it anymore. "Every relationship I've been in, I've... pretty much fucked up."

"What do you mean?" I ask cautiously. Cautiously because I'm not sure I want to know.

"I mean…" He pauses and I can tell that whatever he's about to say is going to destroy our entire night. "I mean I've messed up a couple of times by… cheating."

"*What?*" My face twists as I pull away from him. "And you expect me to want more with *you* after hearing this?"

"Just hear me out," he says, reaching for my hand. "When I was a freshman in high school, that's when it started. But when I dated my last girlfriend, that's when I realized the only reason I do it is because of them. I cheated because they cheated. I always felt it was fair. I wanted to hurt them back."

I shake my head. "What does this have to do with me, Nolan?"

"Everything, Natalie." He clutches my hand but I pull away. He hesitates but that doesn't stop him from sliding in closer. "You were hurt, I was hurt. There's no reason to cheat, but I wanna start over with someone who understands how it feels to be stabbed in the back."

"Cheating is unacceptable in any relationship, Nolan."

"I know." His head falls as he pulls his hand away.

I groan as I stand. I can't go through with this with him. I actually did want to give him a shot at something but now that he's told me this, it's a definite no for me. I can understand being hurt but to cheat period is a huge violation. There's no need for it. I seriously can't tolerate a cheater and imagining more with him frightens me now. I can't do this.

"I think if we do this, it'll help me," he mumbles.

"I can't help you, Nolan. I'm sorry. I seriously don't know what I would do if I actually did give you more and you ended up ruining it."

"But I wouldn't!" He stands to his feet with me. "I wouldn't hurt you because I know you can change me."

My eyebrows furrow. "How can *I* change you?"

"Because… while I'm with you, I can't seem to want anyone else. Trust me, I've tried to get you off of my mind plenty of times I haven't felt this way in a long time—with anyone."

"I'm sure you've said that to the other girls you've cheated on. I'm sure there was one in the bunch who actually wanted to make it work with you but you took her for granted." My eyebrows pull upward.

His mouth seals tight, his eyes broadening. He stares into my irises but I shake my head because his silence answers it all. Even if a girl is faithful to him, he still cheats on her. Just as Bryson did to me. And he really expects me to believe in him?

"Maybe you should just go," I mumble, crossing my arms.

"Natalie—"

He reaches for me but I back away. "Nolan, please."

He stares at me with eyes as wide as golf balls. They're glistening but I refuse to look into them any more than I have to. I can't do this with him. I can't go on a date with someone who I know is a cheater and may have the possibility of destroying my heart even more. What's the point? I'd be the dumbest chick on the planet if I fell for his bullshit.

"I wanted to tell you the truth about me before we got too far," he says. "I wanted to start fresh with a clean slate and let you know all about my flaws before you had ended up discovering them. But if you want me to leave, I will. I can see why you don't want to be involved with me anymore."

As he steps in to kiss my cheek tenderly, heat sparks throughout my entire body and my heart pumps quickly but I don't fall for it. I can't fall for it. I want to pull him back on my bed and kiss him longer, but I find the will to hold off.

Stepping around me, he makes his way out my bedroom door. I listen as the front door creaks open then clicks shuts and I know for sure he's gone. My chest constricts and my throat seems to close in but I hold off on the tears.

Rushing for my bathroom, I start the shower and let the water run over me for about fifteen minutes before I finally decide to get out. But there's not a second that goes by that I don't go over that entire conversation in my head. I should have known he was too good to be true. Maybe he's having troubles that are hard to fix. Maybe he really can't control it. Either way, I can't accept him into my life—into my *heart*. I'm not that strong to hold someone like him up, and even if I were, I'm just asking to be hurt again. It's best to keep Nolan at a distance. I'm going to regret the hell out of forgetting about someone as beautiful as him but I don't have a choice.

I refuse to break again.

Chapter Eleven

The past two weeks have dragged and not one of those days have I seen or heard from Nolan. Although I wasn't expecting him to, I was hoping maybe he would show up at my doorstep or at least call. But he hasn't and that only makes me angrier. I'm not sure why it makes me angry but anger only proves I did feel something for him that I shouldn't have.

I'm hurt he's the way he is. I was actually starting to have fun and forget about Bryson for a slight moment. But that moment only lasted for a second. Now, I can't seem to go a day without comparing the two.

My phone buzzes on my night stand and I groan as I reach for it. Checking the name on the screen, my eyes slightly widen as I perk myself up.

Mom.

Shit. I haven't called her since my first night here… but I have my reasons. I've called my dad and kept him updated. I just hope he actually passes the news on to her. My father is a lot easier to talk than my mom. My mom confuses me sometimes. I'm never sure of what she wants. When I told her that I don't plan on going to a four-year college, she went bat-shit crazy on me. She shouted at me for hours and she didn't talk to me for a whole week.

I told her I wanted nothing more than to write and, with experience, I'll only get better. I'm aiming to write poems I hope people will love to read one day. But she obviously doesn't understand that. She believes I'm wasting my time and that I could do better if I went off to college and faced reality. But I believe my dreams will become my reality. I just need time.

My father understands my dreams completely. He supports my every decision because he had dreams as well. My father wanted to be a mechanic. He didn't have much money when he started but now he makes more than enough. He started fixing cars when he was younger (around the age of sixteen) and when he fixed one man's car at the age of eighteen, that man sent him to a car shop and they hired him on the spot. My father knows a lot about technology, cars, but mainly chasing *dreams*. His only dream was to have grease on his hands, shirt, and even his face.

My mother doesn't understand that dreams are what keep us alive. If my father had given up, he wouldn't be where he is now. I guess he's where I get my boost and my *go-getter* mentality from.

But I guess I could cut mom some slack. My grandmother is a complete bitch to her. My grandmother pretty much planned my mom's life out before she was even born. My grandma wanted her to go to a certain high school, a certain college, and she wanted her to obtain a degree in Nursing. My mom did it, too. She went along with her commands, but now she regrets it.

I know deep down Mom wanted to be a fashion designer. Mom used to dress me up every morning before school and most times I was shocked because the outfits she would buy or pick out for me turned out to be great ones. Every outfit she chose was complimented on by everyone. My mom has a good eye for fashion but, of course, no one will ever know that because she keeps her dreams hidden.

I sit up and press the answer button on my phone. "Hello," I croak.

"Natalie, sweetie!" she chimes through the phone. I pull the phone away from my ear to prevent my ear buds from bursting. "I heard from your father that things are going okay... although I wish you would have told me yourself."

"I wanted to, but Dad said you were still working late and I didn't want to bother."

"Oh." She pauses and her silence reminds me that I always did hate when she worked late or overtime. When I really needed my mother most, she would never be around. On graduation night when I came in with ruined makeup and puffy eyes, I had to be held in my father's arms instead of hers. I would have preferred my mother's arms because she would have understood more about my situation, considering she was once hurt before.

My mom knew everything that went on between Bryson and me. She even knew we were having sex. She accepted him. My father was furious on the night Bryson cheated on me. He wanted to go find Bryson and drag him out of the party so badly but I kept him grounded. My father's large hands would have strangled Bryson to death.

"Well is everything alright down there now? Have you met any new guys?" she asks, aiming to be friendly and hip.

I groan slightly. "No, Mom."

"What about school? Have you signed up for any classes?"

"Mom, no. I will soon."

I knew this was coming. She's going to badger me about school. "Sweetie, stooping down to the level of community college is already too low for you. At least get out there and sign up. I think you deserve more. If you want, I can look online at some two-year colleges that may still be accepting applications. It's never too late, Natty."

"Mom, there's nothing wrong with community colleges. Stop trying to make it sound bad. You and Dad are going tight on money because of the divorce anyway. I don't want my funds to get in the way."

The line is silent and I hear my mom swallow before speaking again. "He told you, huh?"

"Yes he told me. He really didn't have to, though. I'm not blind. I could see the divorce coming from a mile away."

"How do you feel about it?"

"I don't understand it," I mutter as I pull at a loose string of my sheets.

"What is there not to understand, honey? Your father and I clash all of the time. We bump heads way too many times during the day than I can count. I'm tired of bickering and arguing. Your father is too peaceful and too humble to ever want to finish an argument with me. When he leaves them floating around in the air, the tension just builds up between us."

"Dad drops the arguments because he loves you, Mom. He doesn't like to hurt you. You wouldn't understand that because you feel like you're always right," I snap as my eyes roll slightly.

"I do not!" she snaps back.

"You don't realize it, but you do, Mom." I sigh as I push my hair back. "Look, I really want you and Dad to work this out. Dad texts me all of the time asking for advice but I don't know what to tell him. He wants to work this out. Please, just think about this more before actually going through with it. You know he would die if it means you will be happy."

My mom remains quiet for a few unbearable moments. "Mom?" I call after the unbearable moments become awkward. I hear a sniffle and my chest tightens. "Mom. Don't cry. Please." I hate to hear my mom cry. Every night when I lived with them, I would hear her in the bathroom late at night letting out tears. She probably thought I couldn't hear her, but I did. She was crying because her relationship was going downhill. The bathroom was across the hall from my room. When she cries, I feel the urge to cry as well.

"Natalie, I love Frank. He's my world. I'm just afraid I may hurt him."

"The only thing that can hurt him is your pride. Your pride is always in the way. Just let it go and lose a battle for once. I swear it'll make you feel better."

"Yeah," she breathes then sniffles again. "Maybe that's true." A beeping noise rings on her end and muffles whoosh around in my ear. "Well, I have to get back to work. I just wanted to call and check up on you."

"Okay." I don't want this to end. Although my mom can be confusing and a bit pushy, I still love talking to her and nothing felt better at the moment than hearing her voice. I'm surprised she didn't bring Bryson up but I know that's a subject she won't touch for a while. She knows how much I used to love him and how much effort I used to put into my relationship with him.

"I love you, Natty. I'll call you as soon as I'm off tonight. I promise."

"Okay, Mom. I love you, too. Have a good day at work."

"I'll try." She groans. I press my lips before ending the call. Drawing my legs against my chest, I rest my forehead against my knee. My life is truly falling apart. First it was Bryson and now it's this divorce crap with my parents. I seriously don't know what I'll do if they end up leaving one another.

My father has had eyes for my mother for ages. He agrees she can be a bit complicating but he loves her entirely. He loves her more than he loves fixing cars. My mom should know that but I don't know what's causing her to think he's given up. My father isn't a quitter. He'll do everything he can to prove his love to her. He'll fight for her like he has nothing to live for.

I've wanted a guy like my dad. I've wanted someone with dreams, goals, and a huge heart. But it seems like every guy I meet is the complete opposite of what he is. My father is far from selfish but most guys I know are. Maybe it's not meant for me to be with anyone just yet. I'm still young, after all.

Pushing my sheets and blankets away, I step down on the soft carpet and decide to start my day. I make my way toward my suitcase and pull out a pair of crisp skinny jeans, a white tank top, and a pair of black Chuck Taylor's. I head for the bathroom to wash my face, brush my teeth, and then pull my hair up into a loose bun. I refuse to put on any makeup. I don't want to appeal to anyone at the moment but myself.

I guess I could do something with my life by heading to the nearest community college and signing up for classes. I need to do something that'll keep my mind guarded from Nolan and especially Bryson. I put my clothes on quickly, grab my keys, and then head out. Harper is at work which I'm glad for because I'm sure she would be begging me to go out with her like always.

As the door clicks shut behind me, I dash down the stairs to get to my car.

Chapter Twelve

I had to use the GPS my father gave me to find Miami-Dade Community College. To my surprise, it wasn't too far away from Harper's condo. As soon as I step out of my car, my shirt sticks against me. It's blazing today, and for that I had to have my air conditioning on full blast. The air is uncomfortably humid and sticky but I'm hoping it'll pass as I get into the building.

As I step inside, I am fooled completely. It's hotter inside than it is out. I press the back of my hand against my forehead and wipe the beads of sweat away quickly. A few people pass by in just shorts and tanks and I'm glad I have a tank on but I would feel much better in shorts than jeans.

Flicking my hand as I make my way down the hall, I follow the signs that lead me to the admissions office. I spot the line leading to it and groan. There has to be at least ten e people ahead of me. All of them look flushed and some are sweating heavily as they fan themselves with a few papers.

"Next," a woman calls from the front desk with the blandest voice I've ever heard. The boy in front scuffles to her desk and I'm glad the line is actually moving. I stand behind a girl with short brown hair sticking to her forehead and the nape of her neck from sweat. She's softly tanned and petite in her light blue shorts and a pink camisole, as if she enjoys the sun, but only on occasion.

"I take it you haven't been here during the registration periods before," she says, observing my jeans with a soft smile.

I shake my head, looking down with her. "Yeah. First time here." I sigh.

"Don't worry. The lines tend to move fast. When it's that hot outside, the administrators will do everything in their power to get us out of here as fast as they can. For some reason they don't turn the air on during the summer.

"Well I'm glad the line is moving. I don't want it to seem like I've just been swimming by the time I get back home."

The girl laughs softly at my lame joke. "I'm Brittany Lucas. I've just moved here a year ago so I can see how you feel." She reaches a kind hand toward me and I take it.

"Natalie Carmichael," I say as I give her hand a slight shake.

"So what are signing up for?"

"Um... I guess anything that deals with writing or reading." I shrug.

"Ohhh," Brittany says, extending the word. "You're a writer. You kind of seem like one now that you've mentioned it. Most people who want to be writers are usually reserved. I'm a big reader." She pauses while biting on her lip and studying her hands. "This may seem pushy, but if you have anything you'd like to share with someone one day, I'd love to read whatever you have!"

"Really?" My heart flutters ecstatically, surprised by Brittany's remark. She doesn't seem like much of a reader, but she does seem a bit intellectual.

"Yeah!" She nods. "I'd be honored. I've read plenty of books over this summer. Me and a friend are actually having a contest to see how many books we can read before the summer ends and classes start. We started this summer and so far mine is thirty-seven. Not too bad, right?"

"Not at all," I say then press my lips with a nod. "But to be honest, I don't write books. I just write poems."

Brittany's shrill gasp causes the entire line to turn around and look in our direction. Even the women at the desks are looking our way. "Really?" she squeals. "That's even better! I love poets. Believe it or not, my boyfriend and I go to Open Mic sessions every Thursday and Saturday. Most people that show up are poets, singers, or independent bands. You should definitely go one day. They accept new speakers all the time. Plus it's a great way to get started."

"Oh wow," I breathe. "It would be kind of cool to read my poems out loud—but I don't know. I've never done it before. What's the place called?"

"Um..." She thinks on it before her fingers snap. "Haven—yeah that's what it's called. I remember because it's close to the word *heaven*. I go there so much I forgot the name of it." She grins and I do the same. "You should definitely go tomorrow night to experience how it is. If you want, we can hang out and read some of your poems. It would be fun."

"Wow, yeah. I'd love that."

"Great!" she says then reaches to pull her phone out of her back pocket. "Just put your number in here and I can give you directions later on." She smiles as she hands me her phone. I take it immediately and pound my number into her contact list.

"Next," the bland voice calls again. I look up quickly just as I'm handing Brittany back her phone. I hadn't even realized the line died down or that we were standing in front.

"Well, I gotta run, but it was nice meeting you, Natalie. I hope you get the classes that you crave for!" She tosses a wave then rushes for the heavy-set woman behind the desk.

I smile as I stand in front of the line with a heart that's beating gleefully. See, this is all I needed. An escape. I just needed something to occupy my time and I've found it. It's a good thing I took my mom's advice for once because now I have something to do tomorrow night besides sit at home and stuff my face with butter-pecan ice-cream and watch movies. Lord only knows I don't need to fatten myself up again.

****

After about thirty minutes of processing information and signing up for classes that would best fit my needs, I was finally free of that hot-ass hellhole. Bursting through the doors with my registration papers in hand, I rush for the parking lot but before I can set foot on the black asphalt, a soft melody rings in my ears. It's the strumming of guitar strings and along with the beautiful sound of the guitar is a deep, delightful voice. Curiosity piques, and I turn to make my way around the building to see where it's coming from. I've never heard music so appealing—acoustic music at that. It's hypnotically alluring.

Rounding the curve of the brick wall, the first thing I see is his muscular arms and his sculpted chest. He has on a fitted grey tank top and the bare skin that's revealed is glistening with a soft sheen of sweat. A few strands of his hair are sticking to his forehead and I come to a halt as I watch a bead of sweat trickle down and land against his shiny black guitar. I pause as all my breath is gushed right out of me. Even while he's sweating bullets, he is unbelievably gorgeous. His luscious eyelashes touch his masculine cheekbones gently as he stops playing to wipe the sweat away from his guitar first and then from his forehead with the hem of his shirt.

Realizing someone's watching him, he glances up quickly and his grey eyes catch mine.

"Natalie?" Nolan calls as his eyebrows pull together.

Pulling my lips in, I feel the urge to just twist around and rush for my car. But I know if I do, he may chase after me just to talk to me. I've been trapped by his music. A smile sweeps across his lips as he pulls the strap of his guitar around him and steps down from the picnic table. He swings his guitar around to place it against his back, causing the strap to press between the crease of his chest. "What are you doing here?" he asks.

"I um..." My sentence falls short as I observe the way his hips sway in his snug cargo shorts. Sweat is all over him. On his chest, beneath his arms, and even his abs. He might as well take it off because I'm sure by the end of the day, his shirt'll be completely drenched. "I heard you playing. I wanted to see who it was."

"Oh." His head tilts as he meets up with me. "I hope you liked what you heard instead of thinking it sounded disastrous. Your face was kinda twisted when I looked up. Seems like you hated it."

"No," I shake my head quickly. "I—I loved it, Nolan. Where did you learn to play like that?"

"My father taught me how to play when I was six." He sighs. "He was in a band of his own for a pretty long time."

"Oh."

He pulls his arms in to fold them across his chest. He studies every inch of me but I'm sure I look like complete shit. "Do you write your own lyrics?" I ask to distract his sweeping gaze. As he looks away, he places his thumb beneath his strap and slides it along the leather.

"I do."

"Wow. I didn't realize that, um—"

"Realize what?" he asks, his mystic grey eyes meeting mine again.

"I didn't realize you liked to play," I say, completing the sentence I had cut short purposely to prevent any prolonged conversation with him.

"You'll learn a lot about me that you may find interesting, Natalie. I actually wrote a song about you a few days ago. Wanna know what it's called?"

I gulp heavily as a bead of sweat trickles against my forehead. "What?"

"Soul-stealer."

"*What?*" I frown. "Why is that the title of a song about *me*?"

"Because I've been soul-less these past two weeks without you."

"Because of me?" Folding my arms, I take a step away from him. "If anything, you should write a negative song about yourself, Nolan. I did nothing wrong."

"You denied me without reason," he counters. "That was wrong in so many ways."

My eyes narrow defensively. "You really believe that protecting my already shattered heart is doing something wrong?"

"Natalie, you didn't even give me a chance to explain myself to you. I pretty much asked for a chance and you denied me, flat out. Don't you think that was kind of selfish?" His eyebrows shoot up.

"What's selfish is the fact that you cheat on innocent girls. Although it's wrong to cheat period, I can slightly understand why you did it to get back at the ones who hurt you. What I don't understand is why you would do it to the ones who actually wanted to make it work."

"Because none of them kept me interested. But with you," he says, stepping in closer and reaching for my face. "With you, there's something different. There's something here for you that I know I won't get tired of. You're a challenge I know I won't conquer for a very long time and being with someone for a very long time is what I need right now. I need someone who will work with me, not against me. Those girls you think are innocent, aren't innocent. They nagged all the time and accused me of things I didn't do. I got so frustrated that I started putting distance between us and did my own thing. You can't blame me for that."

My skin buzzes pleasurably and I want to pull away from him but I don't because the way he's stroking my flushed cheek actually feels satisfying. I've missed his touch over the course of these few days. I've missed seeing him smile, make jokes, and even him telling me that I'm beautiful. It bewilders me that I can even miss a person like him. Someone who's probably just as low-down and selfish as Bryson. But he's made me happy. I didn't realize it but happiness was there during that *"date"* with Nolan. I felt somewhat complete.

I force myself to pull away from him, though. He stares at me and I clutch my papers in hand before taking a step away. Although this feeling drives me crazy, I can't let the way he is drive me off the rocket. But, then again, I could use this. Spending time with him helps me to forget all I've been through with Bryson. He's like a distraction and to be honest, it helps to think of someone else for a change. This past week has been terrible for me. I was reminiscing so much I felt sick with tears every night. Enough is enough. I can't continue with this depression anymore.

"Do you play all the time?" I ask as I take a look at the head of his guitar.

"I play every night."

I nod as I look over his shoulder to a couple walking past, hand-in-hand. I cringe a bit as I watch them disappear. "Well I'm going to an Open Mic session tomorrow," I state, refusing to let the memories of Bryson get to me. "We should go together to see how it is. Maybe you could play?"

"Oh, no." He shakes his head, waving his hands disapprovingly. "I don't sing for anyone but myself."

"You wouldn't sing for me?" I ask, stepping forward to fill the gap just a bit.

Nolan's head tilts and his lips spread to smile. "Wait—is this you trying to plan a real date with me?" His eyes narrow playfully. "Are you actually willing to help me?"

"*Help* you?" I spit as my nose crumples. "This is not about to be a project for me, Nolan. Just like you told me a few weeks ago. All or nothing. We'll do what feels natural, but that's it. We'll see what happens as time goes on."

His white teeth flash and my heart stumbles before reaching the next beat. His smile only makes me want to step out of my lady-like character and hump him all over this picnic table. He steps in and the space between us is no longer there. Reaching to cup my face, he studies my brown eyes again. His sweat spills through my tank and the heat between us sparks with intensity. It's blazing out right now and I'm sure most would hate to be touched like this while it's so hot, but I love it. I love the way my body is bubbling with more heat than it needs.

"Everything I do with you is out of natural instinct," he says against my lips. "I want this to work, Natalie. There's nothing I want more than to see you every day and to know I can do better. I know I have it in me. It may seem like I'm moving too fast, but I've been thinking about you way too much to just let this go. I can do it."

I nod as he pulls his hands away before they can get too sweaty. "Please… just don't screw it up, Nolan. One strike and I'm done. I swear."

"Of course," he says. "I won't fuck up. Trust me. I promise." He crosses his heart, grinning.

"Okay." I smile as I take another step back. "I picked up some light bread the other day. What do you say to those sandwiches?"

Nolan's chuckle rumbles as he clutches the strap of his guitar. Stepping forward, he drapes an arm around my shoulder before leading the way toward the parking lot. "I still prefer *Natalie* on mine but I guess ham will do just fine for now."

I burn scarlet as I try to keep my face hidden. He has a huge habit of making me blush. But at least I'm smiling. After all, this is what I really wanted… right?

Chapter Thirteen

"So, seriously," Nolan says as he picks at a piece of lettuce on his sandwich. "How did you meet Harper? She's the complete opposite of you."

I reach for my glass of fruit punch from the coffee table before turning to look at him. He stuffs the last corner of his sandwich into mouth before giving me his full attention. "Harper used to live next door to me. We lived in the same neighborhood for ages. We kicked it off on the first day we met." Tucking my leg beneath my butt, I turn to face him, taking another sip of my juice. "Why do you ask?"

"Harper is crazy," he says through a chuckle. "Not like bat-shit crazy, but, like, party-crazy. I always see her bouncing around at club *LIV*. She gave a blowjob to the manager of that club. You know that right?"

I choke on my drink and force myself to keep my lips sealed to prevent any of it from spilling out. "What?" I croak. "Why would you say that? Harper would never stoop that low."

"She wouldn't?" His eyebrows rise smoothly. "The only way a girl can get an underage friend into that club or even get that friend a pass to drink is if she gives him something worth his time. What man wouldn't want something in return, just in case he happens to get fired for allowing underage drinking?"

"You're just making assumptions," I mutter as I sit my glass down. There's no way in hell Harper would suck on a man she hardly knows. The Harper I know would vomit if someone told her to do it. She didn't do it to Bobby so I wouldn't expect her to do it to someone like the owner of club *LIV*.

But now that I think about it, Max (the owner of *LIV*) was pretty hot. He was young and neat with wavy brown hair and a well-trimmed goatee. He had the clearest blue eyes I had ever seen and he kept up with himself really well. He was far from the word 'ugly' but I'm sure Harper has enough respect for herself to not stoop that low... at least I hope she still does. Although Harper and I talked a lot when she left for college, I could tell things with her were different. People change as time goes on, I know that for sure.

"I'm not assuming. I know, Natalie," Nolan reassures me.

"How do you know?"

"Because Dawson walked in on her making out with the owner in the men's bathroom."

This time, my eyes stretch until they are practically popping out of my head. "Making out... with *Max?*" I stand and reach for the plates with the crusts of our bread on them. "So why does Dawson still want to go on a date with her? He doesn't consider her, like, a whore or anything?"

Nolan sighs as he crosses his arms. "Dawson thinks he can make every girl he comes across settle down completely. When he wants a girl, he *wants* her. I'm assuming he hasn't found the right one yet but he's never been unfaithful. He and my brother get on me so much about being a player and being *immature* by trying to get back at the girls who cheated on me. Dawson's like another brother constantly yelling in my ear. They want me to chill out and get serious for once."

"Oh wow," I murmur. "Well, good luck to him with that. Harper is a bit wild and to try and tame her now seems kind of impossible. And you're one to talk. You and Dawson are complete opposites. I can get down with a few parties with Harper but you—" I break off as Nolan's head whips to look at me. His grey eyes depress and I mentally bite my tongue, refusing to blast him about his flaws. "Let me just go take these in the kitchen," I mumble instead.

I place the plates in the sink but as I turn around, Nolan is stepping in. His head is cocked slightly and it looks as if he's about to eat me alive... but there's something else in his eyes. Something extremely seductive. "It's been two weeks since I've felt your lips against mine," he says, taking a small step forward. "Two weeks since I've seen you or tasted that tongue of yours. What are we waiting for again?"

"Um..." I grip the edge of the counter as he takes his last step in and presses his groin against me. My body tenses as I stare into his eyes.

"Does this feel natural?" he asks.

"Does what feel natural?"

"The way I touch you. The way I make your body coil with pleasure. The way your lips pucker when you know you really want to kiss me."

I pull my lips in quickly, realizing they are a bit puckered. I do want to kiss him, and I didn't even realize it. To be honest, I want to do more with him. But we're taking this slowly. We're taking it easy.

"You don't have to resist it anymore, Natalie. Just do it." His lips stretch softly. He's tempting me in every way possible. His voice is low, deep, and causing my legs to quake and stiffen at the same time.

Oh, forget it. I'm going for it. I reel him in but before our lips touch, I see him smile. But that smile is pushed aside immediately as I crush his lips with mine. Wrapping his hands around my waist, he picks me up to place me on the counter. He presses in further, his firm chest pushing beneath my breasts as he pulls me in by my hips. His lips trail from my lips to my neck. I pant heavily, twisting my fingers through his silky hair. He releases a soft groan but he doesn't stop kissing me. Heat slithers from my chest to my panties. God, what is he waiting for?

A door creaks open from the living room and he pulls away from me quickly. Keys jingle and we both try to ease up on our heavy panting but it's impossible. It's almost like we've just run a marathon. It takes only a few seconds for Harper to come around the corner. She spots us and her eyes widen quickly as she clutches her keys in her hand.

Even though she hasn't said anything, I wince. I know it's coming. This is Harper we're talking about. I've been avoiding conversations with her about Nolan purposely throughout the past two weeks but now that she's seeing this, she's going to think I've lied about being upset with him.

"On my counter? Really, Nat!" she screeches. Nolan and I finally breathe again. He chuckles as he pulls away from me and straightens his crumpled tank top. The tank top that I had a vice grip on.

"I'll give you two a minute," he says as he looks from me to Harper who is still scowling at us. He turns to step around her with a smile still glued to his lips. He is truly getting a kick out of this.

As soon as Nolan is out of the kitchen, Harper steps toward me and grabs me by the wrist. "A serious talk in my room. *Now*," she demands as I hop down from the counter and she drags me out.

When we pass the living room, Nolan is sitting on the sofa and shaking his head with a small smirk. He winks and I flush before she rounds the corner, swings her bedroom door open, and then slams it shut behind us.

"What in the hell is going on?" she asks, crossing her arms tightly. "You told me he was a cheating scumbag!"

"I'm sure I didn't say it like that, Harper."

She flicks her hand, pushing my statement aside. "Well whatever. You were so depressed these past few weeks, but I come home to this—to you getting dry humped on *my counter*. This is just weird, Nat."

"It's not weird!" I argue as I smooth my hair down. "I've agreed today and from now on to let things be natural between Nolan and I. You should be happy about this. At least I wasn't sucking his dick!"

Harper gasps, her blue eyes stretching. "What are getting at?" She narrows her eyes.

"Why didn't you tell me about Max?" I ask. "Since when have you kept things from me?" Her face depresses only slightly as she looks away from me. But just in the same amount of time that her face saddened, she perks back up, her face full of life again.

"I'm afraid you'll look down on me for the things I do now, Nat. Most shit I do, I do it out of stupidity. Most times I'm drunk out of my mind and sometimes I don't remember what in the hell happened during the night before. That's kind of why I eased up on taking you out. Because I don't want you following in my footsteps." She reaches for my hand and leads me to her bed. We both sit at the same time but my eyes don't drift from hers.

"Ever since Bobby and I split, I just feel the need to take control. I feel the need to suck-then-fuck every guy I come across. I want each and every one of them to remember how great I am and then regret the way they are. Just like Max. Max has millions of whores in the office of his clubs. He tried to treat me like one of them but I refused. He liked my attitude and asked me to go on a date with him. I agreed to do it. That's how I got the pass for you. It was a few weeks ago, actually.

"Max is a cool guy, but he takes women for granted. He thinks that if he snaps, they'll come running... but not me. I fucked the shit out of Max and then left his house during the middle of the night. I show up at his club just to remind him that he's a dick and that he will never have me. I wanna be hard to resist and hard to let go of. So far, I feel like I'm doing a damn good job at it because they constantly call me. Guys love when you give them a good BJ and then jump on top of them. It's like their fantasy or something. I read it in a magazine once."

My head shakes as I stare at Harp with the widest eyes ever. "But why?" I never would have thought she would turn into a one-night-stand kind of girl. I can't imagine how many men she's actually had sex with during the course of these two years.

"Bobby really fucked me over, Nat. I hate the idea of settling again. It terrifies me to even think about how hurt I was. I don't want anyone to have control over my heart."

"That's completely insane, Harp. You give them your all for one night and then just leave them alone?" My face scrunches. I refuse to judge my best friend, but this behavior is ridiculous. "You don't find that kind of... odd?"

"It not odd. Think about it for a sec," she says, standing from the bed to justify herself. "Men do it all the time. I do it for the fun of it—but don't think I do it every weekend. The maximum number of men I've slept with is seven since I moved here. All of them beg for a real date with me... including Dawson."

"Ugh," I groan. "I seriously need to meet this Dawson guy. Does he know you do this?"

"Yeah," she breathes. "This is what I wanted to keep from you. When I saw him again at that beach party, I wanted to ignore him so damn bad. I wanted him to remember what we shared and how great our sex was but Nat," she says, reaching for my hands to grip them. "There is just something about him that's making me want to stop what I'm doing. I don't get how he can do it to me, but now I regret sleeping with those guys. He practically gave me a lecture about my behavior. I was still drunk when he gave it to me, but I remember every single word he said. He wants to change me. But I can't change. I'm too accustomed to partying my ass of and being single. I'm too used to hurting them for hurting girls like *us*."

As Harper says that, my mind circles back to Nolan. She and Nolan are exactly the same. They can't help the way they are. They're so used to their flaws that their flaws turn into bad habits. I can't believe this. For two weeks, I've been living with someone who hurts others for no reason as well. There's no reason to hurt people who actually want more. But I guess I can understand why Harper is the way she is now. She's broken, just like Nolan. Just like me. She's torn and she refuses to be mended by anyone else until she's ready. But unlike her, Nolan wants to change. He wants the help.

"I think you should give Dawson a chance," I finally say.

Her forehead creases over as her nose scrunches. "Why? He's too... mature sometimes," she mutters.

"Maybe maturity is what you need, Harp. You should do what Nolan and I are doing. Take things naturally, day-by-day."

"Um, I'm sorry but dry-humping and kissing on my shiny counters isn't natural. That's just plain disgusting. I'll be sure not to make my food on that side of the kitchen again."

I chuckle, standing. "I'm being serious, Harp. Nolan is going through something and I'm going to find out more about it. I'm willing to help him, just as Dawson is willing to help you. Give the guy a chance. It won't kill you."

Groaning, she flops backward and her blonde hair stretches across her white sheets. "Do I have to?" she whines.

"You don't have to... but I'm sure you'll love it." *Because I love how things are going already.*

She props herself up on her elbows to evil-eye me. "Okay. But if he gets out of hand with his, I'm calling it quits. I don't want him thinking we're getting serious anytime soon. This will take some getting used to. I know what I do is bad, but it can't be worse than having someone nag at me about the way I am all the time."

Nodding, I turn for the door. I know if she feels that way, so will Nolan. He's still getting used to this idea, but I'm swearing to myself right now that I won't nag.

I know I'm practically setting myself up for failure, but I'll go through with it. I'll do whatever I can to keep Nolan on track. I actually want something with him... big or small. Whatever it is, I'm sure it'll be enjoyable.

Chapter Fourteen

Bryson started to drift away from me about three weeks before he had officially cheated on me. Those three weeks dragged by and made me doubt how strong our love really was every single day. Bryson would pick me up from home to take me to school. We would ride together in his mud-green Jeep Wrangler.

I knew something was wrong. I could feel it. Especially on the night we were supposed to go out for dinner together.

"I have something to do for my mom tonight. We might have to reschedule dinner," he said, parking in front of my driveway. We were coming from Mark's house where we would lie to our parents and say we were having a study session, but in reality, we would be fooling around. But that night at Mark's, Bryson barely touched me. He barely looked at me. That

entire night he played XBOX with Mark until he was ready to drop me off.

I nodded and swallowed the bulge in my throat, reaching to unbuckle my seatbelt. The fact that he wasn't even looking at me bothered me deeply.

"What does she want you to do?" I asked. Bryson's mom is a lawyer. She's hardly ever home so I should have known he was lying to me. I was just too blind to see it. I loved him. Bryson's dad was a complete asshole so his mom kicked him to the curb immediately. Bryson lives with a single parent—a parent who barely spends time with her own son. On graduation day, she told him she was going to be showing up late. After the ceremony was over, we came to the conclusion that she wasn't going to show at all.

"She wants me to babysit some kids of a friend of hers while they go out for quick drinks. I don't know. It's kind of stupid," he muttered with a careless shrug, but he still wasn't looking at me.

"Bryson." I reached for his hand and gripped it. "Are you okay?"

He finally turned to look at me. His emerald eyes pierced through mine as he examined every aspect of my face. It was as if he was debating on whether he should have gone through with the devious plan he started.

I guess he decided to go through with it because he pulled his hand away to place it on the steering wheel. I'm sure he thought it was an unnoticeable gesture, but I noticed everything that was wrong with it.

Usually when I felt something was wrong with him, he would cup my face, kiss me, and then tell me he's more than all right as long we're together. But not that night.

Facing forward, he looked through the windshield again. "I'm alright, Nat. Go ahead and spend time with your dad. I'll call you tonight when the kids are gone."

I nodded as my hand recoiled. He was making small excuses for me just to make his escape, but now that I think about it, he was only trying to get rid of me to most likely spend his night with Sara. It puzzles me now to think he may have cheated on me more than once with her. He had to. I hopped out of the car but hesitated on shutting the door behind me. He was still facing forward, still glaring out the windshield.

"Goodnight, Bryson." As I said it, my chest tightened and I fought to keep the tears back. I shut the door behind me and he pulled off quickly. It was unusual for him to leave that fast. He was out of sight within a second. I watched his Jeep trail down the road until his rear lights grew distant and then

disappeared around the corner. I turned to make my
way up the driveway. I knew my father was waiting
for me inside so I took a deep breath, shook it off,
and headed inside.

I was hoping maybe he wasn't feeling well or that he really did have to hurry off to babysit, but that wasn't the case. Bryson was going to see Sara behind my back. Back then, I didn't even realize it. I made excuses for his stand-offish behavior. I made sure every excuse was a good one and sometimes I would forget I was lying to myself and become dumb enough to believe them. But it was getting out of hand. It was only a matter of time before I was to learn the truth.

****

Tapping my pen against my chin, I stare down at the blank sheet of paper before me. I've been debating all morning on whether to write or not. I decided since I was home alone and didn't have anywhere to go for hours, it was best to get something down. I've had all of these memories—all these confusing thoughts running through my mind. It's all so jumbled up that I feel like writing them down on paper is the best option.

I cross my legs and press the ball of my pen against the paper. I'm sitting at the coffee table of the living room on top of one of Harper's throw pillows as P!nk, Ed Sheeran, and Gavin Degraw play through the speakers. I used to write like this at home when my parents weren't around. I'd grab a stack of papers, place them on the coffee table, grab a beanbag chair, and scoot my legs under the table as jams filled the room. I would then get right down to work.

I cherish the moments that I'm away from you now
You miss what you had; you crave what you've lost
I seriously should just take a bow
Because I took this pain like a woman... like a conqueror.
Like a boss.

Smiling, I read over the lines of my paper over a million times. The last two lines are what catch me. I love them. The fact that I actually do continue to breathe and go on with my life is proof enough that I'm getting through it. It's like taking baby steps. They're gradual but they'll become strides as the days move forward.

I was being suffocated with a plastic bag Bryson put over my head, but now I feel like I can snatch it off and toss it in the garbage. I feel like I can inhale and take a huge breath of relief. This poem proves how much I've been through with him.

I won't pretend he means nothing to me, though. The feelings I have for him will take a while to fade and that's only because he's my first love. But it's happening. I can feel it happening. A pound of all of the weight has been lifted from my shoulders. There's still some massive weight lingering around but with time, I know it'll all be gone.

My phone buzzes on the table and I reach for it quickly, spotting the unfamiliar number.

"Hello?"

"Hi! Is this Natalie?"

"Yes it is. May I ask whose calling?"

"Oh, it's Brittany from Miami-Dade!"

"Oh, yeah! Hi, how are you?" I pull my legs from beneath the table to stand.

"I'm wonderful," she says as I place my pen on top of my paper. "I was just calling, as promised. I want to give you the directions early. My mom knows the manager and she says a lot of people are going to be there tonight. Do you still plan on coming?"

"Of course." I smile. "I actually just wrote something I may share one night."

"Really?!" Brittany squeals. "That's fantastic. I hope to be able to read them soon."

"You can read them today, if you'd like. We can meet up for some smoothies or something and I can bring a few of my best ones with me."

"Oh, no. I seriously don't want to take up all your time," she says, her voice lowering.

Giggling, I make my way toward my bedroom. "Brittany, you're fine. I'm free today—well practically every day until school starts. I don't mind it at all."

"Are you sure?" she asks nervously. "I feel like I've already interrupted your writing. I know how it is for someone to interrupt something important—"

Brittany continues to babble, but I only laugh. She's adorable, really. She's a nervous wreck with a new friend she knows nothing about. I can tell she isn't trying to screw anything up. But I'm not like that. I accept people the way they are. I guess that's a weakness of mine. "It's fine. I swear. What do you say we meet up at Smoothie King?"

"Sure," she breathes out, her voice filled with sweet relief. "What time?"

I pull my cell away from my ear to check the time. "How about three? Open Mic doesn't start until eight tonight, right?"

"Right," she says. "Well, gather those poems and I'll meet you there—at the one on the beach, right?"

"Yup," I say, toying with a hairclip on my nightstand.

"Kay. See ya there!"

I end the call then place the hair clip down with a sigh. I rake my fingers through my hair as I stare at the carpet. If I want to be honest with myself, I'm nervous about the fact that Brittany will think I'm a lunatic for writing such depressing and heart wrenching poems. My best poems are the ones I wrote out of pain or the ones I scribbled down through blurry eyes. I want to share my dreams with someone. I can't continue to bottle up all that I feel inside. My only hope is she actually likes them and doesn't run away from me full speed.

Chapter Fifteen

"So what do you think?" I ask nervously, gripping my cup full of creamy strawberry-banana smoothie. By the creases in Brittany's forehead, I'm not sure what she's thinking. Her eyes are glued to the paper and are scanning each word over and over again. It isn't too long before she stops reading to look at me. Her green eyes are wide and crystal-like as she stares into mine. She seriously looks like she's just seen Freddie or Jason. "Was it that bad?" I ask, wincing.

"Bad?" she asks before her mouth gapes. "Natalie, please excuse me for my language, but this poem is fucking amazing! Who are you talking about in it?"

"An ex of mine."

"Wow," she breathes, reaching for her cup of yogurt. "I could feel your pain. There are seriously no words that can describe what I felt while reading it." She picks her spoon up and slides it into her mouth. "Have you shared these with anyone besides me?"

"Yeah. I have a friend back in South Carolina who loved to read my poems. Her name's Grace. She's the reason I started writing, actually."

"Oh really?" Brittany raises an intrigued eyebrow as she swallows her yogurt down. "How so?"

"Well, she knew I loved to write. She would tell me to just put it all down on paper. I'm kind of glad I did now." I sit back and place my hands between my thighs. "You're sure you loved it?—I mean there wasn't anything on it that makes you want to run away from me while screaming your head off, is there?"

"Hell no," she says quickly, sitting forward. "Seriously, you should think about getting these copyrighted and put out in the world. I think lots of girls would understand this kind of pain. I'm one of them." Brittany's features fall as she reaches for her cup of Greek yogurt again.

"Oh," I mumble. I highly doubt she wants to speak about that right now so I keep the subject on me. "Well, maybe one day. I don't think I'm ready for that just yet."

"Oh yeah! No sweat. Do it when it feels right." Picking her spoon up again, she stares at the pink yogurt. "So, are you coming alone tonight? I don't want you to be, like, a third-wheel or anything. My boyfriend Jordan will be there and I tend to get a little... stuck on him."

A smile snakes it's way across my lips as I watch her almost sink into her sequin green tank top. "Oh, don't worry about me. I have someone coming along that I'm sure will love the Open Mic just as much as us." A wider smile forms on my lips as I lower my head and Nolan comes to mind. He stayed until three in the morning last night. It was wonderful to spend time with him. I don't think there was a moment we didn't make-out. Every hour, our lips were touching.

"Heated cheeks," Brittany muses with a smirk, pointing her spoon at me. "I take it he's a lover of yours."

"No." I shake my head. "Just a friend."

"For now," she counters playfully. "I know that look. I've had it before. You're red all over. You like him a lot."

"Is it really that obvious?" I ask. I kind of figured it was going to get obvious one day.

"Very," she says then sticks her spoon into her mouth to gulp her last scoop of yogurt down. "Is he hot?"

"Very," I say with a slight giggle. She giggles with me then places her spoon in her empty cup before reaching for my stack of poems. She stacks them on the table before tucking them in the yellow folder I carried them in.

"You take these home and really consider reading them for Open Mic sometime. I think the one I just read is the best one—all of them were great but that last one was just... *wow*." I grab the folder with a nod and we both stand from the table.

"Maybe," I sigh.

****

As soon as I step into the apartment, my phone buzzes in my back pocket. I shut and lock the door behind me before pulling it out and checking the screen.

Gracey.

My heart does fifty flips in my chest as a grin sticks to my mouth like glue. I've missed Grace. I haven't talked to her in weeks. She's been on lockdown since she got caught trying to sneak out and go to her boyfriend, Trey's, house. He's the one she met at the infamous house party on graduation night.

I press the answer button and let out a shrill scream through the receiver of the phone.

"Good God, Nat! I hate when you do that!" she complains before giggling. "What's up girl? I've missed your ass like crazy!"

"I know," I groan, slumping down on the sofa. "Your parents finally decided to let you off the hook?"

"Yeah," she breathes. I can tell she's fiddling with something. It's always been a habit of hers when she's on the phone or when she's talking to someone face-to-face. "I think they're realizing I'm not a child anymore. I talked to my mom this morning and she gave me a speech about how pregnancy will cut all the fun out of life and shit like that. It was the same old junk just a different day."

"It took them a little over month to finally let you go. That was way too long."

"I know. It sucks. But screw my punishment. That's over with now. I've got my phone back with a fresh batch of unlimited minutes so spill the beans. How is it down there in Miami?"

I chew on my bottom lip, hesitating. It seems too fast to be back in the game of hearts, but this is Grace I'm talking to. I tell her everything.

"I met this guy," I mumble as I scoot to the edge of the sofa.

"Oh yeah?" she asks. A loud *POP* rings in my ear and I jolt quickly. "Sorry," she says. "This gum is just too damn good to stop chewing. So much flavor! Go ahead, spill it."

"Well he's cute—"

"Describe him," she demands quickly.

My eyebrows pull together as I reach for the pen I wrote my poem with earlier. "Geesh, rush all of the answers right of me, why don't ya?"

"Sorry," she apologizes again. "I just missed hearing your voice. I want to know everything that is going on with you—anything that proves you still have a life outside of that dickhead ex-boyfriend of yours." I know she's just rolled her eyes while messing with the cuticles of her nails. It's another habit of hers, especially when she's trying to be a smart-ass.

"Speaking of," I murmur as I stand from the sofa. I can't believe I'm about to ask but... "Have you seen Bryson lately? Anywhere?"

"Actually, yeah. I saw him with Mark at Target. They were picking up laundry detergent for Mark's mom and you won't believe who else was with them!"

"Who?"

"Sara the Slut." My heart clutches and my mouth lacks with moisture as I stare down at the glass coffee table. "You would think he learned his lesson about being with her after losing you. but he's still an asshole. He tried to act like he was too good to say hey to me while he was with her. I wanted to sock him right in his fucking face for it, too. But Mark said hi and even talked me out of boredom. I seriously think Mark has a crush on me, I'm just afraid to ask him how he feels. He's always been kind of like a brother to us, you know?"

The line goes silent and I want to speak on Mark with her, but I can't. The fact that Bryson is still with Sara has really put me at a loss for words. I mean, it's not like I wasn't expecting it but hearing it fucking sucks. I hate myself for feeling this way about him. I thought maybe he would leave her alone—especially since he tried to see me every single night and apologize.

Was he faking his sincerity? Was he fucking her and then running to me to see if I would take him back? Grace is right. He truly is an asshole. "Um, hello?" Gracey whistles. "You still there, Nat?"

"Yeah." I gulp the bulge of pain down, forcing myself to breathe again. "I just don't get how he can still deal with her. She's worthless."

"Oh, no," Gracey snaps. "You are not about to get mushy right now. I called to talk to my girl—to Natalie Carmichael. I'll be damned if I let you take one sniffle." The line goes silent again and it isn't too long before I'm slouching down on the arm of the sofa. "So tell me about this guy you met. What's he like? How does he look?"

My heart starts to beat in a steady pace again as I circle my mind back to Nolan. I'm going to see him tonight. I seriously can't wait to feel his lips and stare into his eyes. I can't wait until he runs his fingers across my skin. I want to touch him right now. I want him to hold me. Thinking about Bryson makes me feel that way. It's as if I'm getting back at him and letting him know I'm good without him… even though Bryson can't see shit that I'm doing right now.

"Nolan is beautiful, Gracey. He has a body to die for, lips to kill over, and he actually cares. He has his flaws," I note without making it too obvious, "but besides the minor things, I believe something kinda serious might ignite between us really soon."

"Aww," she coos. "That's so cute. Snap a picture of him the next time you see him and send it to me. I need to see the guy who made you forget about Douchebag B."

"Yeah," I breathe in agreement.

"Oh—Nat, I gotta go! Trey is calling. I haven't talked to him all day. I promise to call you tonight. I love you, I love you! Muah!"

The call ends way before I can even fix my mouth to speak. Smiling, I stand to my feet again. I love talking to Grace and I'm so glad she's still the same. Nothing's changed with her. Even though she's boy-crazy, I love her.

But I seriously can't believe Bryson is still fucking with Sara. Sara is hideous and even though I can't stand his guts, he can do way better than *her*. Receiving blowjobs will get tiresome to him soon.

One day, he'll want real love again. Sara can't provide that but I could have.

Screw it.

He doesn't deserve me and I won't sit around and wallow in pity about it. He doesn't deserve any kind of happiness in his life. I do need to get these feelings off of my chest, though.

I grab and throw pillow and sit on it, sliding my legs beneath the coffee table. I grab my pen, a sheet of blank paper from the stack, and immediately begin writing. And I don't stop. Not even when I catch a cramp in my hand.

Chapter Sixteen

About three hours later and Nolan is at my doorstep. And he looks unbelievably hot. Too hot for words, actually. I scan him over in his white muscle T-shirt, snug dark blue jeans, and even his hair that was just how it was when I first met him at the club. It's cropped around his ears and gelled to prevent any strands from touching his forehead. I have to admit it's just like seeing him for the first time again. He looks amazing.

Leaning in, he plants a kiss on my lips and a surge of energy sweeps through me as my eyes widen. I begin to shove him away but once I realize this feeling feels beyond natural, I sink against him, pressing a hand against his firm chest.

"Hey," he breathes as he pulls away.

"Hi," I sayl but it comes out as more of a breathy moan.

I step back to let Nolan in but he doesn't bother to remove his eyes from me. He studies the length of my red-brown hair that I'd just flat-ironed, my mint-green blouse, and then my dark wash jean shorts.

"You look..." He pauses, stepping closer. Somehow, the air seems thicker now... but in a good way. "You look, great, Natalie. Can we skip Open Mic by staying here and fucking all over this apartment?"

My mouth expands into a grin, my cheeks sparking. I bite my lower lip but he brings his hand up to stop me. "You have got to stop talking like that," I say.

"Why?"

"Because *'you have to get to know me before you get to know her,'*" I say, attempting to do my closest mimic to the way he said it during our first "date."

"Oh, trust me," he chuckles, reaching to pull me forward by my belt loop. A surge of heat drowns my entire body and even seeps through my bones. His lips hover above mine and out of instinct, I tilt my head up, craving for another kiss. "Once I get to experience *her* for myself, there'll be nothing that can keep me away." He winks then releases his finger from the loop of my shorts. He takes a step back and I let out the breath I was holding in, folding my arms.

"You wanted that kiss, didn't you?" he asks. One of his eyebrows arc. "We still have thirty minutes."

He steps in again, but instead of reaching for the belt loop of my jeans, his arm curves to pull me in by my ass. I tense as my stomach presses against the bulge in his pants.

"No—Nolan we can't." I push against his chest but he keeps his hold tight. It's seriously turning me on and as bad as I would love to ride him for hours, I can't right now. I've just done my hair and got dressed. I can't go out looking like I've been hit by a sex hurricane. I know that's probably what it'll be like with Nolan. I can tell by the frisky look in his grey eyes—the way he's cupping my ass as if there's nothing else he'd rather hold onto.

"We can't?" he murmurs, leaning in to place his lips against my ear. My skin hums and I melt as the hand that's still pressing against his chest seems to give out and fall against my side on its own. "We're grown, Natalie. We can do whatever the hell we want." Pulling back, Nolan takes a look into my eyes. He studies the desire, the need. I can feel my lips puckering now, but I don't care. I'll go through with anything with this beautiful man.

"But we aren't rushing this, remember?" he asks in a baby voice that's supposed to mimic mine. His eyebrows pull up as he runs his fingers across my cheek. His touch is causing my skin to catch on fire. "I can wait."

"But I can't," I breathe.

"That tense?" he teases. "I can't wait until the day I can release it."

"Why can't you do it right now?"

His face falls as he pulls his hand away from my cheek. "If I do it right now, what'll make you wanna stick around with me? I like the fact I have control over of your body. My dick, my way."

"I'm pretty sure if I were to whip it out right now, you wouldn't stop me."

"I wouldn't?" he challenges, a small smile playing on his lips.

"Nope. Not unless you're just straight-up gay."

His face falls into a deep slant and I cup a hand around my mouth quickly. *Oh, no.* I've pulled the gay card with him again. "I seriously hate when you test me, Natalie," he mutters and before I know it, he's picking me up in his arms and making his way around the sofa. I think he's going to go for the bed of my bedroom, but he passes by it to get to the bathroom.

The door shuts behind us and he pushes my makeup products aside to give my hips space on top of the counter. I'm not even allowed enough time to catch a quick breath before his lips are pressing against mine. Pulling me in by the loop of my shorts again, he presses his groin between my legs. My chest falls against his and he thrusts himself forward and backward against me, getting harder and harder. A trickle of heat slides down and touches my panties and I bite my lower lip as he reaches to pull my shirt over my head. I reach for the hem of his and our lips part for a second before they're reconnected as soon as our shirts hit the floor.

Nolan's lips trail from my lips to my cheek and then down to my neck. With ease, he pokes his tongue out to lick the curve of my breast. His eyes are still closed but once he realizes where his mouth has landed, he yanks my bra down and immediately begins to suck my nipple.

A shrill gasp escapes me as he pulls me in by my hips to keep his erection pressed against the center of my thighs. More heat flushes through my entire body and travels down to my panties. I groan as he moves his lips to my other nipple and sucks it. As he grazes his teeth against them, a spiral of pleasure burns my sweet flesh.

I can't be the only one getting some kind of pleasure, though. I want Nolan to know I'm great in bed as well. I guess all those nights spent with Bryson paid off for something.

I reach down to unbutton Nolan's pants quickly. His eyes fly open as he pulls away and watches my hands go to work. Hopping from the counter, I push him against the door quickly. When he's bumped against it, I stoop down and yank on his jeans.

"Shit, Natalie," he hisses. His voice makes me want to do nothing more than continue. My eyes widen as I pull his boxers down and study the size of him. I grab the length of him and begin to stroke. His flesh is soft, even, and smooth. I hear him suck in a breath and as I look up, the back of his head falls against the door.

After stroking Nolan, I finally figure out something's missing. And then it dawns on me. The strokes aren't smooth enough. He needs something more. I wrap my lips around the tip of him and he quivers, but my hand doesn't stop stroking. It's a pleasurable multitask.

He sucks another sharp breath in, his grip tightening around the door handle. "Fuck, Natalie!"

After a few moments of licking, sucking, and him groaning with a few encouraging curse words, he finally pushes my mouth away, but it's only to pull me up by the arm. He pulls me against him and his erection caves into my stomach. "I wanna finish off with a piece of you," he murmurs against my lips with solid eyes.

Scooping me up, he places me on top of the counter again. He reaches down to unbutton my shorts and I lift my hips so he can yank them down.

His lips trail from the crook of my neck, to my chest, to my navel, then down to my pelvis. He reaches down again to yank on my lacey white panties and as soon as they're off, his mouth seals around me. I inhale sharply, deeply as his tongue strokes the sweet flesh then dips down between the folds. Circling his tongue repetitively, I graze my fingers through his hair, encouraging him to keep going. A finger slides into me, and he growls pleasurably, pulling his mouth away slightly.

"You're tight, babe." His husky voice is seriously going to cause me to explode. "I can fix that, though. You're not a virgin, right?" he asks.

I shake my head rapidly.

"And you're on the pill, correct?"

"Yes," I breathe impatiently. "Just fuck me already, Nolan!"

Nolan bites his lower lip, smirking. The head of him then pokes itself inside me and I gasp because it's been a long time since I've felt something like this. It feels extremely different. Nolan is thicker than Bryson. There's a fuller feeling in my stomach, but I'm not complaining. I love it..

"You want me to fuck you?" he asks, pushing in and out slowly. He glares down at me, keeping his hands hoisted around my waist. One of his hands reaches up to cup my breast but I pant as I stare into his eyes. His strokes are slow. He wants me to beg. "Say it again, babe. I know you want to." He lowers himself to place his lips against my ear.

I sink my teeth into my bottom lip, breathing him in. His masculine body wash and cologne lingers in my lungs before he pulls back to look into my eyes again. He continues his slow strokes and I groan because I don't want to beg, but I hate that he's going so slow. I want it rough. That's what I pictured during my first time with Nolan. Rough sex.

"I can do this for hours, Natalie," he mumbles, his hips still thrusting forward and backward slowly. All of him isn't inside me, only half of it. I want to feel it all. "Say it," he growls. "You've wanted this moment. *Say it.*"

And then, when I can no longer take his teasing or the way his thumb is rubbing circles around me, I decide to let go. "Nolan, please just fuck me. I need this," I beg.

Nolan's lips stretch to smile but that smile fades quickly as he picks me up from the counter without bothering to pull himself out of me. As he turns around swiftly, my back presses against the door and he begins to hammer himself against me, through me, all over me. His hips grind and he grunts while I scream, encouraging him to keep it up. He cups my ass, steadies his legs, and the shift in position leaves me with no choice but to bounce on top of him.

"Fuck!" he growls against my neck.

The more I bounce on top of him and the more we keep going, the more my climax is about to reach its exclusive brink. I try to get my body to control the orgasm that's about to explode all around him, but I can't. He's going too hard, too fast, and he's too damn good not to release. My juices flow and I spot a smile on his lips as I flinch, squirm, wriggle, and write, still bouncing. "Nolan!" I scream. My nails bite into his back as I continuously scream his name. I grip onto him, and to my surprise I'm still bouncing on the length of him.

"Mmm. Glad I can make you this wet, babe," he says against my ear. Even while he speaks, I'm still exploding. I quake in his arms, feeling feeble but I don't want this moment to end. Nolan picks up the speed and continues to pound into me. He then turns around and places my back on the counter. His thumb rubs circles across my center and my legs shake around him, but he doesn't stop.

"Fuck, Natalie!" He grunts again, burying himself within me. I groan, he groans. His thumb doesn't stop working its magic against me and that only causes me to continue with passion-filled screeches.

"This. Is. Mine," he grunts through his teeth with every stroke. I tighten around him even more, nodding. "All. Mine. From. Now. On." He pushes harder and we continue to pant heavily, grunt heavily, groan and moan into each other's ears until

Nolan finally pulls back to drive himself harder and stare into my eyes.

I can feel it coming. The build-up again. I can feel the climax getting ready to implode and I can see his coming from a mile away. Sucking in a breath through his teeth, he tries his best to keep himself going, but after only a few seconds, his head falls back, he lifts my hips up, cups my ass, and a loud growl erupts from the heart of his throat. I yelp and scream from both excitement and the pleasurable orgasm that has just drenched the entire length of him.

"Oh, shit this feels so fucking good, Natalie! Fuck!" he yells, driving himself into me two more times before finally dropping my hips and falling against my chest. I feel the heat of his release splurging throughout my entire body but it's actually satisfying. We breathe heavily, our chests sinking and rising.

Damn. That was un-fucking-believable. I knew he was going to be worth all the sexual frustration he had me through.

Nolan sits himself up to pull out of me then he stares into my eyes. I stare back into his as he runs a warm hand across my forehead and then my cheek. "That felt good," he says then chuckles.

I giggle then reach up to peck his lips. "I could say the same thing."

He laughs before wiping the sweat from his forehead. "As much as I wanted to wait for sex, I've been craving to fuck you since the day I met you. I could only hold off for so long." He shrugs, then presses his lips against mine and if he hadn't gone so soft, I would tell him to bang me again. But I don't.

Instead, I prop myself up on my elbows. "Now that I know you're straight, maybe we should get dressed and get to the lounge before it gets too crowded?"

"Great idea," he agrees as he steps back to let me hop down from the counter. "But the next time you call me *gay* or anything related to it," he growls, pulling me in by the waist. My back presses against his chest as he pulls my hair back to place his lips against my ear. My ears blaze and as he reaches a hand around me to cup my entire womanhood, I melt in his arms. He slides a finger in and out and I whimper as my body tightens once again. *How in the hell can he do this to me?* "I'll be sure I tease you until you can't stand it—until you want nothing but *me* inside *you*. It was fun watching you wriggle just to get me to go deeper."

I can feel the tempting smile in his voice but I can also feel the heat gushing down to my sweet spot again. He pulls his hand away then makes a loud sucking noise. I turn around, only to spot the finger he slid inside me now in his mouth and sucking away. He looks me over with a heart-melting smirk before reaching for his jeans.

Goodness, he truly is something amazing.

Chapter Seventeen

Thirty minutes later and Nolan and I are finally at lounge Haven. And Brittany wasn't lying when she said a lot of people were coming tonight. The parking lot is packed with cars. It takes Nolan almost ten minutes before he finally decides to park across the street at McDonalds.

And then I feel nervous. I'm not sure why I do. Maybe it's because I know I'll have to stand on the stage one day and read my poem to the entire crowd—well, I don't have to, but I want to. I want to conquer my fears and let others hear what I have to say. I spend so much time to myself writing that I don't even realize I love it so much. But I can't imagine how it is to have all of those eyes inside staring at me.

As soon as Nolan swings the door of the lounge open, the sound of clapping floods my ears. I turn to look toward the stage and spot a young man with dark-brown eyes and dark, unruly hair. By the way he's dressed in his loose jeans and tight blue T-shirt with two graphic fingers holding up the peace sign, I assume he's a hippy. By his hooded eyes and soft, lazy smirk, I definitely would put him in that category. This guy is completely stoned.

"I, uh, just want to dedicate this song to the girl of my dreams. She's helped me come from a long way down." He reaches to scratch his eyebrow piercing before scanning the crowd. "Her name's Brittany. I love her and... uh... yeah. This is for her." As he leans back from the microphone to pick his guitar up, I twist my head to find Brittany. I spot her in the middle of the room at a four top table. She's smiling broadly as she stares ahead at the guy on stage. That must be Jordan, her boyfriend.

"This way," I say as I grab Nolan's hand and drag him through the crowded tables. Jordan begins to strum his guitar, clears his throat, and his melody begins to play softly. Nolan and I reach the table and Brittany turns to look at me quickly, her wide eyes now glistening.

"Oh, Natalie! I swear I thought you weren't going to show up!" she says then turns to look ahead again. Man, she can't keep her eyes off of him.

"We got a little caught up," I whisper, sitting in the chair beside her. Nolan sits in the chair to my right and immediately looks ahead at Jordan. I turn with them both, realizing conversation isn't needed because Jordan has a beautiful voice and a lovely melody going on right now.

"If the wind were to take me away," he sings.
That would only leave her heart astray.
I would fly to be by her side
And if I die, at least she knows I tried
I would use all of me
Just to see how happy she'd be
I would fight 'til the break of dawn
I would try to carry on

If a storm comes
I'll be standing in the rain
If a storm comes
I'll just be a call away

I wouldn't give up
I wouldn't let you fall
Cause I have your heart
And I've kept it from the start

If a storm comes
I'll be standing in the rain
If a storm comes
I'll just be a call away, babe

Jordan does his last slow strum on his cherry red acoustic guitar and my immediate reaction is to stand and clap. Nolan does the same and Brittany stands, her face now wet from tears as she cheers and whistles. The other guests of the lounge cheer and hoot as well and a group of guys in the corner chant Jordan's name.

"Thank you!" Jordan says with a toothy grin, leaning into the microphone. "Thank you, guys. I love you, Brittany!"

"I love you, too!" Brittany wails as she wipes her face. Jordan steps down from the stage just as a young woman is stepping up. I watch as he carries himself through the crowd and at first sight, Jordan doesn't seem like much, but as he gets closer, I can see why Brittany is so in love with him.

Jordan is adorable. He's around the same height as Nolan, has beautiful brown eyes garnished with extremely long eyelashes. He has a silver hoop in his eyebrow and from what I can see beneath his blue T-shirt, he must have a body that Brittany can drool all over. His jeans are snug and loose at the same time—if that is even possible—and as he reveals a dazzling smile at Brittany, I smile because it's contagious. His hair is curly and purposely untamed but that only adds to the collection of his simplistic beauty.

"Jordan," Brittany squeals as she takes him in her arms. "I loved it. I'm glad I waited for you to surprise me instead."

"Yeah, I'm glad, too. I was pretty nervous up there but seeing you smile made me go through with it." He leans down to press his lips against hers.

"Aww," she says as she stares into his eyes. For a brief moment, she doesn't look anywhere else. It's like she wants to drag him out of the lounge and into a bedroom. But after a while, she turns to look at us. "Oh, this is Natalie. The girl from school I was telling you about earlier."

Jordan places his guitar down to reach a hand across the table. "I've heard great things. I hope you're stealing that stage tonight," he says as we exchange handshakes.

"Oh, no." My head shakes quickly. "Not tonight. Maybe some other time, though."

"Damn. That sucks. Brittany was bragging about how great your writing was."

"Really?" I ask, a bit self-absorbedly.

"Yeah, dude. Brittany doesn't lie. When she brags, *she brags*." Jordan's brown eyes stretch as he presses his lips together and rolls his eyes playfully.

Nolan shifts to the side of me and Brittany turns quickly to look at him. She was so dazed by Jordan that she didn't even realize he was with me. She stares at him and her glistening eyes broaden.

"This is Nolan," I say as I grab his arm. "He's my date for tonight."

"More like your date for every night," he says with a casual smirk. I flush as I rip my gaze from his to look down at my feet. "Nolan Young," he says, reaching a hand in Jordan's direction. Jordan shakes his hand firmly with a nod.

"Cool. Nice to meet you, dude. Jordan Humphrey. Glad you could join us tonight."

Nolan then places his hand inside Brittany's. "Brittany Lucas."

"Nice to meet you as well."

We all take our seats as the woman up front introduces the next person. "So, how did you two meet?" Brittany asks as she reaches for her cup of water.

"At a club."

"She almost ran me over," Nolan says at the same time.

My eyebrows pull together as I turn to look at him. Chuckling, Jordan reaches for his beer. "You must like hardcore chicks," he says after he takes a swig.

"I kind of do actually," Nolan confides. "I admit she was pretty hard to get a hold of."

Brittany giggles and Jordan chuckles again. "He was pretty easy," I counter, looking through the corner of my eye at him.

Nolan lets out an obnoxious laugh and a few people turn our way to look at us. I stare at them to allow my eyes to apologize but Nolan doesn't seem to care. "If only I was."

"So, how old are you, Nolan?" Brittany asks.

"Just turned twenty-one in May."

"And you, Natalie?"

"Nineteen," I mutter, hating to admit it.

"That just seems impossible. You seem way more mature than your age," she says, eyes wide.

"But that's always a good thing," Jordan reassures. "Immature chicks tend to tick me off sometimes. Have you ever had your high blown because some sloppy drunk sixteen year old vomited on your shoes?" he asks as he sits forward. "It's the worst feeling ever. Especially when you've just bought those shoes."

"Oh, I remember that," Brittany says as she turns to look at her boyfriend.

As they banter on, Nolan's hand sneaks beneath the table to crawl between my thighs. I tense as my legs squeeze together. A burning flash of moist heat slithers down and memories of how great our sex was earlier floods my mind. Oh, the things I would do if we were still at the apartment. It isn't too long before another young man goes on stage with a harmonica. Jordan and Brittany stop talking quickly to watch him but Nolan slides his chair in closer, his hand never leaving. I feel the heat of his body getting nearer and when he says, "In my car would be nice," I shudder. More heat slides its way down and I try to focus on the boy on stage with his lips pressed over his harmonica but as his lips move, it immediately reminds me of the way Nolan's mouth was sealed around me earlier.

My stomach coils as his fingers trail across my bare thighs. "We should go another round," he mumbles into my ear.

God, his voice is so mesmerizing. His voice only causes my legs to tighten around his hand. As the harmonica plays, his finger slides into me and luckily for me, my moan goes unnoticed. I glance around at all the other people but they don't seem to be paying us any attention. Plus, it's too dark. The only light is coming from the spotlight on stage.

I finally find the will to push Nolan's hand away, but it's only to grab it and stand from the table. Brittany's head whips to look at us and it isn't too long before Jordan does the same.

"Where you going?" she asks.

"I just remembered. I have to, um, get home before my roommate gets there. She lost her key." Of course, I'm only telling a white lie. Harper still doesn't have a key but that doesn't mean she'll be home anytime soon. Harper is spending her night with Dawson.

"Oh." Brittany's lips pout. "Well okay. Have a safe drive. I'll call you soon."

"See ya," Jordan says before turning to look at the harmonica player again.

"Okay," I breathe out then turn and make my way toward the door. It's terrible how turned on I am right now. I seriously can't take this. Nolan's chuckle rumbles from his throat as we reach the door and push out.

"Eager aren't we, babe?" he asks, pulling his hand away to take his keys out his pocket. He scoops me up in his arms then rushes for the car. He was smiling, but that smile jut faded and turned into a mask full of lust. His eyes are hard on me as he reaches the car, presses the button on his key to unlock it, and then climbs into the passenger seat. He shuts the door then reaches to pull my shirt over my head quickly. I reach for the hem of his and yank it up. Nolan then begins to unbutton my pants, releasing a low groan. "No panties must've meant you wanted more?" He raises an eyebrow along with a smirk.

I smile then dip in to kiss him. He clings onto my body, pressing his hands everywhere to get a feel of me. I wrap one hand around his face, the other working to get the button of jeans undone.

As soon as his zipper is undone, he lifts his hips for me to slide his pants down. He watches my every move. The way I reach my hand in his boxers. The way I press my lips against the long rock beneath the fabric. I know it's my lips he wants to feel but for now, I'll be a tease and kiss him through the cotton fabric of his boxers.

He reaches a hand down to push my hair aside. Pulling his boxers down, I begin to lick him slowly. He tenses as I reach the head of him and then swallow him whole. "Holy fuucckk," he says through clenched teeth. I do it again, taking a peek up. His hand is around the nape of my neck, encouraging me to go again. And I do. "Damn, Natalie. Please come on," he begs.

A smile creeps across my lips as I pull my mouth away. Although it's cramped in the car, I manage to pull my shorts down and climb on top of him again. But I'm still going to be a tease. I want him to crave for me—for every part of me. I slide down on him gently and he tries to get me to sit on the entire length of him, but I hold off. "You want me to fuck you?" I ask against the crook of his neck, attempting to copy the former words he said to me in my bathroom an hour ago.

"God, yeah," he breathes.

"I want you to say it like you mean it." I lift my hips and straddle the tip of him.

He lets out a deep groan from the pleasure. "You're seriously gonna make me come if you keep doing that."

"Say it." I press my lips against his ear as he cups my ass. "Say you want me, and only me. Promise you won't fuck up."

My hips continue to move on top of him. I know he wants me to go wild right now.

"Natalie, damn it. I promise I won't fuck up. Now *fuck* me," he grunts then smashes my hips down. He slides into me and I let out a loud moan as my hands curl around his shoulders. I begin to ride him harder, going forward, backwards, side to side. Any way that makes him roll with pleasure. "Shit," he hisses through his teeth. "You seriously know what you're doing."

I smile broadly as he pulls a hand away to grab the lever on the side of the seat. The seat falls back and that gives me even more leverage to move. "Oh, fuck, that feels so good," he says as he reaches a hand up to cup one of my breasts. As I continue to go, millions of moans screech out of me. He reaches a hand down to rub the sweet flesh between my legs and as he does that, I know it's coming. My head falls back, my chest sinking and rising, the air in the car thickening.

My grip on his chest tightens and the muscles in my stomach clench as I continue grinding my hips on him. "Nolan!" I scream. "Oh, fuck, Nolan!"

"I love when you call my name," he murmurs. His hips then lift from the seat to pound into me and the shift only causes me to ride him harder. He's completely inside me now. I can feel the entire length of him reaching up to my stomach. "Oh, fuck," he growls through his teeth. His husky voice plays tricks with my head. With my body. His thumb continues to play with me and as we both pant heavily, groan heavily, and call each other's names, that's when I jerk forward, my chest constricts, my legs clamp around him, and I scream his name again.

"Oh, Nolan!"

I quiver around him, but I don't stop, and neither does he. He continues to pump into me, pounding like a hammer on a nail. A loud clapping noise bounces off the walls of the interior of the car and as Nolan clamps a hand around my ass and my breast, that's when a growl erupts from the heart of his throat.

Nolan slams into me one last time before his hips fall and a gush of warmth floods through me. Falling against his chest, I breathe heavily with no intent of controlling it anytime soon.

"Damn, babe," he breathes, pushing a loose strand of hair behind my ear. "I could really get used to this."

Chapter Eighteen

Soft music floods through the speakers as Nolan and I lie on our backs on my bed. It actually feels nice doing this. No touching, no kissing, no sexual feelings... just peace. As of now, the song *I Never Told You* by Colbie Caillat is playing. Listening to the lyrics remind me of Bryson. I hate the fact that I'm thinking about him, especially while I'm with Nolan. I'm glad he can't read my mind.

"So, you write?" Nolan asks as he reaches a hand over to grab mine. His fingers caress the skin on top of my hand. His touch is always satisfying. There's just something behind it—something that proves he actually wants this.

"Yeah, sometimes."

"When can I see?" He turns his head to look at me. I turn and face him, staring into his mellow grey eyes. The fact that he's so humble really makes me adore him even more. I can tell he actually wants to be here and it isn't forced.

"I don't know. You would probably freak if you saw what I wrote."

He chuckles as his thumb strokes circles on my knuckles. "You would freak from the lyrics of my songs so I guess we're a match." Adjusting against the bed, he props himself up on his elbow but he doesn't release my hand. "How about we make a deal."

I sigh, sitting up with him and placing my cheek in the palm of my hand, my elbow propped up as well. "Okay. What is it?"

"You show me a poem, and I'll sing one of my songs for you."

My face begins to spread, but as I think about the power within the words of my poems, my face falls to a slant. I would love to hear Nolan sing for me. He has a beautiful voice, but I'm not ready to show him how I feel. "Nolan—"

"Ah, I'm not done," he says, placing his finger against the fold of my lips. "The song I sing for you will be a song I wrote about you last night. And I promise this one isn't about soul-stealing or breaking hearts."

"You wrote another song about me?" I ask as my heart warms up delightfully and my lips stretch to smile.

He nods. "Yup. I think you would love it... but I'm only singing it if you agree to let me read one of your poems. I think reading them will give me a little depth as to what you're going through."

"How so?"

"Because I write as well, Natalie. Every song I've ever written is from what I've felt. Whether it's pain, heartache, happiness, or just feeling somewhat complete, I write it down. I know you have something in them that'll help me get a better understanding of what you're really going through. I can tell you don't like talking much about your past."

"Yeah, because the past is just what it is. The past." I sigh, lowering my gaze. "I don't like thinking about it."

"But thinking about it will help you let go. Trying to ignore it makes it worse." Nolan's eyebrows arch as he pulls his hand away from mine to stroke my cheek. Pushing a strand of hair behind my ear, he leans in to place a gentle kiss on my lips. "Like I said, I've sort of been through what you're going through, and although I was terrible at dealing with it, I learned how to get over it. That's something I can help you with, but only if you *let me in*. Right now, I'm stuck on the outer part of you. Your interior is where I want to be. I'm sure it'll take some time, but you have to work with me, Natalie. Don't hold off anymore. Okay?"

I nod, my chest constricting. I pull my lips in and bite down to prevent the tears from falling. "I think about this a lot—my life. I want this to work. I've never wanted someone this damn bad. I have to keep you," he murmurs against my lips.

Misguided Ghosts by Paramore begins to play and as soon as the countdown of the song is over, Nolan slides in to lay me on my back. He climbs on top of me, stares into my eyes, and then pulls my hands above my head. His fingers entwine with mine and in only an instant, he leans down to kiss me.

As Hayley Williams sings her lyrics, my only hope is that I can keep Nolan with me. My only hope is if I do let him in, that he won't screw up—that he won't hurt me. It scares the shit out of me and now I can see what Harper means. It's scary to think about having your heart handed to someone else. I don't want to go through it again because I'm still hurting and if I give Nolan my already shattered heart, he can easily crush them.

A tear slides down to my ear but Nolan's lips don't bother to pull away from mine. He releases his fingers from mine to cup my face. His panting is even, strong, yet rigid and powerful. I wrap my legs around him and hook my arms around his neck to pull him in against me. I want nothing more than to feel him, hold him, and never let go. I'm in so deep that I feel like if I allow him to slip once, it's over.

I wouldn't say it's love, but ever since Nolan has come into my life, I've been feeling ten times better about myself. I can tell he wants to make this work and that he wants to keep this going. I do as well, but how long will it be before he finds me just as boring as the previous girls he's dated? I can't be any more different than them. How long will this part of him really last?

Nolan finally pulls away and I stare up at him as the light of the lamp blankets over one side of his face. "We'll take our time, okay? I'll be sure not to hurt you." He pulls a hand up to wipe at the tears collecting at the edges of my eyes.

"You promise?" I whisper.

"I promise." He leans down, kissing me once more. "So is it a deal? I sing for you if you let me read one of your poems?"

"Sure," I agree as he climbs off of me. "But not tonight."

"Whenever you're ready is fine with me."

I smile then pull him in for another kiss. *I can do this,* I tell myself. But if anything happens, I have to be sure this entire thing I'm having with him is worth it.

Chapter Nineteen

As the seagulls caw from above and from the shore of the beach, I flip on my stomach and let out a satisfying sigh, allowing the rays to blanket across my back. Pulling my arms in to rest my head on them, I turn to look at Harper who is still lying on her back with a pair of square brown *Ray Ban* sunglasses on that match well with her gold and brown bikini.

"I needed this," she says, her lips barely moving. I can tell she's just as relaxed as me.

"You and me both," I mumble.

"Seriously, after last night, I needed to clear my head."

I adjust my head on my arm as a cool breeze passes by. "What happened last night?"

"Well for one," she says, twisting her head in my direction to most likely look at me—or at least I think she's looking at me. Her sunglasses are too dark for me to see through them. I reach for my sunglasses and sit them on the bridge of my nose. "—you and Nolan were so loud when I got home. It was kind of disturbing." My sunglasses fall as I prop myself up on my elbows.

"What?!" I shriek, my cheeks filling with blood. "You heard us?"

"Kinda hard not to." She shrugs, turning her head and facing the sky. "But by the way you were screaming, he sounds like he's super good in bed. I could hear you from outside the apartment."

"I thought you came in this morning, though. When did you get back last night?"

"While you two were humping around your room."

Wow. This is embarrassing.

"But don't worry." She sighs, reaching up to push a lock of her medium-length blonde hair behind her ear. "I'm glad you're getting some. You needed to loosen the hell up."

"Did not," I say, flicking a few specks of sand on my towel in her direction.

"Yes you did, Nat!" She props herself up on her elbows. "I swear I thought I was going to have to drown you with liquor every night for the past two weeks. You were freaking me out."

"Whatever," I mutter.

Although I'm not looking in Harper's direction anymore, I can feel the glare and scowl she's giving.

"So, are you gonna talk about how great he was in the sack or what?"

I crush my lips together and try to hold off on a smirk. I flip on my stomach again, turning my head in the opposite direction to keep my smirk hidden from Harper.

Sex with Nolan is un-fucking-believable. I can't believe how good he is. I was looking for a downfall or something that would prove he isn't all-perfect and besides his minor flaws from the past, there's nothing. He has the perfect body, the perfect face, the perfect smile. There's absolutely nothing wrong with him physically. Now, mentally... that's what I'm still unsure about. I still have so much to learn about him.

In the midst of my train of thought, a hand yanks me by the shoulder and I flop onto my back like a pancake. "Damn, Harp! Break my damn back, why don't ya?!"

"I will if my best friend doesn't provide the scoop! Now tell me. I really wanna know. Maybe he and Dawson have something in common." She pulls her sunglasses off her face to wink.

We both sit up and I place my sunglasses back on. "Well, you heard it," I say without eyeing her. I never really understood why it was so hard for me to gossip about how sex with my boyfriends is with my friends. Grace loves bragging and Harper never shuts the hell up about it. I just find it so odd. I guess I'm one of those people who thinks the sex should stay in the bedroom. But, instead, I feel the urge to give in and brag a little. "Harp, he's amazing! There's no need to fake it with him... at all."

"Oh my gosh!" she squeals, reaching for my hands. She slides in and squeezes them. "Go on! What else? Was he big? Did he satisfy you, too?"

"Yeah," I breathe. "To be honest, he satisfies me way before he satisfies himself. I don't know how he does it." My mind drifts as I turn my focus on the body of water beside us. "And yes. He's pretty damn big," I add on quickly.

"Ugh, I am so jealous. I tried to make a move on Dawson last night but he held off on me. He says he doesn't want to rush anything—like we haven't already fucked before." Harper frowns, looking away. "I feel like I've known him long enough. It's been three weeks since we've had sex. Three weeks, Nat! I can't do this anymore. He's really frustrating."

"But?" I ask as my head tilts and she releases my hands.

Her face falls. "But, what?"

"But you're still with him. If you were really that frustrated, you wouldn't still be seeing him, Harp."

She thinks on it for a moment, chewing on her bottom lip. She then looks back up and her blue eyes meet mine. "Well, yeah, only because I wanna do it again. He has the perfect moves. When we make out, I can pretty much feel everything. And when he's turned on, the long rock in his pants is just so hard to not want to take advantage of!"

"That's kind of how Nolan was… but I finally got him to crack."

"How?" she asks as her eyebrows stitch together.

I run my fingers across my orange towel, keeping my eyes down. "Um… I called him gay."

Harper bursts out laughing and I look up quickly just as she is clutching herself. "Seriously, Nat," she says, still chuckling as she swipes at the tears in the corners of her eyes. "You have got to ease up. I'm honestly glad you're happy with him. For a moment, I was afraid you were going to be worse down here than you were at home. I know you've just met him but Nolan is doing something to you that I'm actually glad to see. You should be glad about that, too. I'm kind of jealous."

"You'd be surprised by how glad and scared I am since he's come into my life."

"Scared? Why are you scared?" She uncrosses her legs to swing them straight. Her forehead creases as she eyes me briefly.

"The same reason you are. I'm afraid to let him in too much. Nolan may be great in some ways, but there're things about him that I'm not sure I want to deal with."

"What do you mean?"

I sigh as she lies on her back to soak the sun in again. Her belly ring twinkles and reflects off of my sunglasses. "I don't know—never mind." I shrug it off and lay on my back.

"It's only been a few weeks, Nat. Don't sweat the small stuff. I say count the things you actually like about him. The number one thing should be the fact that he's helping you forget about Bryson the Shitbag."

I giggle as she reaches for my hand to give it a squeeze. Her lips press to form a small smile and I smile with her before looking up at the clear blue sky again. "I guess you're right. I'm going to go grab something to drink. You want something?" I ask, sitting up.

"Sure. Grab me a Sprite."

Nodding, I stand, dusting most of the sand particles off of me. I slide my toes around the thongs of my white flip flops that match well with my white and grey striped bikini before reaching for my wallet and my phone and carrying myself toward the nearest shack. My mother sent money to my card today and I can't wait until tomorrow to go shopping with Harper. I have to get a new wardrobe as well, especially while I'm down here. In Miami, I'll be a new Natalie. I'll try to forget and live on.

As I step into the shack, a cool breeze of air conditioning blows down on me. It feels amazing, considering how hot it is outside.

I make my way toward the counter where a girl with braces and a high bun steps up to the register. She smiles as she watches me approach. "Hi, what can I get you?" she asks.

"Um, I'll take a Coke and a Sprite please."

"Okay," she says, pressing a few buttons on the screen of her register. She tells me how much I owe and I nod, pulling my wallet from the pit of my arm.

"Natalie Carmichael?"

I jolt and tense at the same time as I turn slowly to the sound of the familiar voice. My curls flop onto my back as I face a bright white smile, bright brown eyes, and cropped, slightly curly blond hair. He has on a white tank top with a pair of sky-blue swimming trunks and I swear he still looks the same.

"Mark?" My eyes narrow as I look him over. Mark is still tall with broad shoulders and a very lean chest that I can make out clearly beneath his tank. Something's off about him, though. His eyes are lazier, glazed over. And he's watching me. Hard. Taking a step toward me, he scoops me into his arms. I giggle as I wrap my arms around his neck and he spins around in a small circle.

"Good God I haven't seen you since grad night! Is this where you've been hiding out?" he asks after he's placed my feet on the floor. He pulls away with a large smile glued to his lips.

"Yeah. I moved down here three weeks ago actually."

"Wow," he says through a breathy chuckle. "I can't believe it. Everyone thinks you ran away just to get away from—" Mark's sentence comes to a complete halt as I prepare myself to cringe at the sound of *his* name. Good thing he doesn't say it. "Um, so how have you been?" he asks, changing the subject swiftly.

"Never better," I mumble, pulling four dollars out of my wallet. I turn to hand it to the cashier who seems a bit irritated from my lack of manners. "Sorry," I murmur, forcing smile.

She forces a smile back, handing me my change and placing the bottles of soda on the counter. "Enjoy." She spins around to make her way into the kitchen.

"Nat, I can't believe this right now. You look great," Mark says when I turn to face him. I press my lips to smile lightly. Mark has never been the one to hide his affection toward me. He's had a crush on me since elementary school. I've never considered him anything other than a close friend. After I started dating Bryson, he began to ease up on his flirting, but when we were alone, he would still try to sneak it in. "Come here. Let's catch up," he offers, hooking an arm around my shoulder. The right side of my body crashes into his as he pulls me in and makes his way toward a two-top table.

"So, what brings you here?" I ask as I sit across from him.

"A few of the teammates planned to spend a week at the beach. Bryson thought of the idea and I think I know why he wanted to come to Miami so damn bad now."

My eyebrows stitch. "What do you mean?"

"You're down here, Nat. Means he's trying to purposely run into you."

A tightness sinks from my throat to my stomach. I reach to twist the cap of my soda quickly before gulping a few sips down. "This better be a joke, Mark," I growl, slamming my bottle down.

"Far from it." He looks me over a few times before settling on my eyes again. "He's down here— on the beach actually."

My heart sinks. "Did he bring Sara?" I whisper.

"Yup."

I cringe, just from the thought of them two holding hands while walking along the shore of the beach. My fingers tremble around my bottle of Coke as I think back on how Bryson and I used to walk the shores at sunset. "Okay well I think I'm just gonna head out now," I mutter, grabbing both sodas. "It was great seeing you, Mark, but please do me a favor and don't tell Bryson you ran into me. I don't want anything to do with him."

As I step around the table to get to the door, Mark catches me by the arm. I scowl over my shoulder, but he smiles casually and then steps out into the heat. He drags me toward a tunnel around the corner of the shack and as we meet in the center of it, almost surrounded by darkness, he pushes me against the wall, leaning his head down.

"Mark, what in the hell are you doing?" I hiss.

"Natalie, all this time I've been thinking..." He presses his body in, making sure that his groin is against me the most. "And I've been wondering why you chose Bryson over me. You know I could have done you *so much* better than he did."

"We're friends, Mark." I grunt as I try to shove him away, but it's impossible. He's huge. "Nothing's going to change about that."

"Well how about I change the status of our friendship right now?" My eyes widen with horror and in only and instant, his lips are crushing mine. I drop the sodas out of my hand to try and push him away but his grip is too strong. His hands trail from my face, to my neck, to the curve of my breasts.

"Mark, get off of me!" His lips continue to trail down and even though Mark is attractive, I hate that he's doing this. He's supposed to be my best *friend*. The only explanation is he's drunk. There's no other way around it. As my friend, Mark would never do this.

"I think I've been delusional since I couldn't have you. Kissing you feels too fucking good to stop." Of course I was right. Now I can smell the alcohol on his breath.

"Mark." My voice goes hoarse as I struggle to crane my arms between us. "Are you drunk?"

"It's my vacation, Nat. What do you think?"

"I think you need to get the hell off her," says a deep voice from the light of the tunnel. Mark pulls away quickly and I gasp out of relief as I spot the familiar silhouette.

"Who the fuck—"

Nolan marches down the tunnel to shove Mark away. Mark lands flat on his back while Nolan grabs my hand to storm toward the light. As he continues to drag me out, it isn't too long before Mark comes charging toward us with hardened features.

"You think you can just fucking push me and get away with it?" Mark's eyebrows stitch together furiously but before he can reach up to yank Nolan around by the shoulder, Nolan releases my hand to spin and punch him in his jaw.

"Nolan!" I wail as his grip releases from around me. I rush to help Mark up, but Mark is too out of it. On top of being drunk, his composure is completely worthless. "Stop. He's drunk. It was an accident," I say, but just as I turn to look at Nolan whose grey eyes are glaring down at us, Mark hops to his feet. Mark swings his arms while aiming to reach his fist toward Nolan but the alcohol in his system isn't allowing his actions to happen quickly enough. Nolan ducks out of the way then punches Mark in the mouth.

Blood spills as Mark stumbles back. Nolan pounces forward but before he can hop on top of Mark to beat the living shit out of him, a large man from the shack barges through the doors to pull him off. "That's enough. Stop!" the man shouts as he holds Nolan by his firm upper arms. Nolan jerks away, breathing through his nostrils like an angry bull. He's been tempted by the red sheet, and it was Mark. There's probably no stopping him now.

He looks at me and for a moment his eyes are apologetic, but that sincerity turns into pure disgust as he whirls around and hits the hot sand. His hunched shoulders are all I can see as he continues to drift and right now, I'm stuck on who to go for. Mark is my friend. I can't just leave him lying on the ground drunk and out cold. But then again, he did deserve to be stopped.

I watch Nolan's creased back for a few moments before looking at the large man who's staring down at Mark. "His face's gunna be sore in the morning, huh?" he says. I ignore his comment and reach down to grip Mark by the wrists.

"Help me carry him inside?"

The man grabs Mark by the ankles. "Sure thing. Count of three. One. Two. Three," he counts then lifts. I lift as well and even though Mark is the weight a heap of bowling balls, we manage to carry his body inside and lie him down in a booth. "Don't worry," the man says, his thick Italian accent a bit too gleeful. "He deserved it. Coming onto a pretty lady like you has its consequences. I'll stick around and wait for him to wake up, and when he does, I'll let him know what he did."

I nod, folding my arms. "Uh… thanks."

"What's ya name, sweetheart?"

"Natalie."

"Well, Natalie, this young man right here will feel like shit later on. Go back out and find the other guy before he starts more turmoil."

"Great idea," I breathe, unfolding my arms and spinning for the door.

"Oh, hold on!" I roll my eyes before turning around. Damn it. Will he ever shut up? "Free sodas. I see you don't have yours anymore." He marches behind the counter to open the mini fridge and take a few out.

My attitude disappears rapidly as I step up to the counter and take them from him. "Wow, thank you."

"No problem, sweetheart. Go ahead. Catch your man."

I nod and fight the urge to tell this guy that Nolan isn't my man. "Thank you so much!" I call as I spin around and tumble out the door.

I rush towards the beach, but my heart slows in progress as I watch Nolan stalking the sand, looking directly at me. His shoulders are still hunched and his eyes are still blazing with anger. His fists clench as he meets up to me, slinks his arm around my waist, and leads the way toward the dock. Instead of stepping onto the dock, he goes to the right to get beneath it. We pass by a few large wooden columns until we are so far back that no one can see us.

"Nolan, I can explain," I say, feeling the need to defend myself. By the look in his eyes, I know he has something terrible in mind.

"There's no need to," he grumbles, taking the sodas and my wallet out of my hands to place them in the sand. He steps in closer and I take a few steps back until my back hits the curve of the smooth collections of stones behind me. "I can't believe that just happened, Natalie! Who was he?" he growls.

"He's a friend of mine! I told you he didn't mean it. He was drunk!"

One of his eyebrows shoots up. "Is he your ex?"

"No! Mark is one of my best friends—"

"Friends don't come onto friends, Natalie. I'm sorry to tell you, but it's nearly impossible to have a best friend of the opposite sex. There are always feelings. I know this."

"Of course you know," I mutter, folding my arms. Suddenly, I'm not so glad to have wanted to chase after him.

"Look, I can sit here and complain all day and night, but I won't. I can't tell you what to do because you're not mine yet, and that's only because you don't want to be."

Sighing, he rakes a hand through his hair. I gaze down at his white and green swimming trunks and the bulge sitting between his legs. My eyes then drift up to his lean chest before I look into the clear pool of grey.

"I'm sorry," I murmur. Nolan chuckles without humor and my eyebrows draw in as I watch his shoulders shake. "I'm not sure what else to say to you, Nolan. If you aren't going to take me seriously then just leave me alone already." I reach down and grab my wallet and the sodas then storm around him, but before I can get to far, he catches me by the strap of my bikini top. I gasp as my top falls and I drop into his arms quickly.

"I believe one of those are mine," he says, looking at the sodas I've just dropped to try and cover my bare chest. He looks at me again, his lips inching closer. "And even though you don't think so, I believe you're mine as well."

Wrapping his lips around my nipple, he sucks it greedily. My legs quake as he pulls me up and wraps my legs around his waist. My back presses against the smooth stonewall behind me and then he pulls back, groaning and sucking in a sharp breath. His lips finally meet mine and he attacks them as he grips onto my ass.

"Nolan, what are you doing?" I ask raggedly. Although this is enjoyable, I would never do it in public like this. We're beneath the dock but anyone could walk by at any moment.

"I'm taking back what's mine," he growls against the crook of my neck, reaching his hands down to yank my bottoms off. I gasp as moist heat slides its way down. He pushes a gentle finger inside me and I groan before he pulls out. "I think you need to be punished for making me get crazy like that over you." He spins me around so that my back can face his chest. My palms press against the stone wall as Nolan's erection digs into me. I bite my lower lip and finally give in. I want this so damn bad.

I try to turn around and take initiative by pulling his pants down, but he stops me before I can turn completely. "No." His voice is stern as he pushes against me and my stomach molds around the stones. "This is for me." His breath caresses my ear and I swallow as I hear muffling and then a soft whooshing noise. I push my hips back, wanting to feel him inside me already, but he only presses himself against me. He's teasing me, like always. Pushing my hair aside, he trails kisses from the lobe of my ear, to the crook of my neck, and then down to the crease between my shoulders. I tingle sensationally, feeling myself getting wetter and wetter. This buildup between us is becoming unbearable.

I want to grip onto something because the tension is hard to take. I can't control myself when he gets me like this. All I want to do is be on top of him for hours, maybe forever. After a few moments of debating on whether I should look over my shoulder to see what the holdup is, I finally turn my head to look but Nolan shoves himself inside me from behind before I can even turn my head.

A grunt slides through my teeth as my fingers grip onto the stones. Somehow my fingers manage to find a few crevices.

Nolan pumps into me with heavy grunts as I moan and groan and call his name. His hands wrap around my waist, but his arousal doesn't stop burying into me. I clamp myself around him as he pulls me away from the wall to place me on my knees. He's out of me for only a slight second, but as he cups my ass, he pushes himself into me again and begins his quick strokes.

"This. Is. Mine. Natalie," he grunts through his teeth. I can hear the growl in his voice. This is angry sex. And this angry sex is the best angry sex I've had yet. "I meant what I said." He continues to pump into me, gripping his hands around my thin waist as a loud clapping noise fills the silence. One of his hands reach around to cup my entire womanhood and then one of his fingers begins to circle the nub in between.

The sand grazes my knees and a spiral of pain and pleasure burns between my legs. His hips move at the same speed as the finger that's still circling around me. "Oh, shit, Natalie!" he groans, slapping my ass with his free hand. Pulling his hand away from my sweet flesh, he begins to pound into me without any hands at all.

"Oh, Nolan!" I moan through clenched teeth.

"Yeah, baby." He leans forward, placing his lips against my ear. "I want my name to be the only name you call like this from now on." One of his hands cup around one of my breast, the other glued to my hip, causing the strokes to get deeper.

The clapping noise continues for another few seconds as my juices pour. I tense around him just as he sucks in a low breath then lets out a slight hiss. "Shit," he grumbles pleasurably. He smashes against me one last time before finally pulling out and twisting me around. He lies on top of me, making sure he doesn't squish me as his eyes remain hard. His entire face is dripping with sweat as he pants heavily. Leaning in, he places a damp kiss on my lips.

"I believe you, babe," he breathes.

"About what?"

"About him being your friend."

"Good," I mumble with what's left of my energy. "But why were you so mad?"

"I didn't like that he had his hands on you."

I nod with twisted lips.

"I swear I was about to knock him out, though," he adds on. "I saw him drag you around that corner and I wanted to run, but I couldn't help myself."

"How did you know where I was?"

"I saw Harper lying on the beach and she told me you went to the shack to grab some drinks. I thought I would surprise you, but when I saw that guy twirl you around in his arms, I turned and walked away immediately."

"Why?" I ask, reaching up to push the hair away from his forehead. "I wouldn't do that to you."

"I know but... I thought he was your ex or something. I got jealous and I let the jealousy get the best of me, which is why I came back when I saw him take you down the tunnel."

"No, trust me." I push myself up on my elbows. "Mark will regret what he did to me when he's sober. He'll try to apologize but things won't be the same between us. He'll know it."

Nolan nods before he finally pulls away and helps me to my feet. I reach for my bikini top and he helps me put it on. "Is he from your school?" he asks.

"We went to high school together, yeah."

"What's he doing down here?"

I pause, staring at the columns of thick, dark wood ahead. Good thing my back is facing him because as soon as I think about why Mark is here, Bryson appears in the thought bubble of my head and my face twists with disgust. "He said he's on vacation with a few friends." I won't tell Nolan that Bryson is down here. I just have to stay clear of this beach for a week or so.

"Oh. What do you say we go to the pool? I could cool down after what we just did." His lips spread to grin as he grabs my hand.

"Yeah, that would be great," I breathe, fanning out my hair to get rid of the specks of sand. Nolan grabs the sodas and my wallet and we make our way through the columns of wood until we're close enough to the edge of the dock to come out.

But during our whole walk to get Harper and my things, I can't believe Bryson's down here. What in the hell is he trying to pull? I don't need the drama and I definitely don't need to see Sara. I know if I see her, it's automatically going to ruin me. She'll do nothing but rub it in my face. But if it so happens that we do run into them, hopefully Nolan is with me. At least with him around, they'll know I've moved on with someone hotter.

My lips quirk up as I think about how their reaction will be when they see Nolan. Nolan is fit to be a model. It's just so odd that he wants to be with me.

When you give your all
And in the end, receive nothing
When it so happens that you fall
And your knees scrape while burning

Why do you allow him to let the alcohol
pour?
Why do let him cause you pain?
How can you ask for more
When all that person has done
Was cause the burning in vain?

You want to take the blame

Even when you know that it's not your fault
You want to call his name
But calling his name is like
Trapping yourself in a cult

But as time moves on
You begin to forget
As time carries on
You begin to <u>let go</u>

As the days go forward
That's when he realizes
That he stepped backwards
When you finally find the will to release him
That's when you can smile joyously without
A single word

Chapter Twenty

"What in the hell is this?" Harper frowns, pulling out a gold sequined tunic with blue flowers and green polka dots. I choke on a laugh as I watch her twirl it by the hanger with a face full of horror. It's as if she's watching someone being brutally murdered. "I mean, really. Who would wear this monstrosity?" She shoves the hanger back on the rack before picking through the clothes again. "Are you done shopping?" she asks as I slide a scoop of chocolate ice-cream into my mouth.

"Yeah." I place my container of ice-cream on the bench to reach for my shopping bags by the wall. "Four shopping bags full of clothes is way too many. I wasn't expecting to shop this much." I place my bags on the bench, replacing the straps with my cup ice cream.

"You've got to be kidding me. Daddy gave me seven-hundred bucks today and I'm going to use every single penny. As a matter of fact," she says, reaching for her phone from the back pocket of her pink shorts. There is a brief intermission as she touches her screen a gazillion times while I stuff my face with more ice-cream. "Yep. Still got three-hundred bucks left in the account." She flashes a broad smile, tucking her phone into her back pocket again. I shrug as I flop on the bench while she continues to pick through the rack of clothes.

"So what was up with Nolan yesterday?" She pulls out a red blouse to scan every aspect of it. "He came back kind of pissed after I told him where you were." Her eyes finally meet mine as I swallow my last clump of ice-cream.

"Let me ask you a question," I say.

"What's up?"

"Why in the hell would my ex-boyfriend and a group of his best friends be in Miami?"

Harper's blue eyes stretch as she hangs the red blouse on the silver rail before storming around the rack to sit beside me. "What in the hell? He's *here*?"

"Yeah. I ran into Mark at the shack and he tried to fucking kiss me."

"What the fuck!" She scrambles to her feet and as I look up, a few of the employees of Forever 21 turn our way to look at us. "He kissed you? Mark, of all guys? That's like Bryson's best friend. Was he drunk?" she asks.

"Yeah." I laugh humorlessly. Well, actually, now that I think about it, I am a bit humored by it. It's not like I didn't see it coming. Mark was looking like he didn't want anything else in that shack but me. His eyes were staring directly at me, scanning my body intensely. I could feel the desire, but I was trying my best to ignore it.

Being around him and ignoring his flirting for years has become a terrible habit for me. I knew it was going to come someday. "He had to be hammered because even when Mark takes a few drinks, he wouldn't have done that. He took me down the tunnel, Harp. Where no one could see. Luckily for me, Nolan showed up and pinned his ass down."

"Wow," she gasps. "That's crazy. And I actually thought Mark was sweet." She huffs as she marches for her shopping bags that are in the corner. "Come on. After hearing that, I definitely need something to drink."

Grabbing for my bags, I nod as I clutch the straps and follow her out the store.

"Did he apologize at least?" she asks, stealing a glance over her shoulder to look at me before I can meet by her side.

"Nope."

"What a dick."

I nod in agreement as we pass through the sea of bodies. Some are window-shoppers and some women have just as many bags as we do in their hands, if not, more. My shoulders are about to give out on me, but I did buy a ton of cute clothes I could wear to go out more often.

Making the cut for the food court, Harper whips out her cell and dials a number. "I have to call my mom. She's been bitching about me not keeping in touch with her, but you know how she is. She drives me insane." She gives a slight roll of her eyes, placing the phone against her ear. We make our way toward a table centered in the middle of the food court and it's beyond the word relief when I place the shopping bags down.

"Hi mom!" Harper chirps, pulling her Michael Kors wallet out of her matching Michael Kors handbag. I stretch my shoulders and roll my neck before sitting. "Yeah, total win today. I picked out a ton of cute stuff to wear. I even bought you a new fit. You have to come down to try it on one day—whenever that it." She gives me a sidelong glance and rolls her eyes again. Harper has a good habit of sounding excited. She finally pulls the phone away from her ear to look at me. "She's blabbering. I'm gonna go grab a Coke and a burger. Want anything?"

"No, I'm okay."

Nodding, she puts the receiver to her ear again before shimmying away. I cross my fingers in my lap and sigh. I turn to look around at everyone waiting in line for different food choices. There is a Chic-Fil-A, a Burger King, a place I can tell sells Chinese food, just by their title, and then there's a Subway. I stare at the Subway the longest as memories of Bryson and I flood me.

Bryson loved going to Subway. He would order a sub for the both of us and when they had the five-dollar-foot-long deals, those would be the best. Most times we would share when the deals weren't happening. I stare at the green and yellow letters but as my gaze lowers, my heart clutches and a sudden spur of panic grabs hold of my heart and squeezes it tight.

At first, I'm staring at his back, but as I spot the familiar black hair that's gelled to perfection and purposely tousled, his tight black T-shirt that gives definition to every muscle creasing between his shoulders, back, and arms, I grab the corners of my chair and clutch it.

I gulp as he turns while waiting in the line. His fingers are tucked in the pockets of his camouflage cargo shorts and his eyelashes bat as he scans the area. I want to lower myself in my seat or even better, run away, because this can't be real. *He can't be here*. Turning only slightly to look toward the middle of the food court, Bryson's green eyes meet mine and flicker automatically.

Fuck.

My heart clutches as I begin to stand from the table. I force myself to keep my eyes down and to pretend I didn't see him, but I know he's seen me for sure. It's as if he was possibly hoping to run into me here out of a sheer coincidence.

Holy shit. This cannot be happening. I reach for my shopping bags, but as I look to my right spotting Harper's bags, I groan. I can't carry hers and mine. My thin arms will break for sure.

"Need help?" a deep voice asks from above me.

My heart pounds through my ears as the voice rings with too much warm familiarity. Somehow, I don't want to throw up from hearing him speak. Somehow, in a shame filled way, I've missed it.

Releasing the handles of my bags, I begin to rise slowly. I spot his black Nike running shoes first, his attractively hairy legs that are sculpted athletically, and then his hips. My eyes travel from the hem of his black shirt, up to his firm chest, and then into his emerald green eyes. As I stare into them, they're already smiling at me.

"I'm fine," I mutter.

"Lots of bags there, Nat. You sure you don't need help carrying them to your car?"

"I don't need your fucking help, Bryson," I growl. My fists clench and although my words sound harsh, I could give a shit less. He doesn't deserve any acts of kindness from me. He ripped my heart right out of my chest, sucked all of the life out of me for what seemed like years. To this day, the life is barely there, but I'm close to being alive again and he's not about to ruin it for me.

Bryson's eyes widen, but his lips are still hinting with a smile. Why did I have to run into him here? I thought I'd be prepared for this. I thought if I were to run into him, I would at least have Nolan by my side but Nolan isn't here. He has to work all day.

"Still feisty," Bryson notes. "Still sexy."

I roll my eyes. I know it's too late now. I can't go anywhere. I want to turn into superwoman and take all these bags out to my car, but Harp is still here, waiting in line for her food.

Slouching in my seat, I refuse to make any eye contact with Bryson. Hopefully he'll get the clue that I don't want to be bothered with him, but I know him. I know he has motives. He didn't plan a trip to Miami for no reason. He wants something and I figure that something is me.

He slides into the chair across from me, crossing his fingers on top of the table. Out of curiosity, my eyes slide up to look at him. He's already looking at me, his head tilted, his lips pressed to form a slight smirk, and his eyes soft as he observes me. "How are things down here?" he asks.

"How are things with your slut?" I counter, aiming to be bitchy.

He chuckles, running his fingers through his hair. "She aint as good as you. I'll let you know that now."

My cheeks flush as I tear my gaze away.

"Your eyes were always so pretty. So brown. So deep. They held a lot of things I had to figure out. Right now, you're pissed at me. I can feel it."

Well, duh, dipshit. "Bryson, what do you want?" I force myself to be brave for once and look him straight in the eye.

"You," he replies, grinning.

"Well, you're a little too late." I sigh, folding my arms. "We're done. You've wasted your time coming down here."

"Did I?" Quirking a brow, he licks his lower lip smoothly. My lips press heavily as memories of those beautiful pink lips pressing against mine causes my tough shell to crack just a bit. "There's no denying it," he says. "You were mad about me."

"Well now I'm mad *at* you." His hand snakes its way across the table to reach for mine but I jerk away. *What in the hell is wrong with him?* I can't believe I really fell in love with him—with someone who believes I would stoop as low as Sara the Slut by just falling into his arms and kissing him.

"You know what I heard," Bryson says, kicking his feet up to rest them on the chair beside him. His eyes never leave mine. "I heard that you actually did want me back, but you were holding off. Nat, you have to believe me when I say that I'm sorry. It wasn't supposed to happen. Sara—she came out of nowhere. I was blind sighted."

"What are you telling me this for?"

"Because I still love you." He pulls his legs back to tuck them beneath the table again. Standing, he makes his way around the table but stops right behind me. I can feel the heat of his body hovering and to my surprise, he isn't too close for comfort. "Because I miss making love to you," he murmurs against my ear. "I miss touching you. Kissing you. I'm still craving for *every part of you*."

My skin buzzes and hums like it used to do when we were together. How in the hell is this possible. I hate everything about Bryson... or do I? I realize now that I don't hate him. I don't hate the way he makes me feel, the way he looks, or the way that he treated me while we were happy, but I do hate the fact that he cheated on me. That's unforgiveable. He pulls a few strands of hair away from my ear but I jerk away in a flash, standing to my feet.

"Just stay the hell away from me, Bryson," I snap. "*We're done*. And I mean that." Without bothering to grab for my bags, I stomp through the food court. My eyes burn, but I bite my lower lip and fight the urge to cry.

I rush through the bodies and the crowds, searching for the nearest restroom until I finally decide to just give up and make the turn down a plain hallway where the janitor's keep their cleaning supplies. I duck around the corner and in an instant, tears are blinding me. I try to swipe them away, but it's impossible to stop. I'm heaving, drawing in heavy breaths that I'm sure people can hear, even over the buzzing of the commotion going on.

I swear I had myself under control. It turns out that I'm not completely over him. And to think, I actually thought I was winning. I'm losing right now. Bryson knows what strings to pull, what words to say, and exactly how and where to say them to make me remember, to make the memories come back. Groaning, I bang my fists against the cold white wall. I wish my fists could shatter the blocks, but instead It's almost faint. Not even a thud.

I'm back to square one.

Chapter Twenty-One

I was lucky Harper was talking to her sister and mother on three-way during the drive back to her condo. I didn't want to talk with anyone at the moment. She would have known something was wrong with me and I didn't want to talk about it. If anything, Harper would have made things worse. She would have ratted me out and told Nolan and then Nolan would accuse me of being a liar and probably never speak to me again.

I grab my bags out of the trunk just as Harper is making her way toward the door, her phone cradled between her ear and shoulder, as she carries her bags. Pressing a hand against my forehead, a sigh escapes my lips and I slam the trunk closed. I reach for my bags but hear footsteps scuffling toward me. At first, I can't make out who it is, but once I reach sight of the pressed khaki's, tight green Ralph

Lauren Polo, and the dark hair that's gelled to purposely be messy and sexy, my heart flutters.

It's Nolan.

"Hi, Bunny," he says before stopping in front of me. I begin to speak, but he steps forward to plunge his body against mine. His lips smother mine and for some reason, this feeling is just what I need. I need a distraction. Something to get my mind off of Bryson and I must admit it's working.

Lifting my arms to wrap them around his neck, I pull him in closer until I can hardly breathe. My back presses against the trunk of my Camry and I groan, feeling more than delighted by Nolan and this unexpected kiss.

"Bunny?" I breathe as he pulls away to lean his head down and kiss the crook of my neck. Tingles spiral and I catch a grip of his shirt, wanting nothing more than to hold on.

"Yeah. New nickname I thought of while I was at work." He places a kiss on my cheek then takes a step back. "Soft. Cuddly. Sweet... well when you wanna be, anyway." He grins, placing a kiss between each word. "And perhaps we should greet each other with kisses this sexy every day?"

I suppress a smile as I begin to reach for the bags.

"No," he grunts, pushing my hand away gently. "I got it."

I nod and begin to head for the condo. "How was work?" I ask.

"Just terrific," he breathes sarcastically. "I seriously hate that I took my brother up on that job. Traveling around Miami is starting to annoy me."

"You help your brother with tours, right?"

"Right. My brother's the tour guide. I'm like his assistant—only I believe I know more." He huffs a laugh. "I'm actually working to get a degree in it. At Miami-Dade."

"Wow. That's awesome," I say as we march through the lobby to get to the elevator. I push the arrow pointing up before turning to face him. "So what about music? You don't want some sort of degree in that?"

"Of course I do." He grins. "I want to major in music production and engineering but I want to minor in tourism. Although traveling a lot sucks, I always get a kick out of how people react. Especially the foreigners. They're amazed by almost anything." He winks and just as he does, the elevator doors slide open and a few people step out. When they pass, we step into the empty elevator and the doors draw in to shut.

"I just want to major in creative writing. It's all I'm really good at."

"Not true," Nolan argues then immediately drops my shopping bags. He steps toward me and his grey eyes stare into mine. Dipping his head down, he cradles me into his arms, and then kisses me. A moan gets stuck in my throat, but I don't pull away. I can't. It feels too good. His teeth sink into my bottom lip softly, allowing access to work my tongue around it and let the velvety textures collide.

He finally pulls back, but his arms remain tight around me. I breathe him in and notice he smells different. He smells like he's been outdoors but sprayed a soft sheen of cologne on before getting back to bases. But it's still delightful and it still makes me crave for every part of him.

"You're good at that," he murmurs just as the elevator dings and the doors open. We're lucky no one's around to see us. He steps back, grabs for my shopping bags, and I step out, dazed and somewhat turned on. I trot toward the condo and as soon as I step inside, I spot someone out of the ordinary.

His wavy blonde hair meets just at his shoulders. His chest is firm and sculpted beneath his blue T-shirt. His dark jeans are fit just right for his lean height and as he smiles, his lips stretch and the studs in his eyebrow twinkle. "Nolan!" Dawson says through an unexpected chuckle. "Dude, called your phone ten times today. No answer?"

"Didn't charge my phone last night, plus I was rushing when I got home this morning." Nolan drops the shopping bags on the sofa before his eyes meet mine. "Things got a little... out of hand."

I flush, jerking my gaze away and studying Dawson. He really is hot and now I can see what Harper means when she says he looks good in bed. He has the lean stature—the look that makes him seem muscular in a natural way. He's fair-skinned; a bit tanner than Nolan, but it's most likely from bathing in the sun.

"Well, you're here now. That's all that matters," says Dawson. He then turns to look at me and a slow smile creeps across his lips. "Hot-hot-hot-tie," he purrs.

In a quick snap, my cheeks fill with blood, but to be brave and pretend I'm cool with his compliment, I reach my hand out. "Natalie Carmichael," I say as he grabs it.

He shakes my hand. "No need to introduce. My man here can never shut the hell up about you."

Nolan lowers his head, chuckling.

"Dude, I called today to tell you Harp and I are going to the boardwalk. Care to join?"

"The boardwalk?" Nolan's lips press as he nods. He then turns to look at me. "I don't know. You care to join, babe?"

My heart flutters. He's calling me *babe...* in front of his friend? He must really be taking this seriously. At the thought of it, the flutter in my heart pauses.

I'm still pissed by what Bryson said to me earlier. Look what happened to me when I got too serious with him. With Nolan, the same thing can happen. "Sure. I'll go," I breathe. *Too late to back out now.*

I'm in deep with Nolan. Too deep.

Nolan stares at me, and for a moment his smile fades. Dawson slumps down on the couch, swiping his finger across the screen of his phone. "Cool. Double date then," he says without noticing the change in the atmosphere. I can feel it, though. It's heavier than a block of lead.

"Natalie, do you want these in your room?" Nolan asks, gesturing to my shopping bags.

"Yeah." I nod as I reach for one and make my way toward my bedroom, but as soon as I step in— even before I can flip a switch to turn the light on— Nolan places the shopping bags down and pulls me in by my belt loop. My back hits the nearest wall as his breath caresses my lips and my cheeks.

"What's the matter with you?" he asks.

"Nothing," I mutter as his fingers curl around my wrists to keep them planted above my head. The tip of his nose runs across my cheek before trailing down and nuzzling the crook of my neck. He plants a soft kiss and I liquefy as his groin presses into me.

"There's something wrong."

"I'm fine," I breathe. He leans back a little to look into my eyes. It's not completely dark behind my curtains which gives a little light for me to see his face clearly. His eyes are stern, hard. He then drops my arms from above me but it's only to pick me up by my waist. My hormones thrash within me and I eagerly wrap my legs around him. I fall against the wall again as he sinks against my chest.

"You gonna tell me or do I have to tease it out of you? You know I'll do it."

I gulp. No. Not right now. I can't take the teasing. But I also don't want to tell him. Teasing will lead to sex and right now, I don't need the sex. Right now, I just want to be left alone.

Nolan's lips press against my chest before his head lifts to look into my eyes. His lips peck mine gently, delicately. I groan just as his tongue slides into my mouth. One of his hands cup around my ass as the other remains hoisted around my waist. He rubs between my legs, causing a friction that'll soon drive me crazy. Sooner or later I'll want what's rubbing between my legs, *inside me.*

The pleasure runs through me, coursing through my veins. "Natalie," he breathes. "I meant what I said. All or nothing. Right?"

"Yeah but—"

"No buts," he says, dropping me out of his arms in an instant. He pushes a hand through his hair before turning to flip the switch. The room illuminates with soft lighting but his eyes remain glued on mine. "Is it really that hard for you to open up to me?"

My face falls into a slant. It's not that it's hard to me, I just don't want to. I don't want to get too serious. Yes I meant all or nothing, but I didn't mean every single thing about me. I swear I had myself covered up. How can he tell something's wrong?

"You're transparent," he mumbles, as if he's just read my mind. "I see right through you now. Even though I don't know what you're thinking, I can feel it. Is it about yesterday, at the beach? About your friend that I hit? If so, I'm sorry Natalie. I swear I won't do it again. I was just—"

"No," I say, cutting his sentence short. I step toward him until I'm close enough to feel the heat radiating from his body. "It's not that." I then cup a hand on his jawline. The hardness in his eyes softens and melts into shame.

"I don't know what to do with myself while I'm with you Natalie. I'm trying my hardest not to fuck up."

"You're not fucking up! It's not you."

"Then what is it?" he asks through a ragged breath. "I swear I feel like it's me sometimes. You won't open up to me. How else am I supposed to know?"

"Okay." I pull my hands away from him and square my shoulders. He's right. I have to give something. I can't continue hiding things from him. It'll only turn him away from me... and right now, I need him. I need everything about him. "At the mall, I ran into someone I wasn't expecting to see..."

Nolan's forehead creases but his eyes don't drift from mine. I wait for him to say something but his face says enough. It's telling me to continue. To keep going.

"It was my ex, Nolan."

In an instant he jerks away from me. "Did you do something with him?" he asks.

"No!" I shout as he takes a step back. "I fucking hate him. I saw him and I... I broke down." My head shakes swiftly as the memories flood. The burning in my eyes forces me to tear my gaze away from his.

"Natalie. What did he do to you?" he asks, taking a step toward me.

"He didn't do anything. Seeing him was enough to bring me down again."

Nolan pauses and an uncomfortable silence rings in my ears. I steal a peek at him but his eyes are hard on me, refusing to look anywhere else. "Why didn't you tell me? Why's he down here to begin with?"

"He came down here with Mark and some teammates from high school. Mark's the guy you fought at the beach."

A resemblance of midnight shades his irises. "You knew your ex was down here?"

"Yes, but I didn't want to tell you. I was hoping to avoid him," I plead.

"Natalie—" Nolan breaks off as his head turns to look out the window. "How would you feel if I hid things from you? How would you feel if my ex was down here and I ran into her?"

"I don't know—"

"You'd be pissed, right? You'd hate me and call me a liar and a player because I didn't tell you." He steps in to cup my jawline. He strokes the flesh behind my ears, keeping my head tilted up so my eyes can't look anywhere else but into his. "I want this," he says against my lips. "I want it to work, but it can't if you don't open up to me. Let me in, Natalie. I swear I won't break you. You have to put some kind of trust in me, just like I'm putting my trust in you."

My chest tightens as I shake my head. I bite my lip to prevent any of my tears from spilling... but I can't help it. He's causing them to pour out of me. I feel the warmth trickling down my cheeks, but his lips move forward to stop them. He kisses my tears away then leans down to kiss my lips.

His hands stay firm around my face as his lips crush mine. I taste the saltiness of my tears, but I feel the passion more. He really means it. He really wants this. And I thought Nolan was only kidding in the beginning. By this kiss alone, I've been completely fooled. He's putting all effort into this kiss. This one kiss feels like a million of them combined into one. Perhaps more than that.

He pulls back and my eyes shut briefly. "Look at me, Natalie," he breathes.

I shake my head. I can't look at him. I don't want to break down any more than I have. Not in front of him. It's embarrassing.

His smooth lips press against mine again and cause my eyelids to open slowly. I stare into the mystic grey of his. They're soft, with an edge of steel. His thumb strokes the corner of my mouth as he smiles down at me. He finally pulls his hands away to reels me against him, allowing no space between us. "I'm not mad at you. I understand. I told you, I'm working with you, not against you. Just as you're working with me. I know you'll open up one day, and I promise I won't rush it."

I smile, pressing my ear against his chest to listen to his steady heartbeat. He kisses my hair sweetly and the warmness of his breath tickles me.

Somehow, I know he means it.

Chapter Twenty-Two

"Alright, Nolan. You have to provide me with some kind of scoop," I say before taking a bite of my soft cinnamon pretzel. "I haven't gotten any details on you besides what you like to do and what you want to major in. Tell me about your family. Your brother."

Nolan sighs with a half smirk before taking a sip of his lemonade through the straw. We begin to walk toward the sunset as the water ripples and the seagulls caw. A few boats and yachts are parked against the docks and a few men are turning in for the day. I stare out past the ripples of the water to take in the peace. The sun is sitting on the horizon as the sky blankets with a twist of gold and pink. There's a hint of orange behind the sun, but all together it creates a collection of beauty. With the waves crashing in, it almost seems like the water is made of dark, exotic crystals.

"How about this," Nolan says, lifting a finger. "I tell you a fact of my life, you tell me a fact of yours. We'll make it a game."

"Okay." I nod, my mouth half-full with sweet pretzel. "It's only fair. I'll bite."

"Alright. Ask me a question and I'll answer honestly."

I ponder on it as we meet at the thick wooden rails. We stare ahead as the soft breeze brushes against us. "Where were you born?"

"San Francisco, California."

"Oh wow," I breathe. "What made you want to move all the way over here?"

He pauses, smile hinting at his lips. "I think it's my turn for a question. One at a time, babe."

I blush.

"But if you really want an answer, I moved here to get away from everything… everyone. My mom made the wrong decision. She chose a man over her own kids. It's completely fucked up on her behalf, but my brother and I swore if she chose him over us, we were moving to the other side of America. We took it to the extreme, considering we're now in Miami." He chuckles dryly.

I nod. "So you live with your brother here?"

"Yup." Nolan's eyes don't shift from the body of water ahead. I really want him to go into more depth, but I know I'll be pushing it. He probably doesn't like to talk about it. "My turn," he says, finally looking at me. His eyes scan me as a small smile weaves its way to his lips. "What made you want to move to Miami?"

I shrug. "Just wanted to get away."

"From?"

"My ex." I pause. Although I did want to get away from Bryson, that isn't the only reason I decided to move here. "And from my parents."

His gaze grows quizzical. "Your parents? Why?" I sigh and just thinking about what they're going through makes my heartbeat slow in progress.

"I think the only reason they're still together is because they don't want to disappoint me. I left because I wanted to see if things would change without me."

"Did things change?" he asks.

"Yeah. For the worst." My eyebrows stitch. "I haven't heard from my dad in a few days. I take it as a sign that he's finally giving up. I called my mom to see if she would provide any answers on what's going on between them but she always rushes me off the phone. She never allows me enough time to ask. I know she's busy, but she can't be *that* busy."

"Oh." Nolan's lips seal. I know for sure he doesn't want to touch that subject. And neither do I. I can't think about it right now. My only hope is this situation between them is only temporary.

"So, my turn again." I take a bite of my pretzel and swallow to block the dryness in my throat. "What are your biggest dreams?" I smile, hoping he'll lighten up on the mood with me.

Luckily, he does. Reaching to push a hand through his hair, he turns to face me, leaning his elbow on the railing to sturdy himself. "My biggest dreams?" he asks. "Well, one of them is to hopefully be noticed by a crowd. I don't want to be famous. I just want to be known. I want to leave a mark in this world. I already travel a lot with my brother Mills so that wouldn't be a big deal." His eyes drift from mine to his pressed khaki's. I study the way his features soften and while looking at him, I realize why his softened features seem so familiar. He's a dream-chaser, just as I am. Just as my father is. He wants his dreams to become his reality.

"I can understand where you're coming from," I say. "I want the same thing. For my writing to be seen. Picked up and published, even."

"That can't happen if you don't get yourself out there, Bunny. Open Mic is the perfect opportunity."

"You're one to talk." I giggle, leaning in to punch his arm playfully. "You don't sing for anyone but yourself, but you want your dreams to come true. That's impossible. How else will people get to know you if they can't *hear* you?"

His eyes drift as he thinks on it. "True," he finally says as his lips press. "I've been thinking about singing the song I wrote for you during one of the Open Mic nights. But we have to make a deal," he inquires.

I lean against the wood rail, crossing my arms. "You're full of deals. Let's hear it."

"At the next Open Mic session, I'll sing the song, but only if you read one of your best poems." His gaze grows serious but it can't be as serious as mine has just gotten.

"I wasn't planning on reading one of my poems so soon. That's only three days away."

"Three days to practice."

Sighing, I push from the rail and pace in front of him. I take my last bite of pretzel before tossing the wrapper into the trash bin. "I don't know, Nolan. It's nerve-racking to read in front of all those people. What if they don't like me? What if they don't understand it?"

"A part of attending an Open Mic sessions is to have an open mind. Most people who go plan to dig deep—explore. They put themselves in one another's shoes. I believe every person who attends Open Mic sessions has a dream. Why else would they show up? There has to be a reason behind it."

"Which is why you were so willing to go?"

"Yup." He grins. He pushes from the wooden rail to make his way toward me. His hips swing with nothing short of masculinity before he comes to a halt, stopping barely an inch away from me. Centered on the path of the entire boardwalk, he stares into my eyes. I stare back into his and somehow, I become lost in them.

"How about we share our dreams," he murmurs against my lips. He presses his fingers against the nape of my neck and my skin scorches from his touch alone. My hair is pinned up, but a few strands blow with the gentle breeze. With my hair up, this only allows me to feel everything.

"How can we do that?"

"We'll work together on it. I play a guitar, you read poems. I could play a melody to go along with each and every one of them—but only if you want to. It would be an easier way for me to hear what you've written." I tilt my head back and his lips inch even closer.

"But I still want you to sing," I breathe.

He chuckles. "I will." He stares into my eyes for a few more seconds and then his lips find their way to mine. He doesn't even hesitate to slip his tongue into my mouth. I savor the taste of him—the sweet and tangy mix of lemonade on his tongue. His fingers press harder on the nape of my neck to pull me in closer. My fingers braid between the locks of silky hair at the nape of his neck.

I just want to feel him. I want my senses to take in the way he touches me so I can remember it all. I want his imprint on me, his aura. I would never have suspected that he'd hurt anyone. Nolan just doesn't seem like the type who would cause damage to another person's heart.

His free hand glides its way from my shoulder blades to the small of my back. His fingers stroke their way around until they reach the button of my shorts. His hand then slides into my pants and a moan erupts from the heart of my chest. Inching his fingers along my pelvis, his feet begin to move and my feet move backwards until my back hits against the trunk of a thick tree. Then, as he slides a finger inside me, my eyelids fly open, but his are hooded.

His head falls forward and he sucks the crook of my neck gently. Fuck, this is so erotic. He really is making me enjoy having sexual relations in public. But right now, I don't think sex is the cure. Right now, I just want to be with him. I just want him close.

"Nolan?"

He pulls back, jerking his hands out of my shorts and looking into my eyes. "Yeah?"

"I don't think tonight is really a good night for sex."

He bites back on a smile, nodding his head. "That's cool with me, babe."

"You aren't mad about it or anything, are you?" I ask, in hope that he isn't. I don't want it to seem like I've just turned him down.

"Bunny," he breathes, pressing his erection against me. I choke on my next breath as the rock in his pants makes the sweet spot between my legs clench. "I'm gonna have blue balls, yeah, but that doesn't mean I'm mad. I respect what you want. If you don't want sex tonight, we won't have sex tonight. Although, I was hoping for a good fuck against this tree."

My mouth gapes and his eyebrows shoot up. "Right here?" I screech. "People could walk by and see!"

He shrugs nonchalantly. "I don't mind."

"You do know sex in public is illegal, right?"

He chuckles, revealing all his perfect, square teeth. "It would have been worth it to break the law."

I giggle as he presses his lips against the crook of my neck again. God, I love when he does that. It turns me into a pile of sweet mush every time. It's delightful.

"How about you two get a room!"

Nolan pulls away quickly and I gasp, spotting Harper and Dawson walking along the brick path toward us.

"You guys are a load of freaks!" Dawson adds on with a broad grin, watching me hurry to button my pants.

Nolan laughs and I bite on a smile.

"The lady here wants to grab a bite to eat. What do you say to Buffalo Wild Wings?" Dawson looks down and squeezes Harper's hands. She smiles up at him, revealing all her teeth. Wow, she really likes him. I've never seen her smile so big at a guy. Not since she was dating Bobby.

"That's cool with me," Nolan says, reaching for my hand. "Cool with you?"

I nod. "Yeah. I can chow down on a few good wings."

"Cool shiz," Dawson says with a lazy, surfer vibe. He turns around with Harper's hand still in his and they walk toward the parking lot a few feet away. I step ahead and begin to follow after them, but before I can get to far Nolan stops me, gripping onto my hand and reeling me in by the waist.

"Think about it tonight," he murmurs into my ear, positioning his groin against me. My legs tighten as his voice causes my ears to blaze. Heat sinks down between my legs and I stifle a moan, clutching the shoulder of his shirt.

Hmm. Perhaps sex with Nolan doesn't seem like a bad idea after all.

Chapter Twenty-Three

Buffalo Wild Wings was too crowded so instead Harp and I ran to the store to grab a few groceries that would make a meal of tacos while Nolan and Dawson kicked back and watched the game at Nolan's apartment. We decided dinner at his place was better since he had a large patio with an even larger table we could eat on.

Scrolling through the aisles of the grocery store, I scan each product until I see the bags of cheese. I grab two of them and toss them in the buggy. My phone buzzes in my back pocket and I reach for it quickly.

Gracey.

A wide smile glues to my lips, but almost immediately thoughts of Mark come to mind. How am I supposed to tell her about Mark? Grace may have never admitted it, but I could always tell she had some sort of feelings for Mark for a very long time.

I hesitate, but end up answering and pressing the receiver to my ear.

"Hello?"

"Hey baby doll!" she chimes. At least she sounds happy. Takes a load off of my shoulders.

"Hi, honey bear."

"Listen," she says and right after is a loud popping noise. "Sorry. Good gum," she mumbles. "I called Mark last night. Guess what he said!"

Oh, no. I gulp, pushing the buggy forward. "What?"

"When he comes back, he wants to go on a date with me!" she squeals.

I frown. "What? What about Trey?"

She groans loudly. "Fuck Trey. I hate him. He just wants me for my ass. But Mark... he is just too beautiful for words. I decided to be bold and send a text to Mark telling him to be straight-up with me. He told me the truth then immediately asked me on a date."

My eyes roll slightly. "Listen, Gracey, there's something I have to tell you about—"

"He told me he ran into you down there."

This time guilt burns the heart of my chest. "Oh really?" I gulp again, swallowing the brick in my throat. "What did he say?"

"That you look better than ever without Bryson. You know, I find it beyond weird they're down there of all places. I could have sworn they said they were going to Myrtle Beach for their summer getaway."

"Yeah. So I thought. Look, Grace—"

"Nat!" Harper screeches from behind me.

I spin around to face her as she smiles widely with a case of *Ferrero Rocher* chocolate in her hands. "They have it! I've been craving for this!"

I nod before she dips around the corner to continue her snooping around for snacks. It's like she's a child in a toy store. "Who was that?" Grace asks. "Harper?"

"Yeah. Look, I'll call you tonight, okay? I'm going to be spending some time with Nolan." Plus, I keep getting interrupted and I take that as I sign that I shouldn't be telling Grace about the altercation with Mark.

"Yum. Snap a pic for me for real this time!" she says. "I'm gonna call Mark."

"Grace, don't call him."

"Why not?" I know her eyebrows have just raised and her hazel eyes are wide with a spark of confusion.

"Because..." I hesitate. Somehow this has become harder for me to say. "Mark *kissed* me."

"*Kissed you*?" she spits. A low growl erupts from her throat before she huffs. "What the fuck? I used to see the way he looked at you but I always ignored it." She groans and silence fills the line. "I guess I have to find someone else then, huh? Too fucking good to be true."

"I'm sorry, Gracey," I mumble, twisting my buggy around to walk down the aisle and look for my other best friend.

"Did you kiss him back?" she asks.

I scowl. "No, Grace! You know me better than that. He came onto me. Nolan fought him."

"Nolan!" she screeches in more of a joyous shrill than anything else. She giggles heartily. "I bet he whooped Mark's ass bad. I gotta see this Nolan guy. Send me a pic tonight. I'm serious. But, Nat, I gotta go! Mom's calling for dinner. I'll be expecting a picture from you."

The line ends and I sigh, pulling the phone away from my ear and placing it in my back pocket. I turn and make my way down the main aisle but as I spot the straight, pale-blonde hair, the bright blue eyes, and the way her hand is placed on her hip as she talks to the brunette in front of her, I come to a screeching halt.

Sara Manx! What the fuck is she doing here? I begin to turn around, reeling my buggy in the opposite direction but as Harper yells, "Nat!" again, I freeze. I turn to the sound of Harper's voice and spot her standing in the middle of the main aisle with a bottle of Coke and two packs of cherry flavored Kool-Aid.

"Kool-Aid or Coke?" she asks, her lips pouting indecisively. "Lazy," she says, lifting the bottle of Coke. "Or hard working wifey-material?" She lifts the pack of Kool-Aid with a coy smile.

I push the buggy her way, keeping my eyes solely on her. Gripping her by the wrist, I drag her toward the nearest aisle.

"Is that really Natalie Carmichael?" the familiar voice that I absolutely cannot stand asks before I can even make it out of plain sight.

"Who the hell is that?" Harper asks, tugging her wrist away as she takes a step back. "Who the fuck are you?" Her eyes narrow at Sara.

I find the strength within me to be bold, removing my sweaty palms from the handle of the buggy and stepping back with Harper. I stare straight into the heavily mascaraed light-blue eyes of Sara. It's a shame. She still looks the same. Still disgustingly hidden behind a bag of make-up.

Sara cracks a laugh, tucking a pack of carrots beneath her arm. "I must say, Natalie, you look somewhat... incomplete."

"You still look completely shitty," I mumble through clamped teeth.

Harper tenses at my side, clutching the bottle of Coca-Cola in her hand. "Is this the bitch Bryson cheated on you with?" she asks. She then laughs, scanning Sara's extremely mini-skirt, tight pink tank top, and her bone-straight hair. "You've got to be kidding me, Nat. Did he really stoop this low to this worthless broad?"

I nod. "Mmhmm. Sad isn't it."

Sara stops just a foot away from us as the brunette comes to her side. As I stare at the brunette, I realize who she is. Madison Brewer, Mark's ex-girlfriend. I smile at her devilishly, remembering why Mark had broken up with her. Mark realized if he couldn't have me, he didn't want anyone. He said it to me one night while he was drunk but I've never said anything of it.

"No, what's sad is the fact that I have your boyfriend," Sara says. I cringe but Harper shakes her head as she places the Coke in the buggy.

"Listen here, bitch," Harp says with more pleasure than anger. "You have five seconds to get the fuck out of our faces or I promise your blood will be all over this floor. You don't want that, do you?" Harper's lips press to give a sarcastic, but full smile.

Sara bursts out laughing. "A shame, Natalie, how you always have to have one of your friends stick up for you. Grace the Whore was already enough, don't you think?"

"Sara, I'm not in the mood for you or your shit."

"What are you gonna do?" She places a hand on her hip again. "Call Bryson? Which side do you think he'll take?"

And then, just as the anger blinds me, just before I can charge forward and pounce on top of Sara, I spot Nolan strolling through the store, scanning the aisles. *What in the hell?* What is he doing here?

"Why are they here?" Harper whispers in a hiss. "I really wanted to beat this bitch's ass with you."

Nolan's head whips to look in our direction as Dawson follows behind him. At first, he's smiling, but as he gets closer and realizes how flushed my cheeks are and how drawn in my eyebrows are, his smile fades. He switches glances between me, Harper (who is still clueless as to why Dawson and Nolan are here) and then to Sara and Madison.

"Natalie, what's going on?" he asks, stepping forth cautiously.

"Uh…" I shake my head swiftly as Sara and Madison spin around to the sound of Nolan's voice. As soon as they reach sight of him, their eyes broaden with a mix of bewilderment and adoration. Spotting the way their drool spills is priceless. I step through Sara and Madison purposely, bumping shoulders with both of them before getting to Nolan. "It's nothing. Why are you here?"

"Who are those girls?" he murmurs so only I can hear.

"Some… dumb bitches," I grumble.

"Are they stirring up trouble? If we're interrupting, please ignore us. Dawson and I love a good cat fight." His lips spread to grin and speaking of Dawson, he steps to the side of Nolan with his eyes hard on Harper.

"Harper, baby," he coos. Harper practically melts as she rushes for his arms.

I turn to look at Sara and Madison who're still staring at us, eyes wide. As a sneer sneaks its way to my lips, I turn and kiss Nolan. At first, he stiffens but as he realizes he loves when my lips are against his, he softens and kisses me back.

"So pathetic," Sara hisses beneath her breath but I can hear the jealousy brewing within her.

I pull away from Nolan to turn and look at her. "Do me a favor," I breathe.

Sara and Madison's eyebrows shoot up at the same time, their eyes still wide. "Tell Bryson that unlike him, I've done better."

Clutching Nolan's hand, I turn around and grab the buggy. As soon as we start walking down the aisle Nolan lets out a roar of laughter. Dawson does the same and Harper giggles as she meets up to me.

"Oh my fucking God, Nat!" she squeals. "That was so fucking brilliant. You made Bryson look like complete shit! I know for sure she's gonna go back and tell him exactly what you said."

I giggle as Dawson steps to her side. "Is that how it was for you in high school?" he asks.

"Worse," Harper and I say at the same time.

"Well don't worry, Bunny. You showed her. I'm glad I came. We were coming to tell you, you forgot your wallet." Nolan's hand slides into his back pocket to retrieve a teal pleather wallet. "Can't pay without money, babe."

My cheeks spark with heat as I take it away from him. We continue strolling through aisles for a few more items, but I can't believe how good I feel. I feel like I've really won with Sara the Slut. With her, I've always felt like she was knocking me out cold and stepping on my toes purposely. She has a natural habit of being a bitch... something I wasn't back in high school.

But now, I feel better. Now I feel like I can say, *"fuck Bryson and fuck Sara."* But just as my rein of happiness comes to surface, a rush of nervousness comes as well. We can't run into Bryson. Knowing Nolan will fight if he sees him touching me terrifies me. If he fights for me, he may end up leaving me.

Nolan is too mature to deal with me—a girl who's just graduated high school. Sooner or later he'll tap out and say he can't deal with me or my past that's haunting me. Back there with Sara, that's what it felt like. Like I was back in high school and being immature by showing off in her face or flaunting my new boyfriend. In fact, this time around it had to be worse.

I just have to stay out of sighting. I can't run into Bryson again.

Chapter Twenty-Four

Dinner was completely satisfying.

As I collect the last plate from the small patio table, a long pair of arms wrap around me from behind. The heat molds from the crook of my neck, to the crease between my shoulder blades, and even against my hips.

"Need some help, Bunny?" Nolan's breath trickles across my earlobe, causing heat to spark within every inch of my body.

"I don't think you can help me from back there."

"I don't know," he says, taking a step back. I spin around and watch as his eyes scan me. "I kind of like the view from where I am." I bite on a smile as I turn around again. He presses against me, wrapping an arm around my waist. "Dawson and Harper went to take a walk on the beach." Before I can react, he grabs my free hand and spins me around to face him. I stare into the abyss of grey before me as my chest sinks against his. His eyes are softer than ever before, but there's something else within them. Perhaps a craving for lust. "Did you think about tonight?" he asks, leaning in to place his lips against my ear.

"Tonight?" I repeat. "I thought about it quite clearly."

"And?"

"And I think tonight should be sex-free."

Nolan pulls his head back to look at me. At first, there's a hard glare, but after only a few seconds, he presses in until my butt hits the edge of the table and a smile sneaks its way to his lips. He kisses my neck tenderly and my skin hums. His lips then trail to the V of my tank top before making their way up to mine. I practically melt in his arms.

"Don't hold off, babe. You can't tell me this doesn't feel natural."

"Just because it feels natural, doesn't mean it should happen," I whisper, aiming to keep my composure.

"Oh really?" One of Nolan's eyebrows elevate. He then picks me up in his arms. He clears one side of the table completely then lies me down. His lips immediately crush mine as a groan throttles against the back of my throat.

When he catches me completely off-guard it's so hard to hold off and I hate that he knows it. He snatches his lips away quickly, trailing them down to my chest as he works to get my pants undone. As my pants unzip, he towers over me. I reach forward quickly to unzip his pants without taking my eyes off of him. His eyes have suddenly turned as hard as steel. I can see the tension he has built inside. There's a fire brewing within him and radiating strongly from his body.

"Wanna take this to my bedroom?" he asks, cupping my cheek.

I nod quickly. A warm smirk graces his lips before he reaches for my hand and leads the way toward his bedroom.

Making the turn for the hall, Nolan steps ahead, but when someone says, "Need me to leave?" we both whirl around quickly.

Standing in the kitchen is a tall man with similar features as Nolan. He has the same dark hair, but unlike Nolan's grey eyes his have a hint of green in them. He is just as fit as Nolan—if anything fitter—with a red T-shirt and cargo shorts on. As he stares at us with a smile, that's when I realize who he must be. Nolan's brother.

"Mills?" Nolan raises an eyebrow and steps in front of me to guard me of his brother's vision. "What in the hell are you doing here? I thought you were hanging with Lorie tonight."

Mills shrugs. "Eh, we got into it again. I took off before she could get too angry. Who's your friend?" He reaches for a soft taco, takes a bite, and then his eyes meet Nolan's again.

"Natalie. I've told you about her," Nolan says through his teeth.

"Well, I mean you've had so many over before. It's kind of hard to keep up with them all," Mill quips with a mouth full of food.

A slight shudder corrupts me as Nolan squeezes my hand. "Mills, don't start."

"What?" Mills shrugs, taking a step forward with a large smile on his lips. I happen to see everything that's going on in front of Nolan and I'm beyond uncomfortable with where this conversation is headed. "Natalie, is it?" he asks.

I nod. "Yeah."

"Nolan treating you good? He's not fucking up yet, is he? He tends to fuck up a lot with the ladies. My only hope is he learns how to control that dick of his soon."

"Mills, just shut the hell up," Nolan says through a sigh.

"No, seriously. Did he provide you with a clean slate? Did he want to start fresh?" Mills grabs a glass out of the cabinet beside him. "I told him, if he wants to really settle with someone, start clean. Don't fuck up, don't lie, and don't cheat just because he feels like it'll be a great way of payback." Placing his glass down, he pulls the handle of the fridge then dips down to look inside. "Outta sweet tea, huh?"

"Maybe I should go," I murmur from behind Nolan. Nolan twists around quickly and clutches my hands in his.

"Don't let him get to you. He calls these things "*tests.*" He wants to see if you'll run away," he grumbles. "He sees it as if you run away, you're not the one. He'll think you're not strong, but if you stay, perhaps you have heart. He can be a dick that way."

"Don't act like I'm the one who started it," Mills butts in. "You fucked with Lorie for what seemed like years before she actually started to like being around you." I force a smile, looking over Nolan's shoulder at Mills who's now gulping down a glass of water.

"But I was only kidding," Mills breathes. "I was expecting you to smack my baby brother upside his head. Good thing you stood your ground. But that was only *one* out of many tests." He steps out of the kitchen and his eyes flicker at us. "The next few won't be so easy. Gotta make sure you're actually worth his time... or, better yet, if he's worth yours." He winks, trailing off to the living room. "Oh, and nice panties by the way. Sorry to have interrupted. Is the patio table dirty enough yet?" Mills chuckles before finally disappearing around the corner.

My cheeks drain of color as Nolan lets out a sigh. "Seriously, Bunny, don't mind him. He's a chill guy. He's just kidding around."

I nod with a breathy laugh. "I know. It's okay."

Nolan smiles then grips my hand before pecking my lips with his. "Let's go get your pants. I guess sex really isn't meant to be for tonight. We'll just cuddle."

I giggle and he chuckles as we make our way toward the patio to retrieve my pants.

Chapter Twenty-Five

It's a Thursday night and my legs are curled up beneath the coffee table again. Adjusting myself on the throw pillow, I sigh when I can't get comfortable enough. But there's a real reason why I'm not comfortable. It's because I'm expecting a call from my father today. When he'd text me, my heart had practically stopped beating.

Dad: Serious talk tonight, Natty. Make sure you answer your phone.

I'm pretty bummed out right now. All I can think is the negative. My dad wouldn't just text me and say that. If he were happy, he would have added one of his silly smiley faces. But not this time. No, he's upset about something.

As I tap my pen against my chin, I finally find the right words to say:

Love is still there,

Even when you feel blinded by it
Love is forever strong
Even when you want to try and hide it

My phone buzzes on the table, interrupting my next few lines. I gulp heavily, spotting the name *Dad* along with his picture on the screen. Dropping my pen quickly and rushing to my feet, I grab my phone and march for the patio door. I slide it open and as soon as I gulp the night air down, I answer.

"Dad?" I breathe.

"Hey, Natty Bear." I know he's smiling on the other end.

"Are you alright?"

"Never better, baby." He pauses and I chew on my bottom lip until it hurts enough to stop. "Look, I won't keep the tension in the air. Your mother and I talked last night... and I mean *really* talked." He sighs through a breathy chuckle. "We talked about us—about what was really going on between us— and why we were mad at one another in the first place. And you want to know what we came up with?"

I gulp again, forcing myself to keep my eyes on the guardrail of the patio to prevent any dizziness from taking over. "What?" I ask.

"The conclusion is we don't know why the hell we're arguing to begin with. At first, I thought it was me. And then she thought it was her. She blamed me for wanting a divorce but when I really looked at her—when I really took in how she felt—I knew what was wrong."

My eyebrows stitch. "What do you mean?"

He sighs. "I mean your mother doesn't want this. She doesn't want a divorce and she doesn't want to separate. She just wants me to fight back. She feels as if I'm careless when it comes to our relationship but in all reality, I love your mother. She can win any fight that goes on between us and I'll still love her the same. She can knock me out cold and give me a black eye, but she'll still be my wife. When I said the words "'til death do us part," I meant every bit of it. I'm not leaving Darlene, Natalie."

As my father finishes his rant, my heart does ten glee-filled flips in my chest. I can't believe it. "So you're not going through with the divorce? Is that what you're saying?" I ask, squeezing my phone against my ear.

"Hell no," he grumbles. "I grew up to love one woman, to never let her go, and I'm doing just that. I love my wife and last night I took her in my arms and made it clear. I guess that's what she was waiting on. For me to give it to her straight." He sighs and I know for sure he's just raked his fingers through his greying hair. "I just don't understand why she would think I stopped loving her. That's nearly impossible for me."

"Yeah." I slouch down on one of the cushioned patio chairs. "I don't either. To be honest, I think Grandma Minnie is putting thoughts in her head. Grandma hates you and of course mom listens to everything that woman says."

"I can't stand that woman," he growls. "If she weren't family she'd be in a cardboard box on the side of the road somewhere."

I giggle, pulling at a loose string attached to my tan camisole. Dad chuckles with me for a brief moment before the line goes silent. "So, does this mean I don't have to worry anymore?" I ask.

"Not at all, Natty. I swore an oath to your mother—to you—and I'll be damned if after all these years, my marriage goes down the drain."

"Well, good. I'm glad, Daddy." Right now, a smile is stuck firmly to my lips. I'm smiling like a big goof but I can't feel any better from hearing this. It's a big relief on my behalf. I was dreading being on the phone with him, but now I'm glad it's happening. I'm glad my dad fought for what he truly loves. And that's my mother, Darlene Missy Carmichael.

"Yep," he sighs. "So how are things down in Miami? When are you going to pay us a visit again? Your mom misses you."

"Things are actually great right now, Dad. And I'm not sure. Maybe around Thanksgiving."

"No… er… boyfriend or boy problems, are there?"

I giggle and I can almost imagine him trying to keep a straight face. "None, dad. Everything's fine. But I am seeing someone."

"Name?"

"Nolan."

"Is Nolan a *"hottie"* as you and Grace used to call those guys on T.V.?"

I giggle just thinking of how Gracey and I used to squeal over Jason Mraz. He had a voice to die for. "Nolan is really cute, dad."

"Well just don't get hurt by this Nolan character. Remember, I was a guy once. We strive for one thing at such a young age."

I groan. "Okay—enough, Dad. I think I got it." I shake my head as I stand from my chair.

"I'm just saying, Nat. Back in the day, looking at your mom would make me just wanna—"

"Oh my God! Dad, stop!" I squeal, trying my hardest to bite back on a smile.

He chuckles as I step back into the condo. "I love you, Natty. Your mom should be calling you later."

"I love you, too, Dad. Kiss her goodnight for me."

"I plan on doing much—"

Giggling, I end the call way before he can even finish his sentence. My dad never used to hide the fact that he and my mom had tons of sex.

Sometimes it was okay because they understood sex is natural, but when they started talking about it, I had to dismiss myself from the room because things got pretty awkward. Heading back to the table, I tuck myself beneath it and begin to write again, this time with a happier purpose.

****

Rounds of applauds filled the room, and although I didn't win, I was proud of the winner. Kelly Sparks. Long legs, beautiful, curly brown hair, nude pink lips, and a body I would die for. To top it off, she was as sweet as candy. She deserved it.

Clunking my way off the stage with my high red sequined heels that matched well with my ruby red dress, I turned for the girl's locker room. I grabbed my things without even bothering to change. I was just ready to go home. After a whole days work of practicing and running in fourth place of the pageant, I was exhausted. I didn't think fourth place was too bad. I was just glad I was a few spots before Sara.

Before stepping out of the locker room, I spotted Sara bawling her eyes out as her minions/best friends Madison Brewer and Danielle Lucas rubbed her back.

"Get the fuck off of me," Sara growled, pulling away from them. "I should've won that shit. I should've just cheated my way to the top, like my mom told me to do. That ribbon and tiara should have been mine! I'm way higher than seventh fucking place."

I quietly pulled the door open, smiling to myself the whole way through the halls. Some people gave their condolences and said "congrats" and "great job," but I was more than relieved that all of the attention wasn't on me.

Kelly deserved it. She wasn't popular at all, but she was beautiful. She wasn't a cheerleader or a flirtatious chick. She was just a normal girl involved in the yearbook committee and even the debate team. She had goals, dreams, and that's what I loved about her. Her speech was touching and her focus was on herself, her future, and the futures of the underprivileged.

Flickers and flashes of cameras were going off and at the moment, I just wanted to see my mom. My dad was there. I saw him in the crowd looking as lost as ever. I should have been upset about my mom not being there since she was the one who made me audition and she was the one who chose my dress and shoes and had the appointment set up for me to get my hair done. I could have been mad at her, but I wasn't. Seeing my father was kind of *enough and in a way, I didn't want her to be disappointed. My mom always strove to be a winner. Nothing less. Even when I told her I came in fourth place, she wasn't satisfied with it and I knew if I could get another year in school, she would have made me go just to audition again.*

But I didn't mind it. I was glad to be in the top five, at least.

As I stepped out, the fall air was brisk, but a jacket wasn't necessary. I stumbled around the corner, clutching my keys in hand and making my way toward my white Camry, but just as I was nearing it, someone was already standing there.

He had on dark jeans, a black Rolling Stones T-shirt, and a grey baseball cap on his head that hooded his eyes. I couldn't see anything but his mesmerizing smile that caused my heart to stumble over the beats. As he pushed from the car, his shoes pressed against the asphalt and his hand wrapped around my waist. He took my things out of my hands to place them on the trunk of my car then immediately crushed my lips with his.

His tongue tasted like beer and a mix of peanuts. I immediately pulled away from him and tilted his baseball cap back to get clear sight of his eyes. "Bryson, have you been drinking?"

"Just a little," he murmured, his lips still graced with a grin.

I bit on my bottom lip as he pulled me in closer. "You drove here drunk?"

"I'm not drunk, Natalie." Just as he said that he staggered a bit. "Just... tipsy I guess."

"You're not tipsy. You're drunk," I snapped. I turned to scan the parking lot and spotted the silver chrome of his motorcycle his mother had given to him as an early birthday gift. My head whipped to look at him again. If he drove his motorcycle it only meant he was hanging around Moe's with a few older friends who were in college. At Moe's, they don't check I.D. They ignore the policy.

"Bryson, I think I should drive you home. We can pick up your bike in the morning." I pulled away from him to grab my things off the trunk but before I could make it to open the back door of my car, Bryson pressed against me and my chest pushed against the glass. "Bryson," I struggled to say. I could hardly breathe. "What are you doing?"

"I wanna do it. Right here, Natalie. I've been waiting all night for it."

"No." I shook my head then turned around to face him. I don't know how I managed to spin, considering there was minimal space between us. Bryson's hands pinned on both sides of me and barricaded me in. His emerald eyes were hooded but hard. His eyes scanned their way from mine to my chest then to the curve of my breasts in my dress.

Usually when I spotted him looking at my cleavage I would find it cute, but this time, I was afraid. He was looking at me as if I were a piece of meat. "Bryson, seriously. Come on." I tried to push my way past him while also aiming to keep my voice steady, but he stayed in front of me.

"You're not taking me home, Nat. Right here. Now," he demanded. I gulped as tears crept to my eyes, but as soon as he spotted them he titled my chin with his forefinger. I kept my gaze down to hold the tears back. "Don't cry, Natalie. You love me right?" he asked.

Like a love-struck idiot, I nodded.

"Then why can't we make love right here? Right now... In your backseat? There's plenty of space. I just need to release. I need to be inside you. I've missed you."

I nodded again. Although I didn't realize it then, he was only using love as an excuse. He knew I would do anything for him—that I would go through with whatever he wanted. I was a fool in love. I only wanted to be wanted by him.

"Okay," I breathed through another nod.

"That's my baby," he said, pulling me against him and opening the back door of my car.

Chapter Twenty-Six

It's no surprise I woke up with tears in my eyes. All night I had been thinking about it, and all night I realized the truth. What Bryson and I had wasn't real love. We weren't in love and he couldn't have valued me because a lover wouldn't have forced themselves onto someone they shared their heart with. I'm such an idiot. I hate I did that to myself.

Snatching a towel from my basket, I rush for the shower. After about fifteen minutes of basking beneath the water, I step out and wrap the towel around me before blow-drying my hair. As I gaze into the mirror that's when I realize I'm crying. I have been since I stepped foot into the bathroom.

It's a shame that after everything is over is when I want to face facts. I've been lying to myself for four years just to cover up for Bryson. I wanted him to be the perfect boyfriend, the perfect friend. I didn't want any of his flaws to get in the way so I ignored them. I ignored everything about him that made me uncomfortable. If I would have known how fucking stupid I was making myself look, I would've broken up with him way before two months ago.

I rush for my room and grab my phone quickly. I dial Grace's number and she answers after the second ring.

"What happened to my picture?" she whines.

"Sorry, Grace. I forgot."

She groans. "Forgiven. I take it he's just really ugly and you don't want me to see him yet. It's okay if he is. Ugly guys usually have the kindest hearts."

I would usually laugh at something like that, but I don't. "Grace, I have a question and I want you to be completely honest with me right now."

She pauses. "Okay."

"When I dated Bryson... did you notice anything... wrong?"

"What do you mean?"

"I mean... did he seem controlling, edgy, manipulative? Did I seem like his puppet?"

Grace's side of the line goes silent. I wait for her to answer for almost ten seconds before saying her name again.

"Grace, please be honest with me."

"Nat, I never wanted to say anything. Bryson had a fucked up alpha edge. It's only hot until he gets carried away with it. He never hit you or anything—at least I hope he didn't—but when he said come, you came. When he said run, you ran. When he said jump, you jumped. He owned you in his own little way. You did everything he said. Sometimes it scared me. You brushed me off too much—too much to the point where I didn't like speaking on it anymore. You were in love, Natalie. It's what happens. We're blind for months—years—and we don't even realize it."

I want to speak. I want to say something to that, but I can't. Something's keeping the words trapped. Perhaps it's my dry throat that's suddenly become scratchy. Or maybe it's my tears that are blinding me once again. I slouch down on the corner of my bed as the tears pour uncontrollably. I can't believe myself. I can't believe Bryson.

"It's okay, Natalie," Grace coos. "It's a lesson. I'm glad you got out of it. I was afraid one day he would have actually ended up hitting you. Then I would have had to beat his ass."

I choke on a sob and a giggle. "I just feel so fucking worthless, Grace. I loved him—"

"You thought you loved him," she corrects. "It wasn't love, Natalie. He just wanted you to believe that it was. I'm sorry to say it, but Bryson has that kind of effect on girls. He had you wrapped around his finger with a glittery pink bow."

"But all I can remember is the good in him."

"That happens," she notes. "We only store the good. Never hold in the bad. It's a part of being human. We don't want to face reality so we block it out and try to hold on to the best that we have."

I shake my head. All this time I've been some sort of blow-up sex doll for Bryson. Now that I think about it, Bryson and I had sex almost every other day. Even during my first month of meeting him, he asked to make love to me almost everyday until I finally gave into him. We were only freshmen, but I still find it odd that he can be that way after so many years. And it's a shame because he didn't change at all after taking my virginity. From freshman to senior year, Bryson was himself. As years passed, he became worse.

I can't believe I compared him to Nolan. Nolan is nothing like that. Of all the times Nolan and I are together, not once has he pushed himself onto me. He could be manipulative and try, but he doesn't. He can make me as horny as he wants—he can tease me until I can't take it anymore—but he never goes against my free will.

Wow.

As it occurs to me, I hop from my bed and rush for my dresser. "Grace. I'm gonna have to call you later." I end the call, not even allowing her enough time to get a word in.

Although what I'm about to do may cause damage to myself even more, I have to. I have to go.

Chapter Twenty-Seven

As my tires roll near the curb, a slight panic consumes me. The beach house is two-stories high with patio on top of patio. Various cars are swamped around the house along with a few motorcycles. Stepping out the car, I place my hand over my eyes to block the sun. I gulp the brick in my throat, spotting the mud-green Jeep Wrangler parked in the driveway. It's a shame how his car is the one that stands out most.

"Okay," I breathe to myself. "I can do this."

Clutching my keys in hand, I weave my way through the cars and bikes to get to the porch of the house. It's around ten-thirty in the morning and I'm sure no one's going to be up considering the fact that when graduates party, they do it like there's no tomorrow, but I don't have any other choice. I refuse to wait because if I do, I'll think about it too much and I won't make it happen. I'll regret my decision.

As I meet the tall white door, I hesitate on my next step. I push my bangs away from my eyes, take a deep breath, and then step forward to knock. At first, it's silent. I can't hear a thing inside. But after only few moments, I hear footsteps and with every one of them, my heart thuds against my ribcage.

The locks on the door clink, the chains slide, and then it swings open rapidly. Spotting the sculpted chest and the white basketball shorts that are riding low on his hips, I jerk my gaze up quickly to meet the light-blue eyes of Mark.

"Hi," I breathe.

With a busted bottom lip, Mark smiles and leans against the frame of the door. He folds his arms, looking me over in my white shorts, custard-yellow tank top, and my purposely-messy bun. "Took you long enough."

"Whatever," I mutter. "Don't think you're forgiven, because you're not."

He sighs as his smug smile fades. "I know. Natalie, I'm sorry. It's like I remember it, but I can't believe I actually did that to you."

I keep my mouth sealed, refusing to speak on it. "Bryson here?"

He raises an eyebrow. "Is that what you called me for this morning? Bryson?" he grumbles.

"I have to speak with him. It's important."

Mark steps away from the frame, unfolding his arms. "Well, good luck with that. He's upstairs with your *'best friend.'*"

I frown, knowing he's being sarcastic and referring to Sara. "Can you just get him and tell him to come out or something?"

"What, so I can get Sara's claws in my back while I sleep?" he quips. "Don't think so. Come in, Nat. We won't bite... but Sara might."

I bite my bottom lips, debating on whether it's worth it to go in. If this weren't so serious I'd say fuck it and bounce. But it's serious to me and I need to talk. It almost feels mandatory. "Fine." Mark steps aside and I brush past him.

As soon as I'm in, I spot a few bodies lying on the carpet. Red cups and glass bottles that I'm sure were once filled with alcohol are scattered around the hardwood floorboards. Clips of marijuana blunts and joints are lying in ash trays of every table along with butts of cigarettes. It must have been one hell of a party last night.

"Ignore the mess," Mark says, stepping past me. "Follow me." He leads the way upstairs and I follow him, but suddenly I'm not so sure about this plan anymore. I feel like I'm being led toward a dungeon full of dragons. I know for a fact Sara is lying in the same bed as Bryson and at the thought of it I shudder because if he hadn't fucked up, that would be me lying in his arms.

Dragging my way behind Mark, he continues up another flight of steps and as soon as we're up, he starts down the hall until we reach the last bedroom.

"Oh, fuck yeah, Bryson!"

My eyes widen immediately as I come to a screeching halt in the middle of the hall. *Was that Sara?* Just thinking about them two together rips me in half.

"Shit," Mark hisses beneath his breath. I begin to turn around, planning on rushing down the stairs, slamming my car door behind me, and speeding home with tears blinding me, but Mark stops me before I can reach the stairs.

"What the fuck are you doing?" I growl. "Let me go."

"Bryson! Oh, God! Go faster!" Sara screams.

Listening to her makes me want to throw up and cry at the same time. I try to shove Mark out of my way but he barely stumbles. His hand remains tight around my arm as I scratch and claw for him to let go.

"Mark, get off me!" Tears sting my eyes, but I force myself to keep my eyes focused on Mark's large hand that's still clasped around me.

"Nat, chill! I'm not letting you go out like that. You have to get over it. You have to get over *him*! It's been two fucking months!"

I scowl at Mark's hand. Although he's right, it's easier said than done. I want to forget about Bryson so damn bad. I want to toss all feelings aside and just stand up to him like a real woman should. I want to face my fears by talking with him privately, but I can't. I hate that another girl is touching him because not too long ago, he was mine. Not too long ago, we were together and we were happy… or so I thought.

Mark pulls me in and holds onto my tightly. I'm still bothered he came onto me two days ago at the beach, but I decide to fall against him because he's my only option of remaining sane at the moment. He was my best friend, after all. Things like that don't just fade.

The tears spill as Mark coos and shushes me. "Nat, it's alright. You want me to drag him out?"

"No!" I snap, yanking away from him. "No, Mark. You really think I want to talk to him after he's been fucking *her*? Hell no!"

"Either way you would have been talking to him, Nat. He's been fucking Sara since he's gotten here. You knew that way before you came. Don't be dramatic."

My eyebrows stitch as I bore holes through Mark. He shrugs, but that's when I realize Sara has stopped her screaming and moaning. The door unlocks and my heart leaps to my throat quickly. I want to back away and clamber down the stairs but as I spot Bryson with his shirt off, revealing his healthy abs that come along with a sheen of sweat, somehow I can't. His green eyes are wide as they meet mine and as he spots Mark, he rakes a hand through his spiky, dark hair. He shuts the door behind him quickly before meeting up to us.

"Nat, what are you doing here?" Bryson asks in a whisper, and right after he narrows his eyes, lowering his head. "Are you crying?"

"No point in whispering," Mark says as I swipe the tears from my eyes. "You and Sara have practically woken up the whole house."

Bryson gives Mark an edgy look but Mark just shrugs and turns for the stairs. Right now I wish I was doing what he was doing. Leaving. Now it just feels hard to talk, to speak, to breathe. I still can't believe that I went through with this. Only a fool would put herself through this again. I must think I'm dreaming. Perhaps I need to be pinched extremely hard to know how stupid this decision was.

As Mark clunks down the stairs, I turn to meet Bryson's confused gaze again. "I think I'll just come some other time," I mutter before turning. As I do, Bryson catches my hand.

"Natalie." We lock eyes. "Don't leave. Please. I didn't know you were stopping by."

"Doesn't matter."

He swallows, pulling his hand away. "What'd you come for then?"

I shake my head because by his tone, I know he's trying to get under my skin. He's trying to get me to feel guilty for showing up. "I wanted to talk to you about our relationship."

"You want to date again? Nat, I've wanted to talk to you about that since—"

"No, Bryson." I shake my head, cutting his sentence short. "That's not what I came to talk about. I don't want you back. I never will." Moments after the words have flown out, that's when I realize how harsh they actually sounded.

Bryson's green eyes become glossy as he stares at me. Raking his fingers through his hair, he presses his lips until the skin around his mouth pales. "So what did you want to talk about then?"

I pause, looking from him to the door of the room he stepped out of seconds ago. "I don't wanna talk here. I'll give you three minutes to get ready and to meet me in my car." I spin around and clutch my keys before taking a step down. I glance over my shoulder only to spot Bryson still staring in my direction, his mouth slightly ajar. "Hurry," I demand before completely disappearing out of his sight.

Chapter Twenty-Eight

The rattling sound of dishes fills my ear buds, along with the whooshing sound of my blood. I grip my strawberry and cream Frappuccino and meet Bryson's eyes. Of course he's already staring at me, but his face is unreadable. I can't tell what he's thinking because every feature on his face is lacking with emotion.

"So should I start talking or what?" he asks.

"No." I shake my head. "Just finding the right words to say."

"I'm sure you already have what you want to say on the tip of your tongue, Nat. You were never the one to hold off on telling it like it is."

My lips press around my straw as I gulp slowly. Ice trickles down my throat before fading into smooth heat. "Okay," I say, placing my cup down on the two-top table a little too aggressively. "Why'd you do it?"

He raises an eyebrow.

"Better yet," I say, correcting myself. "What was wrong with me?"

"Nothing was wrong with you," he says quickly. "I promise, Nat, I didn't know what to do. You know how it is for me. People look up to me. I was the star quarterback of West Ashley. Every college was riding my dick just to get me to sign to them."

"That has nothing to do with why you cheated, Bryson," I mutter through partially clenched teeth.

"Nat—" He breaks off, his green eyes drifting from mine. He stares around the coffee shop before turning to look out the window as a few pedestrians pass by. "Okay. You wanna know the truth?"

I fold my arms. "Please."

"There's nothing wrong with you, Natalie. It's all me. I know it sounds cliché as hell, but it was me. And that's the truth. I love you, but things were flipping upside down. My mom was barely there for me to talk to and all those house parties got to me. Sara and I didn't start messing around until the first house party I threw. I was heading upstairs to find you, but I couldn't. When I checked my mom's room, Sara was laying on her bed half naked. She was wasted. Mom's room is off limits so I tried to get her out, but she threw herself at me—damn it,

I'm a guy, Natalie. If a girl just so happens to pull our pants down and suck our dicks, we aren't gonna stop it."

His green eyes flicker and I cringe. I tear my gaze away from his almost immediately and stare at my Frappuccino instead. I did notice he was acting a little strange that night. I asked him what was wrong and if he wanted to end the party early but he said no. He told me to chill with Grace while he acted as the host. But I should have been worrying. Now I feel like it's my fault because he couldn't find me. Instead he found Sara and fucked her. The first party her threw was during our junior year.

"I just don't understand, Bryson. You swore you loved me but you fucked her constantly behind my back?"

"Natalie, I'm sorry. I promise I tried to stop." He reaches across the table for my hand and surprisingly I don't pull away. "Nat, what I did was wrong, and I know you're thinking that since I'm with her, I didn't care for you much, but I fucking love you. I love you from the bottom of my heart. I just want to make amends. I want you to forgive me or this shit'll be on my chest for the rest of my life.

"It's hard to focus as an athlete. It's hard to be faithful when women just throw themselves at you. Do you think it's easy to walk around town and have every woman know my name? You were more than enough for me, but I was a fucking idiot. Every day, I think about you. And every day I know I fucked up by losing you. I miss you, Nat. I want you back so damn bad... but I know you don't deserve someone like me."

My eyes widen and sting with tears but I force myself to bite my lip and look down at my lap to prevent them from falling. I pull my hand away from his, twisting to my right to look outside. A few bodies pass by, but it's all a blur. I'm not thinking right now. I don't know how to feel. I loved Bryson, but I know for a fact *we* will never happen again. I know for a fact he's going to continue what he's doing. He's not going to change. And that's okay because he doesn't have to do it for me anymore. It'll be for himself. If he really wants the change, he'll make it happen. Maybe it's a good thing I got out of the relationship.

And then it all comes back. Nolan was Bryson once, but he wants the change. He wants to make himself better... with me. Wow.

I sigh as I look at Bryson again. "I forgive you," I say. His face lifts as he reaches a hand toward me again but I pull away, holding mine in front of me, signaling for him to stop where he is. "I forgive you, *but* we're not getting back together, Bryson. I understand you want to change and I'll always have love for you, but you tore me apart. You pretty much killed me inside. You made me feel lower than shit."

"Nat, I'm sorry," he pleads.

"Don't apologize."

His mouth seals and his hand recoils.

"I always wanted to remember the good in you. I always wanted you to be the highlight of my days—and you were—but now that we're apart, I realize how fucking stupid I was. I didn't know what to do with myself. At times, I would just beg to sleep forever. But now that I'm without you, I know for a fact what we had wasn't love, Bryson. You manipulated me millions of times and I'm obviously an idiot for coming to the realization of it now—after we're already over."

"What?" His face twists. "Manipulated you? I did nothing wrong."

"Yes you did!" My voice raises a notch and a few people whip their heads in our direction. My mouth clamps shut before I meet eyes with Bryson again. "Yes you did," I whisper in a hiss. "I was practically your bitch. You'd say you love me and then fuck me. You'd look me right in the eye and say it. That's why I thought it was real. I thought we were real."

Bryson sighs, folding his arms and looking away. "That's a fucking lie," he growls.

"Is it?" I snap. "Why are you getting upset about it then? If I'm lying, why are you getting so defensive?"

"Because you're fucking lying!" he roars. This time the entire coffee shop looks at us, even the employees. "I never did shit to you, Natalie! I fucking love you! I fucked up *one time* and you're gonna shove that in my face?"

Bryson's chair scrapes against the floor as he pushes back. "I don't even know why the fuck I came here with you. I knew you were just going to blame me for everything. You know I fucking love you so don't feed me that bullshit." He storms around me and before I know it, the bell above the door rings, letting me know he's out of the coffee shop.

My mouth gapes into a half-circle as I stare down at my drink. I can't believe he's trying to flip this on me. But now that I realize it, he's always done this. Whenever I would confront him, he would always run from the fight or make me feel like it was my fault. All this time, I've been blinded. But from what? *His dick?* Was I really that lost in lust that I couldn't see what was clearly happening? It was right in my face the entire time but I didn't even comprehend it.

My heart clutches and my palms become clammy as Bryson makes a turn around the corner of a building. It kills me to know what we had, wasn't real. Now I just feel stupid. The only reason he's so upset is because he knows it's the truth. He knows what he did to me for four years was wrong.

But instead of sitting around, I push away from the table and storm out of the coffee shop. I rush around the corner of the building that Bryson turned on until I spot him marching down the alley to make his way toward the beach.

"Bryson! We aren't done talking!"

He spins around swiftly with his fists clenched. "What the fuck do you want from me, Natalie?"

"For you to tell me the truth!" I rush toward him until I'm only a few inches away. His emerald eyes are blazing with intensity. His jaw ticks rapidly as he glowers down at me. "I wanna know if you were really in love with me. If you just tell me I can drop it and forget bout it."

Raking his hand through his dark hair, he huffs and takes a step back. I allow my eyes to plead for me because I really do want an answer. I need to know if what we had was more than lies, bullshit, and more lies.

"There was a point in our relationship where I was in love with you, Natalie," he says, and then sighs. "But as we got older and I started to get noticed, it faded." My stomach clenches because hearing it is worse than actually thinking about it.

"Freshman, sophomore, and the beginning of junior year, I knew I was in love. But during the middle of junior year through senior year, shit started to get tough between me, my family, football, and even *faithfulness*. I just couldn't be faithful to you anymore. It's not that you were a terrible girl—you were amazing and still are—I just knew I didn't deserve you. I knew I wasn't the one for you. I could never figure out the right things to say to you so I tried to stay distant. I tried to just go with the motions. I wanted something to happen so you could leave me. I couldn't hold it in anymore. I didn't want a relationship with anyone. But now I regret it... Nat, you won't believe this, but I've lost my scholarship."

I blink rapidly before my eyebrows stitch. "*What? How?*"

"Sara and I went binge drinking while driving. We got arrested but my mom bailed us out. Good thing she's a lawyer, huh?" He sighs as his eyes travel up to look over my shoulder. "I fucked up, Natalie. And I'm sorry. I miss you like hell, but even now I know you don't need me. I came back to tell you how I felt—to get it all out and off my chest. It kills me to know you despise me because at one point, you loved me. Everything about me. And I loved everything about you. But sometimes all relationships don't work out.

"I'm sorry for wasting your time. I'm sorry for being a complete asshole to you. I loved you, but not in the way you loved me. I was in love at one point in our relationship, but it faded. Afterwards, I only had love for you. You were a girl I knew I could have as a friend... and nothing more. I was tired of disrespecting someone as sweet as you."

As he lets the words flow, my heart skips a beat. I choke on a gasp and my next breath as he reaches for my hand. "I'm sorry, Natalie. I never meant to hurt you."

I continue my stare at him and that's when I realize my sight has grown blurry. Everything's fuzzy and for a moment, I feel completely and utterly useless. Tears trickle and crawl along my cheeks as I finally find the will to take a step back and heave in a deep breath.

"I understand, Bryson," I murmur.

He nods, watching me swipe the unwanted tears from my eyes. "None of it was intentional. Life and reality just got in my way," he whispers. "I know you'll never see me the same, and I'm sorry. I screwed everything up. Losing someone like you will be one of the main things I regret in life." Bryson then does the unexpected. Pulling me in by my waist, he wraps his arms around me. He squeezes me against his chest and, just like that, I'm bawling again. I've missed his hugs. I've missed his touch.

I've missed everything about him. But I can't continue to hold on. At least I got the answers I'd been thinking about constantly. At least now I won't have to lie to myself about what his problem may have been.

I always thought I was the problem, but I was completely wrong. He was his own problem. Every day I wanted to kick him in his balls, knee him in the gut, and smack his face. Every day I wished bad upon him because I always felt like I was worthless to him. I felt like *nothing* since he'd cheated on me with a bitch that had nothing on me.

"I promise I'll always love you, Nat. Letting go will be hard for the both of us, but I want you to forget about me and start over with someone worth you and your time. I'm not worth the heartache."

I nod against his chest and thoughts of Nolan immediately come to mind. My eyelids fly open as I pull away from him, swipe the tears from my eyes, and clutch my keys. "I have to go," I mumble. "There's something I have to do."

"Sure. I'll call Mark and tell him to pick me up," he says as I begin to take gradual steps backward. I nod then dash off to get back to the parking lot.

****

I slam my car door behind me and rush for the wooden stairs. I clamber up until I'm in front of apartment **C**. I knock heavily, allowing my fists to pound out of adrenaline. Right now, I'm not thinking. Right now, I'm just doing what feels... *natural*.

The door unlocks and as soon as it swings open, I step in. Nolan's eyes broaden as I shut the door and then hook my arms around his neck. I crush my lips against his and pour all that I have into him. All I want is him.

Not once has Nolan fucked up. Not once has he made me feel like I couldn't be myself. He wants to be loved, just as I do. I was just so afraid, so terrified, and so worried that he would be worse than Bryson. But with love, there comes a price. Either it's worth it, or it's not. I just hope Nolan is worth way more than all I've been through.

Nolan finally pulls his lips away, but his hands cup jawline and he strokes the pad of my cheek with his thumb. "Natalie, what's wrong? Why are you crying?"

I shake my head, hating myself for showing him my tears. I've been at it all day. I'm just an emotional wreck. Hearing Bryson say those things have really put me at a loss for words. "Nolan, I'm sorry for holding off," I sob. "I'm sorry for being stingy with my heart. I want to give it to you now." His grey eyes are still confused, but he doesn't release my face. He leans in to place his lips against mine and I tingle sweetly. Our chests mold as we breathe and pant with urgency. With passion. With love.

It isn't too long before Nolan has me in his arms and is carrying me toward his bedroom, our lips never parting. I wrap my legs around him as he pulls one hand away to open his bedroom door. He places me down on the comforter gently, letting our lips part only once before reconnecting them again.

My tears continue to flow, but I want this. I need this. I grab his face and kiss him with what seems like all the life within me. As my legs hook around his waist, his erection presses into me.

Our clothes disappear piece by piece and as I lay on his bed with nothing but my bra and panties on, he stares down at me, his grey eyes softer than ever before. He reaches a hand down to wipe the tears that have collected in the corners of my eyes.

"I've been trying to find the right words to let you know I feel more for you, Natalie." He strokes my cheek then places a kiss on my lips. "*I love you*, Bunny."

I pull my lips in, bite down on them, but they're soon released as he trails kisses from my neck, to my collarbone, then down to the heart of my chest. His fingers entwine with mine as he plants kisses on every inch of my bare skin. A few seconds later, my bra has disappeared. Moments afterward, his boxers and my panties have been discarded.

Nolan's lips collide with mine as I wrap my legs around him again. He cups my face and his lips trace my cheek and the crook my neck. A moan brushes past my lips as his thick arousal presses against the sweet spot between my legs. "Tell me you feel something more for me, Natalie. This has to be more than what it seems."

I sit up and pull his face in my hands, staring into his grey eyes. "I love you, Nolan. I know it's way more than it seems."

He smiles, and I melt pleasurably. He finally pushes himself inside me and I groan as my nails dig into his back. His strokes are simple, sweet, tender. He grunts against my ear and my fingernails claw into his skin the deeper he goes.

I feel it. I feel all he feels. We're not just having sex. *We're making love*. And it's amazing because this is exactly what I wanted.

He plants gentle kisses on my lips, on my cheek, and on my chin as he reaches his hands beneath to cup my ass. The switch in position only causes him to go deeper. His teeth graze my lower lip and soon my head falls back and my body arcs into his. I'm allowing myself to give everything. I want to let go—I need to. I have to forget. I have to release. I want him to feel all of me.

"Oh, Nolan," I breathe.

"I'm not going anywhere, Bunny," he breathes back. His breath tickles me, and my nails claw into his blue sheets. "I told you, you were mine. I told you I wanted this."

"I know." He strokes into me deeper, slower, passionately. His body tenses, his panting rigid.

"I want this to last," he groans into my ear. I hook my arms around his neck as he begins to pump faster, stronger. His actions are sweet, but swift. His hand continues to cup the cheek of my ass, his other hand lifting my leg. I can feel him in my stomach now. I'm spiraling in the best way possible. I can feel my climax coming, building its way up.

I screech his name again and as I do, I shudder around him. He shudders as well and we both groan with deep pants, tense against one another. Nolan collapses against my chest, pressing his lips on my collarbone along the way. "Hopefully that was proof enough that I'm here to stay," he says, laughing.

I giggle as he pulls out of me to meet my lips. He hovers only inches above me with all his teeth revealed. His smile is so adorable. I stare at his lips, reaching a hand up to push his hair off his forehead. "Meeting you was all the proof I needed."

He leans down on his elbows and kisses me again before sliding his tongue into my mouth. I refused to let him slip and I'm still holding on. One drop and it's over. One screw-up and this entire thing can be depleted.

I hate to think negatively, but anything can happen. Nolan is beautiful, both mentally and physically, but he's still a *guy*. He still has dreams and if he's going to start pushing to reach them, there'll be sacrifices. He's still young and he has plenty of options.

Bryson sacrificed our love just to keep his rep, but in the end lost it all without me. My only question is what will Nolan sacrifice when it comes down to me? What would he choose?

Chapter Twenty-Nine

The strings of Nolan's guitar strum gradually. His finger movement is graceful. I try my hardest not to stare at him, but it's impossible. As he plays, it's nothing short of beautiful. The way his eyelashes touch his masculine cheekbones and the way his eyebrows pull together slightly as he concentrates proves he's been doing this for years. I know this is something he admires. It's something he loves.

"Go ahead," he says as he finally gets the melody right. It took us almost an hour to get the right tune with the poem. I step from my bed and take a deep breath. "Remember, you don't have to look at me," he murmurs, continuing his melody. I force a smile, but beneath my heart is pounding erratically. This is so nerve-racking, but only because this is Nolan. He hasn't read my words but hearing them may have a stronger impact than anything else.

"Okay," I breathe. Turning my back to him, I decide to look into the mirror attached to my dresser instead. I can still see him but it's only his firm shoulders and right arm. I can deal with that. As long as I don't see his face, I can do it. "Should I start now?" I ask.

"Whenever it feels right."

I nod, replaying the words in my head. I've read over this poem so many times—too many times to count, actually. It runs through me, pumps through my veins and my blood. Remembering it is just like breathing because it's the one I've related to the most thus far.

I allow my eyes to shut and breathe in. My body sways out of instinct and I roll my neck, allowing the tension to be released. As soon as Nolan hits the right chord, I let the words flow.

And with each word, I can feel it all. I know what I'm letting go of and what I'm holding on to. I know I deserve to be happy again—to be myself. These words have a meaning, a meaning so deep I can't even breathe until I'm finished. They're strong, but reassuring.

Hard to hear, but good to think about.

My eyelids fly open but as I stare into the mirror, tears blind me. I swipe at them quickly and then I hear Nolan placing his guitar down to get to my side.

"Natalie." He cups my face, crushing my lips with his own. "Don't be ashamed," he says against my lips. "That poem just told me everything." His lips stretch to smile before they crush mine again. I hook my arms around him and we collide. Our bodies plunge and I swear this is the best feeling ever. I'm glad he doesn't think I'm insane. I'm glad he's accepting the way I am. Reading that out loud proves a lot. It proves I've come a long way from what happened two months ago. Two months ago I wouldn't have been able to even look at the poem. I would have thrown up from reading the first few lines.

"What did you really think?" I ask as soon as our lips fall apart.

He pauses, stroking the pads of my cheeks with his thumbs to get rid of my tears. "I think you still need time to grow, but I can help you get there. Hopefully I can heal the pain with *time*." I smile as he presses his lips against my forehead. "My turn?" he asks.

"No." I shake my head, pulling away. "I want you to sing tomorrow, at Open Mic. I already called Brittany and Jordan and they've jotted our names down. Tonight, I need to get out. Harp wants to go to a club and quite honestly I could use a few drinks." I wink as Nolan looks me over.

"She doesn't plan on going to club *LIV*, does she?" His face falls immediately. He's thinking of his best friend at the moment.

"Max won't be there. She's made it her goal not to run into him again."

Nolan's shoulders fall as his eyes soften. "Well, cool. Wanna go back to my house and help me change clothes?" He presses in, thinning the gap between us before completely closing it by pulling me in by my belt loop.

"Sure," I giggle. "But maybe we could do more than change clothes."

"Mmmm," he hums, leaning forward and pushing my hair behind my ear. He kisses the crook of my neck and a surge of tightness seizes me. "You know I'm always down for more."

"Have been since day one," I mumble.

He pulls back to stare into my eyes. "What does that mean?"

My eyebrows pull together as he glares at me. "Nothing. It was just a statement."

"Was I not supposed to be interested in you since day one?"

"What are you talking about?" I frown. "I never said that."

Nolan pulls away completely, taking a step back. "Then what are you saying exactly? I know there's

always a hidden message behind your '*statements.*'"
He uses his fingers to make quotation marks.

"I didn't mean it offensively Nolan. You're being dramatic." I force myself to look into his eyes but deep down I'm kind of worried. There has been something off about Nolan today, but I can't put my finger on it. He's been moody. At moments, I would feel all of the love he has for me but then at some moments, it seems like he doesn't want to be around me.

Raking his fingers through his hair, he sighs and takes another step back. "I think I'm gonna bail out on going to the club."

What the fuck?! My eyebrows stitch heavily as I look him over. What in the hell just happened? "Nolan. What's wrong with you? I really didn't mean it that way."

"Mills told me I was moving too fast. I just didn't want to believe him. All day I've been thinking about us, Natalie, and it's fucking hard. All day I've been wondering if you're the right one for me. Sometimes, I don't even know if I'm right for anyone."

"What are you getting at, Nolan?"

He sighs as his eyes finally meet mine. "We're moving back to California." My heart clutches, my eyes growing broad. "My mom is sick and her boyfriend left her. We've just found out she has lung cancer and she needs us. As much as I couldn't stand her for letting us go over a guy, I still love her. I have to take care of her."

I pull my lips in and bite down. Fuck, this hurts. "So you're saying you're not staying? Is that it?" I look up at him.

He nods, his eyes lowering shamefully. "But I can still do long distance, Natalie. I can visit you often and you can visit me. Nothing has to change. I already have a job there with Mills ready for me. Maybe you could move to Cali with me."

"Hell no!" I spit. "I moved away because I knew being here was going to keep me sane. I knew *meeting you* was going to keep me somewhat all right, but now I just feel like a fucking idiot, Nolan. How long have you known you were going to be leaving?"

"I found out a few weeks after we met, Natalie. We were in too deep and I didn't know how to tell you without letting you down. I didn't wanna lose you."

"Deep or not, you could have told me, Nolan!" I growl. "Instead you continued to carry it on. Where did you think this was going to go?"

"I don't know!"

"What do you mean you don't know?" I screech, feeling all the anger boiling its way out of me. "When you first met me, what did you really want?

I'm sure it wasn't my heart! You wanted something else entirely but instead, *this* happened. This is what you got."

"I just... I wasn't expecting to fall in love with you," he mumbles.

"But you told me when you first saw me, you knew I was hurt. You said you wanted me to help you, Nolan. I don't understand what's going on right now!"

"Okay, you wanna know the truth?!" he roars, taking a large step forward. His chest bumps against mine as he grips my face. I can feel the anger boiling off of his skin. I can see the tense heat scorching in his eyes. "I just wanted to *fuck* you, Natalie. I just wanted you in my bed. I didn't care for your feelings or how you felt. I was just running game. I didn't care for a relationship or if you were hurt. But that night when we first went to the beach, shit changed. I felt like I could be myself with you. I felt like I could really talk and relate with you. No girl has ever spent personal time with me the way you did. No girl has ever made me feel guilty for wanting just sex. That's never happened to me before.

"You were different, yes. You're beautiful, which is why I wanted you in my room on the first night we met but, Bunny, I couldn't go through with it. You were so hurt, so lost. You were drowning yourself so much that I felt bad for thinking that way of you. It backfired on me. Talking to you that first night made me realize it wasn't fair. It was time for me to change. I couldn't fuck you over like how I planned on doing. I told Mills about the mix of feelings I had for you and he told me it was a sign to just try and settle down with someone right. It was a sign to let go of the immature shit to become better. *Mature.*"

A tear trickles down his cheek but he jerks away quickly to wipe it away. His eyes then torn on me and not once does he bother to look anywhere else. "I've never—in my entire life—felt anything like what I feel for you, Natalie. Meeting you has changed my life drastically and as much as I don't want to fuck up, I can't stay here. I want this to work, but I have to go, Nat. My mother needs us and if I refuse to go and she ends up dying, I'll regret the fact that I could have helped her, but didn't. I need your test of faith right now, Natalie. I fucking love you and I refuse to let you go."

A warm wetness runs down my cheeks, but he steps forward and pulls me against him. His arms wrap around me as he places his nose in my hair. I choke on a few sobs, my tears soaking his shirt. "I just don't want you to leave me, Nolan," I sputter out.

I feel his head shake as he sniffles. "I know, I know. I'm sorry. But I'll always be here for you. I mean that." He pushes me back by the shoulders gently to take a look at me but I refuse to look at him. I feel like a mess. I haven't cried this hard since graduation night, but if I want to be honest with myself, it's worse this time around because what Nolan and I have is real. I can't deny it. I've wanted to ignore it for so long and hold off from him but I knew there was going to be a time when I had to give in.

"Babe, look at me," he murmurs, tilting my chin up. I force myself to meet his eyes. "I'm going to come back. I'm not going to leave you stranded and hurt like the last guy did. I mean that. It's time for me to man up. I wanna make this work, not only to get better, but because I love you and I can't allow *this* to end." He leans down, placing his damp lips against mine. This time, I savor him. I want to feel this right now. I never want to let go. It's been so hard for me and I feel like I won't be able to breathe correctly without him around me.

I love Nolan Young and I want nothing more than to be with him every day. I want nothing more than to hold on to him, laugh with him, joke around with him, but most of all, *be happy* with him.

I know he isn't lying when he says he wants to make this work. No matter what his past consists of, it is just that. The past. It was only a matter of time for him to get rid of it and I'm thankful I'm the one he wants to start fresh with.

Chapter Thirty

It's the day of Open Mic.

I twist my fingers in my lap and repeat my lines constantly. My head twists to the right to take a peek at the time. It is now 4:58 PM... almost two hours away from the Open Mic session tonight. As a contestant, I have to show up early. I have to be back stage and ready. But am I truly? I felt more than ready a few hours ago. This morning, I was somewhat rejuvenated and a bit relieved that Nolan didn't runaway screaming his head off.

Instead of hitting the club, Nolan, Harper, Dawson, and I just chilled at our condo and watched Netflix movies. After what Nolan told me last night, drinks weren't needed. Drinks would have most likely made the situation worse. But at least he stuck around with me after telling me he had to go. It meant something.

I want nothing more than to have him close to my heart than anything else. We deserve each other, whether we see it or not.

I hop from the sofa to make my way toward the kitchen. I pull a glass down, fill it with ice, and then drown it with water. I gulp a few sips down before placing my glass on the counter and taking a deep breath. When I was nervous back at home, I would call my mom. That was the one thing she would make time for me. If I had a nervous spell going on.

I rush out of the kitchen, dipping around the corner until I'm in my bedroom. I scramble for my cell on top of my nightstand and immediately call her.

"Natty," she breathes.

"Hi, Mom."

"What's the matter?" she asks quickly. "You sound... flustered."

I pause to gather my thoughts. "I'm going to an Open Mic session tonight at a lounge. From what I've heard, there are going to be tons of people there. The number of people grows every weekend."

"Okay," she urges.

"I'm going to read one of my poems tonight, but I'm nervous, Mom. It's about Bryson."

"Bryson?" I can hear the anger behind the shrill of her voice. "No disrespect to you, sweetie, but you need to put that asshole in the garbage. Rid him of your memory bank. He's not worth speaking on."

"But it's not exactly a good poem. It just expresses how I really felt after what he did to me."

"Mmm-hmm." I know she's nodding with her lips pressed. "Frank told me you met a guy down there. Why didn't you tell me?"

My words trap in my throat. Why haven't I told her? When Bryson had asked me out freshman year she was the third person I told. Gracey and Harper were the first two. "Because I don't want you thinking I'm moving too fast."

"I wouldn't think that," she argues. "You sound happier, Natty. I'm sort of glad he came your way. Your father showed me the pictures of you and Harp down there and you look amazing. Happy."

I grin, lowering my head. "Thanks."

"As for the poem. You're going to nail it. I've always had faith in my baby. And you never know. Someone may be there to notice your talent and take you far. Never pass up a beautiful opportunity. Never stop chasing your dreams. You see what happened to me when I gave up on mine." She sighs. "I don't want you going through the same thing. I want you completely happy."

"Okay, Mom. I'm just—I feel like they're gonna look at me like an idiot. My words aren't clean. They're kind of crazy."

"Some of the craziest people in the world are the most creative, sweetie. Albert Einstein? Dr. Seuss? That's never an excuse."

I purse my lips, trotting out of my bedroom. "I guess you're right. I'll tell you how it went tomorrow. Hopefully I can catch you and Dad on three-way."

"Sounds good, Natty. Good luck, and I love you!"

"I love you, too, Mom."

I pull my phone away from my ear, slumping down on the leather sofa. I shut my eyes briefly and try to imagine a peaceful setting. I want to be somewhere where I won't have to worry. Where I won't have to feel like I have to live up to everyone's expectations. Surprisingly, behind my eyelids, I'm envisioning myself with Nolan.

We're on a faraway island with white sand and crystal-clear blue water. We're walking along the shore, hand-in-hand, as the sun is on its horizon. It's beautiful and right now I want nothing but that vision to be real. All I want is Nolan.

My phone buzzes in my hand, interrupting my peaceful daydream. Checking the screen, my eyes broaden as I stare at Nolan's name.

Nolan: *Ur gonna rock it tonight, Bunny. I got ur back.*

I grin as I reply.

Me: *U got mine, I got urs. Love u.*

Nolan: *Pretty nervous as well. Hearing that it's going 2 be packed 2night.*

Nolan: *And u know I love you more, Bunny.*

I giggle again.

Me: *Can't wait 2 see you 2night. If we do good I may have a pleasant surprise for ya. ;)*

I wait for him to text back for almost ten minutes. At one point, I'm nervous and thinking maybe he didn't like that line. I begin to chew on my bottom lip—that is until my phone buzzes gain.

Nolan: *I'm all about surprises. I'm gonna rip Open Mic to shreds tonight, babe. As for that surprise? Can we talk arrangements?*

A smile sticks to my lips.

Me: *I'm down. :)*

Nolan: *Can't wait Bunny.*

All my teeth reveal as I stand from the sofa and tuck my phone into the pocket of my grey hoody. That mini conversation has just given me a boost of confidence. I can do this because not only will I be on stage with Nolan, but I'll also be facing my dreams. People will finally hear what I've been storing within me. It may not be the whole world, but a crowd is good enough for me. We all have to start somewhere, right?

****

This is it.

It's so gut wrenching, so intense. I weave my way through the tables, spotting Brittany and Jordan at a lounge area big enough for more than ten people. Harper and Dawson came along and that makes me even more nervous because they're so close to me. It's the people who are my friends that I'm really afraid to face after the show.

"Natalie! You're finally here!" Brittany sings, hopping up from the plush sofa to get to me. I nod, swallowing as she hooks her arms around my neck and reels me in. "You look fantastic. I love the dress! All black with diamonds and lip-gloss. Beautiful." Brittany studies my outfit but I can't help but study hers. She looks amazing in her coral sundress. Her short hair is now wavy from most likely washing it. She's applied more makeup and has on gold sandals that match her gold studs.

"Thank you." I smile.

Jordan steps around Brittany to look at me. "All prepared for the show. They're gonna love you," he says.

"You think so?" I ask nervously, scanning the sea of people chatting amongst themselves. "There are so many people here. This doesn't make you nervous?"

"Nah." Jordan shrugs. "It did at first, but I've been doing Open Mic nights for so long that I don't really care whether they hate it or love it. It just feels right to do for myself... and Britt." He grins at her, kissing her cheek.

I nod with a boggled mind. I turn to look over my shoulder and spot Harper and Dawson making their way through the crowd. "Nat! Where're we sitting?" Harper screeches from across the room. God, she can be obnoxious.

"Over here, Harp," I say, pointing to the reserved lounge area. There's a perfect view from the sofas to the stage. Nothing is standing in the way. We have front row seats with unlimited drinks and cozy sofas. Nothing can top that. I'm glad Brittany's mom knows the manager of this lounge now.

Harper stumbles her way through with a white and gold sequined dress, gold heels, and freshly applied makeup on. Her hair is slick and straight (as always) but she looks beautiful. Unlike her, I decided to curl my ends and make myself seem a bit classier. It isn't too long before Dawson casually makes his way up to stand beside Harp in his dark jeans and collared blue shirt. His hair seems much curlier than its usual wavy. His dark eyes meet mine before meeting Brittany's and Jordan's.

"Harper and Dawson, this is Brittany and Jordan. Brittany and Jordan, Harper and Dawson," I announce.

"It's really a pleasure to meet you guys. Nat can never shut up about you two. She says you got her into stepping out of her shell."

Brittany and Jordan look at each other, smiles hinting at their lips. "You could say that," Brittany says. "It's always good to get yourself out there. From what I've read, Natalie has true talent. I love the way she writes."

I blush from both the compliment and from the fact that all eyes are now on me. "How about we have a seat?" I insist

"Loving that idea," Dawson says, stepping around me to slump down on the curved sofa. Harper takes the spot on the left of him and I take the spot at the end. Brittany and Jordan sit on the sofa across from us with bright smiles glued to their faces.

"So, where's Nolan?" Brittany asks.

"I'm hoping he'll be here momentarily," I murmur. I thought he would beat me here since he said he was getting dressed before me. It takes guys no time at all to be ready, so now I'm nervous.

"I can't wait to see which poem you've chosen," Brittany says, reaching for a drink. "I hope it's my favorite one." She winks.

"No spoilers," Jordan teases. He leans forward to kiss the tip of Brittany's nose and she grins broadly before kissing him back.

"I won't spoil it for you."

Watching them causes my heartbeat to snag. I whip my head to look toward the entrance of the lounge and it's just my luck I see him.

As he steps in, my belly heats. His grey and white T-shirt fits to every curve of his upper body. His dark jeans are snug and fit all too well against his swaying hips. His guitar is strapped around him, dangling in the back as he steps through the tables. His grey eyes scan the crowd but once he turns his head and meets my gaze, he smiles. Damn, his smile. So beautiful.

I hop from my seat, silently thanking him for actually showing up. "You're here."

One of his eyebrows shoot up, confused. "Why wouldn't I be?" he asks.

"I don't know." I shrug. "I got kind of... nervous that maybe you weren't going to show up."

"Bunny, I wouldn't miss this for the world. I know this is your start. It's mine as well. I'd never do you like that."

"I know—sorry. My mind is just everywhere right now."

"Nolan!" Dawson calls, sliding his rear to the end of the sofa. He stands and his eyes become chinky as he grins at his best friend. "Looking swell, man. Looks like you're gonna crumble that stage."

Nolan chuckles, placing his thumb beneath the leather strap of his guitar. "I practiced all night and this morning. I feel like I'm ready for anything."

Dawson laughs with a nod. "Good luck, dude—to you both," he says as his eyes meet mine. I know you're gonna kill it."

"Thanks, Dawson."

"Thanks, man," Nolan says right after me.

"Attention," a woman calls through the microphone on the stage. "We need all speakers, poets, singers, bands, and story-tellers that have signed up for tonight's Open Mic Jam to please meet us back stage. The show will be starting in less than five minutes."

A whirl of panic corrupts me as I squeeze my hands together. *Okay, breathe, Natalie. You can do this*, I tell myself. A gentle hand presses against the small of my back. Whipping my head upwards, I stare into Nolan's soft irises.

"We got this, babe. Remember, you got my back, I got yours? You're gonna be fine."

"What if they hate it?" I whisper. "What if I make myself look worse than what I already am?"

"There's nothing bad about you, Natalie." He leans forward, placing a kiss on my lips. He then laces his fingers through mine and steps forward. "Jordan, can't wait to see what you have in store for us tonight," he says.

Jordan chuckles, grabbing hold of his cherry red acoustic guitar. "I think I'm more excited for you two than anything else."

Nolan chuckles as Jordan straps his guitar around him and leads the way backstage. I swallow the lump in my throat and my grip tightens around Nolan's.

I have to do this. It's a must. It's far too late to back out now. And I feel much better with Nolan by my side. At least if I fuck up, he'll be there to comfort me and to tell me to start over.

Chapter Thirty-One

"If you feel the words blurring together, look into my eyes and I'll smile. That smile will be my way of reassuring you that you got this, Bunny. You got this. Chin up."

Those are the exact words Nolan said to me before we stepped onto this stage. And right now, my heart has never pounded so heavily. All eyes are on me, from behind and in front. Every aspect of my body is being put under the investigation of whether they'll like what I have to say or not.

Turning my head only slightly, I glance over my shoulder to take a peek at Nolan. His fingers are already prepared to play on his guitar. He's just ready for me to speak.

"I love you," he mouths.

My lips press as I look away and face forward again.

"Hi, everyone," I say through the microphone, trying my best to keep my voice steady. "My name is Natalie Carmichael, and with me is Nolan Young who will be performing a solo later." I turn to look at Nolan who has just nodded his head and is now smiling at the crowd. "I'm a poet and writing runs in my blood. It's what has kept me sane throughout these past few months—well that and a few other things," I say, immediately thinking of Nolan and grinning. "Tonight, I'll be feeding you the words of one of my best poems. Nolan here will be playing a melody to it that we've worked on. I hope you all like it."

As soon as I stop speaking I clear my throat and Nolan begins his melody. The strums start quick but begin to slow down into a brief, soft flow. But as soon as his melody picks up again, I begin to pour the words out of me. The words that I have memorized since day one of writing them and the words that explain my entire relationship with Bryson and even how I feel with Nolan.

I asked to be loved
You gave it to me
I asked for your heart
You handed it to me

Every day, there was happiness
Every night, there was love
Every day, I felt blessed
But soon, every night was tough

I felt it happening
I felt you changing
I felt us fading
I felt you slipping

All I wanted was devotion
All I wanted was your touch
But now I'm going through the motions
I'm trying not to think so much

But without you, it's hard
Without you, it sucks
Without you, I wasn't smart
Without you, I felt no luck

But with time, I blossomed
With time, I grew
With time, I lost some
But without you, I knew

I learned how to live
Without you
I learned how to love again
Without you

In order for myself to move on
You had to be let go of

In order for myself to be reborn
You had to lose my love

Without you, I found him
Without you, I found <u>life</u>
Without you, I wasn't on my last limb
Without you, I've learned to fight

We're over now
We're completely through
I'm forgetting about you now
Because I <u>never</u> needed you

I finally open my eyes to the sight of blurriness. Nolan strums once more before placing his guitar down, standing up, and meeting to my side. The whole lounge applauds, but I hear Brittany and Harper screaming the most. Chills crawl along my spine... but they're soothing. I can't believe it. They actually loved it—and I actually did it. I swipe my tears just as Nolan turns me around to face him. He kisses me tenderly, passionately, and the crowd cheers even harder to root on our kiss.

"I love you, Bunny."

"I love you, too," I whisper before colliding with him again.

****

Jordan performed with a revamped version of the song that he sang on the first Open Mic night I attended. He had a drummer and a pianist playing along with him. It was amazing, but what I was really waiting on was for Nolan to play. He was the last on the list. I guess it's true when they say save the best for last.

As soon as he steps on stage, I perk myself up and prepare to listen. He doesn't even hesitate to lean forward and place his lips near the mic.

"What's up every one!" he says with a broad smile. The people cheer, as if Nolan is some rock star and everyone knows him. I smile as he watches everyone clap. "I admit I've been holding off on myself and my talent. I've been playing the guitar for fifteen years. My father taught me when I was only a kid and when he died, I promised I would never give up on it. I play every day and night and the older I get, the better I am. The song I'm about to sing not only goes to my dad, but to the girl who has caused a massive impact on my life. She's made me a better person over the course of these few weeks and I'm glad I met her because loving her comes second to none. With her, I'm alive. The song is titled *Grew on Her* and, Natalie, this is for you."

My heart flutters as his grey eyes land directly on mine for a brief moment before he brings his leg up to sturdy his foot on the bar of his stool. He places his guitar on top of his thigh, hooks his arm around it, and begins his sweet melody.

"Oh my gosh!" Harper squeals, hugging my arm.

I turn to smile at her, but then Nolan's lyrics spill and my head whips to give him my undivided attention.

Verse 1:

Since I was just a boy
My father told me how to love
To love not only my toys
But all things above

But I ignored him
I thought nothing of it
I dismissed him
But now I hate that I did

Then there she was
Craving for a change
There she was
Causing me to change . . .

Chorus:

And I did
I moved on
Yeah, I did
I grew on her

There is love
I accepted it
Yeah, I did
I grew on her

Ohh . . .

Verse 2:

I don't know what I would do
Without you
It tears me apart when
I can't see you

It breaks my heart
To know what he did to you

Bridge:

I promised I would stay
I promised I wouldn't leave
I'll always take your breath away
I'll always be here to please

Ohh . . .

Chorus:

Cause I did
I moved on
Yeah I did
I grew on her

There is love
I accepted it
Oh, I did
I grew on her
I grew on her

Hook:

And I won't let her go
No, I won't leave her alone
I'll always be here
Please don't shed anymore tears!

Yeah, I did
I moved on her
Yeah, I did
I grew on her

I've matured
Yeah I moved on
I love her
Yeah I know she's the one.

Nolan's eyes open slowly as he pulls back from the mic. I stand quickly and cheer as hard as I can, clapping, whistling, and chanting his name along with Dawson and Jordan. Nolan stands, scans the crowd, but when his eyes meet mine, he smiles. My heart thunders against my chest as I stare back at him.

"I love you," I mouth. He flashes another bright smile before leaning into the mic again.

"Thank you. The support is greatly appreciated." The crowd continues to cheer madly, even when he's stepping off stage and making his way toward us. A few women ogle him but his eyes are on me and not daring to look anywhere else. I love the fact that he only has eyes for me at the moment. The song was beautiful and it says a lot. We may have been together for only a few weeks but this feeling is something beyond that. The spark I'm feeling right now isn't just a simple love. We're *in* love.

His lyrics have proved he'll do nothing more than carry me in his arms. He'll do nothing more than make me happy. So far, he's been faithful to his word.

"Dude! I've never heard you sing like that before! You destroyed that stage!" Dawson says as soon as Nolan meets with us.

Nolan smiles, grasping the hand Dawson is holding out and then giving him a brotherly hug. "Thanks, man."

They let go of each other but as he does, I spot tears forming at the rims of Nolan's eyes. He's going to miss this. He's going to miss hanging with his best friend. That song was something fantastic for him. Saying my poem has made me feel completely different but for him, I know it must feel surreal.

Setting his guitar down, Nolan begins to make his way toward me but as he glances over my shoulder, his eyes widen. "Mills?" he calls.

I spin around quickly, only to spot the phenomenal Mills making his way through the tables and chairs. "You seriously thought I wasn't coming, bro?" he asks, meeting up to us. "Wouldn't miss it for the world. I've been waiting for you to get out of the box." They hug one another but this time Nolan's tears fall without hesitation. He squeezes his eyes shut over his brother's shoulder as Mills rubs his back with nothing but love. "Proud of you, man. Never let these dreams slip. Dad would be proud of you, too."

"I know. He's why I did it."

"And her," Mills says, pulling back to look at me. "She gave you motivation. She must really be the one. I promise all my tests are done with," he jokes.

I giggle as Mills opens his arms to me. I step in and hug him briefly before pulling away to hug Nolan. "You did good. I loved it."

"You swear? I was nervous about it."

I push him back by the shoulders and stare into his wet grey eyes. "Loved it, Nolan."

He grins. "Thanks, Bunny."

Mills clears his throat as he looks us over. "How about celebrating over some wings, beer, and an intense soccer game. It's still early enough to catch a few seats at Buffalo Wild Wings." Mills looks over Nolan's shoulder to see everyone else. "We all could chill together," he offers.

"Dude, some honey-barbecue wings with beer sounds like the shit right now!" Dawson says before his eyes meet Harper's. "Right, babe?"

"Yeah." Harp grins as Dawson pulls her into his side.

"I could go for some beer and wings," Jordan says, shrugging. "Britt and I are free for the rest of the night."

"Cool," Mill says with a small smile before turning around. "Let's make it happen."

Chapter Thirty-Two

Dinner with everyone was fun. I didn't want it to end, but of course it had to. We couldn't stay there all night. During dinner, I was still lingering on Nolan and his song. I still can't believe it was about me. I can't believe he actually put in time to write a song about us. It fit so well, there were no flaws at all. Just mere perfection.

As soon as we're inside the condo, Nolan reels me in by my waist. "Did you have fun tonight?" he asks.

"Yeah," I murmur as he places his lips against my ear. My skin is screaming for more of his touch right now. "Thank you."

His head tilts back to look me over. "For what?"

"For stepping out of your box with me and singing. For pushing me to see my dreams come true."

"Don't thank me for that, Natalie. It was bound to happen one day, whether I was around or not. But you did good. I could feel the emotion, the pain, the heartache." He reaches a hand up to push my hair behind my ear. He then grabs my hand to lead me to the bedroom.

The door clicks shut behind us and it isn't too long before his hands are cupping my jawline. He strokes me cheeks and the flesh behind my ears. I breathe him in, wanting nothing more than to hold on. As he pulls back, his grey eyes stare down at me. "I have to tell you something."

"What?" I ask.

"Mills and I are… leaving… tomorrow."

My heart practically stops beating as I stare at him. He takes my hand so we both can sit on the edge of the bed. "Tomorrow?" I repeat. "But why?"

"My mom is sicker than we thought. She can't even move and she has no one to take care of her. She doesn't have enough money to pay for a nurse so Mills and I have to leave. He already bought tickets."

"Is that why Mills wanted to celebrate tonight?"

"Yeah," he says, chuckling dryly. "He wanted to celebrate for Open Mic but he also wanted me to enjoy my last night with you. He told me before we all departed from Buffalo Wild Wings."

"Wow." I shake my head, my eyes still wide and my face still struck with what's most likely terror. "Tomorrow—Nolan that's too soon. I can't stomach the thought of you leaving yet. I thought I'd at least have time to cope with the idea of it."

"I know, Natalie. I'm sorry. But it's okay. I want you to go to school, work your ass off, and keep writing. When you miss me, write. When you're thinking about me, write. When you're lonely, write… and then call me." He smiles softly before leaning in to kiss my forehead.

My eyes burn but I shut them to allow them to cool. "How long do you have to stay?"

"I don't know but I promise to visit. There won't be a day that goes by that I'm not thinking about you."

I choke, realizing I'm crying. The tears pour as I bury my face in his chest. He clutches me in his arms and strokes my back. "I love you, Natalie. You're my world and I didn't even know it until now. I'll never let this go." He pushes me against my shoulders to get a look into my eyes. "Do you hear me?" he asks. "I'm never letting *this* go."

His stern eyes search my face and although I don't know what he's searching for, I know he's found his answer because his lips crush mine. He lays me on my back, pushes his way between my legs, and begins to trail kisses from my lips to my cheek, and then down to my collar bone. One of his hands sneaks its way down to grab my thigh gently while the other strokes my cheek continuously.

"It's only temporary, Bunny," he says against my lips.

I nod with my lips pulled in. I try my hardest to control my tears but at this moment, it's impossible. I'm going to miss him more than anything. It feels as if we're letting one another go. It feels as if we're breaking up... maybe worse. But we're not. He's always going to be here for me. Bryson couldn't say that.

After a few seconds, my dress has disappeared. His eyes stare and scan every bare inch on my body. As I lie before him in just a light blue bra and lace panties, I can tell he wants nothing more than to make me his. He dips down, kisses me, and I reach down to unbutton his pants. He pulls back again to tug his shirt over his head and as soon as his pants and boxers fall, he slides his arousal into me.

A gasp escapes my lips from both pleasure and pain. But that pain boils into nothing but pleasure as he slides in and out with swift strokes. They're even, defined, and every single one of them is giving me a dose of his love. His lips press against mine sweetly and my lips part, allowing him to taste me.

He plunges into my deeper, harder all while kissing the crook of my neck and growling against it.

"I love you, Natalie," he whispers in my ear. He lifts me upright, pulling my legs around him so we can remain chest to chest. Here's my chance to return the love. I move forward, backwards, slowly all with my legs strapped around him and his hand grabbing hold of my ass. I want to cherish this. I want to cherish all of him.

We're heart to heart, chest to chest to chest, nose to nose. My head falls back as he drags his lips from my jawline to my collarbone. I then smash lips with him, pecking them lightly and delicately as my hips continue to grind. As he grunts, he whispers my name with a few mild curse words.

"I love you, Nolan," I breathe. He grunts and I moan before we both hit our climax. Bursting with ecstasy, I quiver before wrapping my arms around his shoulders and hugging him. I inhale, taking in the pleasure of his sweet sweat, his masculine scent.

"You're my baby. My Bunny. Distance will never change that," he murmurs.

Tears stream, but I smile because I know he means it.

Chapter Thirty-Three

My eyelids flip open quickly. I reach for my phone to check the time and it's now 9:26 A.M. Snatching my blankets off of me, I clamber out of the bed. "Oh, no," I mumble, searching through my dressers. I'm late. I scramble through my drawers until I pull out a pair of blue jean shorts, a brown camisole, and a bra.

I rush to the bathroom, struggling to pull my shorts over my hips. After yanking my shirt over my shoulders, I reach for my toothbrush and give them a quick brush. With my toothbrush hanging out my mouth, I hook my bra then reach for my shirt to pull it over my head. I rinse my mouth then dash out of the room to slide my feet into my brown Toms.

Clutching my keys, I rush out of my room and head for the door.

"Nat!" I spin around only to spot Harp stepping out of her room with a silky pink robe on and mangled locks. She has the sleepy eyes, proving she was up late last night. "Where are you going?"

"I have to get to Nolan."

"Nolan?" Her face pulls together. "You were just with him. What's wrong?"

"He's leaving today, Harp. I have to go."

Her eyes widen but I don't allow her enough time to ask any more questions because I am out the door and clambering down the stairs in a heartbeat.

****

Twenty minutes later and I'm at the airport. Bustling through the busy streets, I don't stop until I am at the glass doors. I'm moving so fast that I almost got ran over—twice. As soon as I swing the doors open, there's a line of people waiting to walk through the security monitor. I groan as I stand on my toes to see if the line is moving quickly but it's just my luck that it isn't. I spot an opening to my left where a few security guards are passing by to get to the other side. That's when my body goes into play. Without thinking, I dash toward the gap and rush through.

"Hey!" one of the security guards call. I ignore him. "Hey!" he calls again. I can hear his footsteps but I decide to walk faster. I spot a crowd of people ahead and rush for them. Sliding my way between, I let my hair down and it falls into curls against my shoulders. Hopefully he won't notice me with my hair down. I'll be harder to find without a bun.

I crash into a few people just to make my way through, but I don't stop. I'll fight if it means I'll make it in time to see him. I promised him last night I would meet him here before his flight. Arriving here a few minutes before his departure isn't enough. I should have set a damn alarm like he said.

The crowd finally begins to die down but then I'm greeted with a fork hallway. I groan as I clutch my keys in hand. I spot a young woman behind the counter and rush for it.

"Can I help you?" she asks.

"Yes. I'm looking for a departure to San Francisco, California at ten."

"You're looking to catch a flight to California in less than five minutes?" she asks, her eyes broadening and pretty much calling me an idiot. "Sweetie, sorry to tell you, but there's no way in hell you can catch a flight now. This is an airport. These places are constantly booked."

"No—I'm looking for the flight that leaves at ten!"

"Oh!" She nods as she clicks the mouse of her computer. "Let's see here," she says, tapping away at her keyboard.

A groan rumbles at the heart of my throat. *I don't have time for this.* I push away from the counter and cross my fingers while speeding down the middle hallway. My only hope is he's down here because if he isn't, I'm screwed and I won't see him again for another few months. I can't deal with that. It won't last.

As soon as I hit the end of the hall, I scan the area. I spot a few people sitting on benches and a few people waiting in line for coffee. My heart pounds against my chest but once I spot the cropped dark hair, the worried grey eyes that are scanning the area just as much as I am, and the bags in his hand while he waits in line, my heart beats rapidly.

"Nolan!" I scream as he takes a step forward. He's next in line. One more step and he would have been on that plane. His head whips in my direction and his eyes land on mine. He rushes out of the line, passing through the crowd of seated people.

Then, dead in the center, our bodies clash, collide and our lips don't dare to be anywhere else but against one another's. My fingers braid through his hair as he picks me up in his arms and squeezes me. He finally drops me, but he doesn't bother to remove his lips from mine. His gentle hands cup my face and tears streams down my cheeks. He pulls back to study my face and take me in for what will be the last time for a very long time.

"I got worried," he says.

"I wouldn't have missed this moment, Nolan. I love you."

His lips spread and reveal a row of beautiful, white teeth. He kisses me again, cradling my face in his hands. And as I kiss him back, I can feel it. I can feel everything. The love, the power, the passion. It's all there. Nolan and I have been through battle grounds during this love game. But it's no longer a game to us. It's real. It's here. And it's speaking to us more clearly than ever.

I was always told that love comes during the right time. At times, I didn't believe in love and at times, I swore I would never fall again. But he's changed my mind. He's changed my opinion of love. At one moment, I hated it. I hated everything about it. But now, I can say it. Now I can admit that *love* is just what it is. *Love*. And without it, there is no point in living, in breathing.

We're all destined to be with someone. We're all supposed to meet that one person who will change everything. Whether we're put through heartache, pain, or even grief, it'll come.

I fell, but was picked up in his arms. I was blessed with his love, with his heart. And I swear to never drop it. I swear to never lose it in all of this madness. Our love will blossom and grow. With time, we'll be more than one.

Just when I thought he would be completely hard to keep a hold of—just when I thought he would shatter me even more than my past had—he's actually made me better.

This love was hard to control.

This love was hard to keep hidden.

This love was hard to go through with.

But this love was going to happen one way or another because it was completely and utterly *hard to resist*.

The End...?

Hard to Hold On (the sequel to Hard to Resist) is now available on all e-book platforms.

Harper and Dawson's spin-off novel will be released early 2014. It has not official title yet.

GIVING IN

A poem dedicated to *Hard to Resist*

By: Stina Rubio

I dream of your touch
Sliding down my thighs, it's rough,
Stealing my breath away,
Making my whole body sway,
Singing out in ecstasy,
All the while your kisses lingering,
Sliding in and out, its slick,
Your name escaping my moaning lips,
Grasping my hips so tight,
You lift me up and slide me on just right,
Fitting perfect like a glove,
You and me making endless love,
Hardly able to hold it in,
This feeling is nothing short of sin,
Kissing my breast and licking your lips,
Stroking my ass with soft finger tips,
Not wanting to stop, not giving in,
The feeling building, to explode within,
As I shatter, as I shriek,
Wanting to scream out but I'm too weak,
Falling forward onto your chest,

Sated and satisfied and also blessed,
Your kisses teasing at my neck,
All the hopes and promises that you kept,
Hard to resist, but I'm giving in,
You and I were meant to begin again.

About Shanora:

New York Times & USA Today Best Selling author, Shanora Williams considers herself one of the wondrous, down-to-earth authors who's all about romance and the paranormal... but of course she always makes room for the many other genres out there.

She's a huge lover of Starbucks and a big kid when it comes to Haribo Gummy Bears. If she could swim in Coca-Cola she would. She's a very avid reader and a huge fan of many other independent authors.

Follow Shanora (S.Q. Williams) for the latest updates.

Facebook

Goodreads

Twitter

Blog

I am always responding to emails from fans and readers. Don't be shy! If you want to contact me, feel free to do so. I love to connect with those who read my work, whether it is through Facebook, Twitter, email, or even my blog. I appreciate and love you all. Your support and feedback is beyond amazing.

Thank you,

Shanora

77436395R00198

Made in the USA
Middletown, DE
21 June 2018